CONFESSIONS OF
AN **ORGAN DONOR**

SHANNON McCRIMMON

MC
SQUARED

Published by Shannon McCrimmon
www.shannonmccrimmon.com

Copyright © 2018 by Shannon McCrimmon

Design: Popcorn Initiative • www.popcorninitiative.com

For Mom and Dad: I love you and miss you.
And for Jacob Farley: you are inspirational.

PROLOGUE

"Irregardless": it's not a word, even though Webster says it is, and this guy who's rambling like a derailed train has said it three times now. He's also said "supposedbly," which we all know isn't a word, either. Strange that people say these kinds of things. In this day and age, it's not hard to Google something on the internet to guarantee you don't sound like an idiot.

You can call me Ishmael. Not really. I just finished reading *Moby Dick* and think the opening line is overrated. I'm in the minority on this one, since all of those literary scholars rate it as one of the best opening lines in literature. What do they know? Not sure what they're comparing it to, but I don't see it. Anyway, I digress. You can call me anything you want, but I may not answer.

My name is Beckett Wentworth – the third, mind you. Everyone calls me Trip, because, well, for obvious reasons. Maybe it's not obvious to you. The name Trip comes from triple, and I'm (waves) the third. At least I'm not a Trey. One out of five children is named Trey, at least according to Them. You know, the elusive *Them*.

This guy is a chatterbox. I know I should be paying attention to him—he's giving me, well, all of us, a stern lecture— but he lost me at the third "irregardless."

"This is a very serious matter. I don't think you kids realize that," he says.

A kid is a baby goat. Not a human guy or a human girl. Why do people insist on calling other human beings by that term? Did you know that a mother goat will communicate with her baby by bleating? It's a unique call that only the two share. Can you imagine if humans did this? Sometimes I wish I had my own special calling mechanism. I guess that's what cell phones are for, with the variety of ringtones. My mother doesn't know this but I use "The Imperial March" for her.

"You're in a lot of trouble," he adds with a hardening glare from his beady brown (or hazel, I can't tell) eyes. His eyes squish into his round, puffy cheeks.

I think we all know we're in trouble – no need to state the obvious. It's not often (let's say never) I find myself sitting in an interrogation room with two police officers playing good cop/bad cop (just like the cheesy 1980s cop dramas), treating me like I'm some sort of vandal hoodlum who goes around causing a ruckus. They're even recording us. Millicent has waved at the camera at least three times now, which made Puffy Cheeks irate.

I knew there would be trouble the moment Millicent Huxley entered my life. Sounds cliché, doesn't it? It's like a line from one of those 1930s movies. I picture myself wearing a fedora, talking real fast, and referring to ladies as "dames" with "gams."

You know when your instincts tell you to run for the hills? Yeah, that's what mine told me when I met her. But I still got sucked into her like a vortex. Bad pun, but Millicent is like that: she lures you in. You want to breathe the air she's breathing. Maybe being the most gorgeous, yet bizarre girl I've ever met has something to do with it. All I know is I wouldn't be sitting here with two trigger-finger cops if it weren't for her.

"You don't have any proof that we've done anything wrong," Millicent says.

The one cop laughs in a smirky, grate-on-your-nerves kind of way. "I'd say that stolen casket in your truck bed is proof enough."

CHAPTER 1

High School: to some, it's the epitome of hell. To others, it's their milestone, which is pathetic given the span of our lives. For me, I don't know yet. I'll have to see. It's been a long time (like more than a decade and then some) since I've stepped foot inside a public school, and now here I am standing inside Ambler's Fork High School. Tada! At this point, I can't really tell if I'm going to like it or not.

The only thing I can see is that there are way too many steps to climb and everyone is a walking advertisement for American Eagle. Meanwhile, I'm sporting a Pink Floyd t-shirt. I might be the only guy who is wearing an homage to a vintage band and not to a clothing store. I feel like Kevin Bacon in *Footloose* sans the tie and funky hair. My hair is too curly to spike like his, and I don't like wearing ties.

My mom and I have to go through a checkpoint in order to enter the main office. It's like TSA but worse since the old man who is scrutinizing my mother's license moves like a snail and can't see very well. The fact that he's using a magnifying glass to read her license doesn't give me much confidence in his ability to keep me safe from harm's way should some creeper try to break into the school.

"Type in your name," he croaks to Mom.

She clicks the keys on the keyboard. A sticker with the word "Visitor" prints from the nearby printer. He hands it to Mom, and she applies it to her chest, then gives him a look as if to say, "Anything else?" He gestures to the fireproof doors, hits a button that causes them to open, and we walk into the front office.

A few students are seated in blue upholstered chairs. They're all texting: faces down, fingers moving at the speed of light. They look up when we enter, stare us both down for a millisecond, then go back to texting. I hear some chattering, and a few whispers of, "Who's he?" But no one attempts to strike up a conversation or offers me a smile. Not that I expect a welcoming committee offering me bundt cake and warm apple pie—I'd choose the bundt cake, by the way; apple pie is so 1994.

We move to the front desk and are ignored by the harried receptionist, who's trying to answer endless calls. Mom drums her fingers along the counter, which was made to emulate granite, only it's laminate, so it looks really cheap. It's like cubic zirconia: fake and looks that way, too. Fakes are fakes and will always be… well, fake. I know, very sage of me.

Mom keeps tapping her fingers against the counter. It's an annoying habit I've learned to ignore, but to the lady who's trying to answer the phones, it's a feat. Mom's a ball of nerves. She's been like this since I woke up this morning.

"I wish you'd change your mind," she said with a frown as I ate my favorite cereal. I have to have fuel for the brain, and I can't start my day without Toasty Oats, which is a generic version of Cheerios. Dad is frugal and won't buy anything but generic products. Mom draws the line at toilet paper, though. That's a relief.

"A deal is a deal." I picked up the bowl and slurped the last of the sugar-coated milk.

"I never should have agreed to it."

I set the bowl down on the table. "You're not taking me to Rikers."

She formed a defeated frown. "It feels that way to me."

I turned the big whopping eighteen last week, and to celebrate the momentous occasion of entering adulthood, my parents agreed to my one request: that I attend public school this year. (I also purchased my first lottery ticket, and surprise, I didn't win. What's the statistic on winning: one out of a billion or something like that?) Anyway, I was tired of wondering. You know when you obsess over something, constantly thinking about it to the point that it's all you can think about? That was me about public school.

I'm appreciative of my one-on-one education from my private tutor because it is stellar, but I lack the comradery. Sure, Mr. Finley is an interesting guy, but you can't jive with a man three times your age. He was keen on me leaving the trenches anyway. When I told him I wanted to take the leap, his exact words to me were: "You should have done this years ago. It's unhealthy for a boy your age to be around an old man day after day."

"You're not old," I argued. Seasoned might be a more apt description.

"A boy your age shouldn't have a friend three times his age."

"Who said we were friends?" I teased. "And, I have friends."

He narrowed his eyes to mine. "Online friends don't count; neither does your music teacher. She is old, too."

"Don't tell her that," I say, deciding it's futile to defend myself. The sad truth is I don't excel in the social department.

So, today, I'm hoping to change that. I'm starting summer school. Not that I need to go to summer school – I have enough credits – but it is part of the compromise. If this doesn't work, then I don't come back in the fall. No way am I going back to being homeschooled. It's like living in sunny Florida and then moving to Alaska.

Mom has tried bribing me since I told her what I wanted. "I bet you'd like a brand new car," she said with a devious grin.

"Nah. I'm good," I'd told her, much to her chagrin. Not that she and Dad would be buying me a brand new car anyway. I know a fib when I hear one.

I wasn't even tempted by her offer anyway. Not in the least. I've wondered for so long how the rest of the world does it; I can't keep living my life guessing.

The receptionist looks up at my mother, fights hard not to glare at her, and says, "Can I help you?" There's subtle irritation in that tone of hers, but Mom is oblivious. She's too busy fidgeting and has that apprehensive look on her face that all mothers wear because it's in their blood to worry.

"I'm Trisha Wentworth, and this is my son, Trip." She points to me. I wave and half-grin at the receptionist. It doesn't charm her like I'd planned. (I've been told I have a decent smile.) "We have an appointment with Mr. Buckley."

The woman offers her a subtle nod and is about to say something, but there's shouting coming from the adjacent office, which causes us all to look in that direction.

"Can you explain to me why it's okay for me to miss class because I'm supposedly scantily clad?" I hear a girl ask. Kudos to her for the use of 19th-century vocabulary.

"Watch the tone," the man says to her. "We have a dress code policy here, Miss Huxley."

"And I'm following your Fascist rules," she says to him.

Gutsy and smart.

"Straps, Miss Huxley, are supposed to be this thick."

"So, let me get this straight. I'm being sent home because these straps aren't wide enough?"

"On page fifteen in the school policy manual, it states: 'straps are to be two inches or the size of two fingers.'"

"In what context of two fingers? Because if you compare your two fingers to mine then it's an unfair comparison."

"Two inches," he says with a resounding sigh. "The point is, you're not in dress code, and either you need to don a sweater or jacket to cover your shoulders or go home and change."

"I don't have a sweater or jacket to *don*," she exaggerates the word. "It's still summer if you haven't noticed. That's not the point, though. I still don't understand how it's acceptable for me to go home because of my wardrobe, which any reasonable person would agree is not unsavory. I'm missing a very important lesson in Mr. Marshall's class because we're having this discussion."

"You know the rules, Miss Huxley. I don't understand why you can't abide by them. We certainly never had any issues with your uncle Luca."

"Well, I'm clearly not Luca, now am I?" she retorts. "Just because I know the rules doesn't mean I understand or agree with them. It seems odd to me that Mr. Adams was even paying attention to what I was wearing. Shouldn't he be busy helping you run the school? And secondly, half the boys on the cross country team, basketball team, and any other sports team around here run around without their shirts on, but that is okay? How is that appropriate, but spaghetti straps warrant missing an hour of my education? If you had a daughter, would you want her to be subjected to this hypocrisy?"

"We're finished with this discussion."

He comes out in a huff, his face red as a beet and veins

protruding. "Have a seat here." He points to one of the empty chairs.

She marches out of his office, and it's like one of those scenes from the movies except her hair isn't blowing and there isn't a fog machine. She's... perfect. Too pretty to be real, almost ethereal. She's what the French would call au naturel. Her dishwater blonde hair is tied into a semi-braid that looks like it could unravel any moment, but I'm willing to bet she wouldn't care. She seems like the kind of girl who doesn't spend much time primping but still looks like a million bucks.

She stands with a purpose in front of the chair, looking like a petulant child. She's not dressed how I imagined she'd be, how I'd hoped she be. I'm not a perv, but given the principal's reaction, I thought she'd come out showing a lot more skin. Like maybe a string bikini, a thong, or something of that nature. The dress she's wearing is pretty conservative. All I can see are her tanned and toned shoulders and legs. Ironically, I'm a leg man, and this girl has long ones.

She catches me staring at her, brings her hands to her hips and says, "You done looking?"

CHAPTER 2

"No, spin around," I blurt to the smarmy little activist, which is quite brazen given that I did just get caught ogling her like a horny construction worker.

She shoots me a dirty look, and I give her a bored one in return—I have to maintain the cool facade and can't let her know she's gotten to me so easily. So, I turn my head and look at the inspirational art hanging on the drab walls. *"Team: Together Everyone Achieves More!"* I don't feel motivated by this kind of quote. Do other people? And if they do, it's pretty sad that a poster is all it takes to get them pumped up.

The man, who I assume is Mr. Buckley, feigns a smile at Mom and me, then whispers to the receptionist. She gives him a nod, side-glares The Activist, then begins punching the keys on her keyboard, a little deliberately, as if hitting the keys harder will infuriate the girl.

"This is Mrs. Wentworth and her son. They have an appointment with you," she says to him.

He fakes another smile at us and extends his hand to Mom and me. I give him a limp handshake in return. His hand is moist— I hate that word—but I don't know how else you'd describe the dampness of his hand. I wipe my hand on my shorts, trying hard not to grimace from thoughts of what germs might lurk on on his clammy hand.

Shaking hands in this day and age is stupid. The ritual comes from the Medieval Times and was a way of showing that you and the other person weren't carrying weapons. Now it's polite practice. But given the germs people carry, it's a sure way to get sick, and something tells me Buckley doesn't wash his hands the length of "The Birthday Song" like he's supposed to.

"It's nice to meet you. Please come with me," he says to us. He points to his office and stands at the threshold, allowing my mother to walk in before him.

"Please have a seat," he says, all prim and proper.

As I make my way to his office, he averts his eyes and glances the other way, which is what some do when they see me. People want to look at anything but me because they're ashamed, scared or realize they're jerks for being that way. I'm tempted to wave my hands in a frantic fashion, then point to my leg and say with crazy eyes, "Have a look. I know you want to."

I glance at The Activist again. She's still standing in front of that chair. She reminds me of the Lorax or one of those tree-huggers who chain themselves to a tree to fight off the mighty evil corporations who are intent on demolishing it.

As I find my way to an empty chair, I turn and peer over my shoulder, watching The Activist twirl her dishwater blonde hair around her finger like it's a piece of thread. Buckley closes the door, and my view of her is gone.

His office is full of accolades: certificates of achievement and pictures of him with people who I assume are a big deal since he's showing them off like they are. There's a framed photo of him and his family, and the family pet, a Siamese cat. The photo of him and his family is facing the opposite side of his desk, which is strange considering he doesn't get to peek at it. I guess I'm supposed to feel comfortable and willing to warm up to him because I see he loves cats and is a family man.

"I'm sorry you had to bear witness to that earlier incident," he says. The roots of his hair are white but the rest is a reddish brown. Upon further inspection, I see his mustache is also dyed. "As you heard, we have a low tolerance for disrespect." He rambles on about house rules and such – things I'm supposed to do, like keep my nose out of trouble and dress appropriately. Do my work. Mind my P's and Q's. Be on the up and up.

"You'll find this is different from being homeschooled," he adds. "We have rules that must be followed."

I refrain from rolling my eyes at him, but I can't help but have the typical teenage reaction. When adults start adulting me and talking at me instead of to me, it irks me. It's like they forgot they were once young.

"We have an elevator," he says.

"I can climb the stairs," I say, which is true, but you know how slow a New Orleans funeral is? That's about the speed I run when climbing.

"He'll need extra time," Mom interjects. Why does she do this? Sure, I move slower than the average guy, and I burn half the amount of energy than someone with two working legs, but this—having these type of requests made for me like I'm a special case—isn't what I wanted.

"Certainly," he says. "We will accommodate you as best as we can."

The thing is, I don't want to be accommodated. I want to blend in. This was kind of the whole point in me being here.

"How long do the students have to get to class after lunch?" I ask.

"Five minutes, but," and he leans forward like we're sharing some kind of secret, "we can certainly give you more time should you need it."

"No, five minutes ought to do it. If I'm late to class, it's not because of this." I tap on my thigh, then look him square in his shifty eyes.

"Well, we will see how it goes." He forces another disingenuous smile at me, then proceeds to speak to my mother like I'm a nonentity.

After a few more minutes of discussion, he ushers us out of his office. "Mrs. Sims will meet with you shortly to schedule you," he says. I nudge my mom to leave because it's bad enough having her walk in the school with me like I'm a little boy on his first day in kindergarten. It makes me feel like a big pansy. She fights me to stay, but I'm pretty persuasive when I want to be. So, she reluctantly hands me a ten dollar bill and leaves the school.

The Activist is standing against the wall, waiting. I catch her looking at me. "Did he offer you some sage advice?" she asks me. Her eyes dart toward Buckley then back at me. She's chewing gum like those girls in the movies who have "the tude." "He's great at giving advice."

I doubt the sincerity of that statement.

I don't answer her because he is standing within earshot and my snarky reply wouldn't give a good impression.

She places her right hand on her right hip. "I'm sure he relayed the rules. Their sticklers about rules around here. Can't do this. Can't do that. Half the school is addicted to prescription drugs, but as long as they're dressed appropriately it doesn't matter," she says loud enough for everyone in the office to hear. She blows a bubble, then it deflates, touching her lips. All I can think is, I want to be that gum.

"Miss Huxley, stop fraternizing with the other students," Buckley says. He turns to face me. "Mrs. Sims is ready to meet with you now." Everyone is a mister or misses with Buckley. I bet when he comes home from work he greets his wife by saying, "Hello, Mrs. Buckley." During the Victorian period it was common for people to address each other by their last name, but in today's age, isn't it a bit pretentious? I gather the sentiment is supposed to convey respect, that I am supposed to feel respected because I'm being called by my last name, and in turn, have to address him by his. But give a man a suit, comb his hair and call him Mr. So and So, if he's a jerk, he's still a jerk. Like a turd on a silver platter.

She ignores him and continues speaking to me, "Anyway, what's your story?" She moves closer to me and waits for me to answer. "We already know you've got a staring problem." She gives me a sly grin. Is she flirting, or is she doing it to piss me off? I'm not good at reading signals, especially from women, who seem like they're another species... because they are.

"I was just trying to figure out what I was looking at," I tell her before being escorted into the counselor's office.

CHAPTER 3

One of the worst things about being new is not knowing what to expect. Everyone else is going on about their business, and I'm trying to figure out which way is up. Another bad thing about being new: walking in late to class. It's one thing to slyly sneak in before the bell rings and find a seat in the back all suave so no one notices you, but to come traipsing in a good hour after class has been in session is like I'm skywriting my presence. "Hello! I'm here! Everyone look at me!"

I open the door and silence fills the classroom. Mr. Marshall, the teacher, shoots me an annoyed look because I've just interrupted his important lesson, then glances down at me, noticing the leg. His expression changes, because I guess people aren't supposed to be mad at people like me. Whatever. I hate it when people treat me differently just because they think I'm delicate.

All eyes are on me, and I hear a few hushed voices. I hand him the schedule Mrs. Sims gave me. He reads it, making sure I haven't made a mistake about my whereabouts and says, "Nice to have you in class, Beckett." He gives me back the piece of paper. I fold it and slip it in my pocket.

"It's Trip," I tell him.

"Trip?" He twitches his long pointy nose, and a line of wrinkles form across his forehead. "That's different."

I don't get into the specifics about where the name came from. No need to elaborate.

"Why don't you have a seat next to Oliver?" He points to the one empty desk in the back of the bright, colorful classroom. Posters cover every inch: some are the kinds that are supposed to pump you up or make you feel inspired to get out there and do something (give it the old college try and whatnot); others are math-related with quotes like, "Three out of two people have trouble with fractions." Haha. I'm not much for math humor. Is anyone? Maybe Stephen Hawking or some other genius.

The guy, who I assume is Oliver, gives me a subtle head nod—the kind that most guys give because we'll look like jerks if we wave Miss America style. Usually, this kind of nod is accompanied by a fist bump and a "What's up, boss?" or "Hey, bro!" Two terms I've never used. A boss is a person you work for, and a bro is an actual blood relation. Why do guys do it?

I know his face from somewhere. He's grinning at me like he knows me, too. I'm trying to make the connection, but my memory is failing me. I don't get out much, and it's not like my social life is thriving with lots of activity. I'm not even that active on social media. Well, by not active, I mean I'm not on it.

I walk down the narrow aisle. The desks are really close to each other. It's like one of those scenes in the movies where everyone is watching me even though the teacher has gone back to teaching. I should catwalk or strut or do something fanciful (yes, I just used that word), but I'm too busy looking down, avoiding a landmine of backpacks making sure I don't trip.

I maneuver myself into the seat. The desk hits my legs. Did I mention I'm tall? Being tall is not all it's cracked up to be. Try finding pants that don't hit you at the ankles or sitting in a Mini Cooper. Or getting fitted for a prosthesis. It's a shitshow for sure.

He nudges me. I turn and look at him. "Psst. Hey," he whispers. "I know you. You're that guy who's got the leprosy."

I make a surprised face. Leprosy? Hmm. "I think you're

confusing me with someone else."

"No," he shakes his head emphatically. "You're Trisha and Beck's son. I deliver hamburger meat to them dogs of yours. Right spoiled dogs if you ask me." His Southern twang is strong, and he's got hat hair. There's a John Deere ball cap attached to his belt loop, and he's wearing a faded t-shirt and a pair of scuffed leather boots. Stereotype aisle four.

"Your dogs eat better than I do," Oliver goes on.

He's come to our house to deliver meat for our ten German shepherds. That's right, ten. We had twelve at one time, but once they're trained and fit to be placed, they leave us. I don't take part in my parents' dog training shenanigans. Nor do I weep when the dogs leave.

These dogs learn commands in German, Dutch, and French. Evidently, German shepherds are multilingual or are capable of learning basic words in many languages. You want to have low self-esteem? Try standing next to a German shepherd while your mom's barking commands in Dutch and see the dog react while you scratch your head in confusion.

Mom and Dad's business is a lucrative one. I guess because there aren't too many people who are multilingual like they are and want to spend that much time with furry creatures who piss and shit all of the time.

"Whatcha you doing here anyway?" he asks me.

"Getting enlightened."

He shoots me a look. "Nah, I meant, why are you *here*? I thought you were holed up in that mansion of yours 'cause of the leprosy."

What is it with leprosy? I doubt he knows what it means because if he did, he'd be hauling ass away from me. And, I'd hardly call our house a mansion, but when you live in a two-story Italian-style villa, while some of the others are plain ranch style homes or double wides, then, yeah, I guess someone might view it as a mansion.

"I get out," I defend.

He gives me a skeptical look. "I never see you at the lake or in town." He leans back into his chair and folds his arms across his chest. "You've been locked up in that house, haven't you?"

"It's a requirement when you're in witness protection," I tell him, hoping he catches the sarcasm, which he does because he lets out a loud, boisterous laugh, which makes Mr. Marshall glare our way.

"Boys," Mr. Marshall says to us. "Quiet."

We immediately stop talking since he's the type of man you don't want to mess around with and start paying attention to his lesson. When the bell rings for lunch, I get up and follow the crowd outside.

Cattle move in herds; so do America's high school students. I'm surprised we're not all mooing our way down the hall as we head toward our troth. Some students stop in the middle of the hall to gossip, forgetting that there are people who are trying to pass them by. Others make out by their lockers like they're in the back seat of their cars. It's either a sign of too much testosterone or being an exhibitionist. I'm not sure which. I mean, if I had a girlfriend, sure I'd want to kiss her, but I wouldn't be shoving my tongue down her throat in front of a bunch of people with one minute to spare until my next class. Kissing is like an art; it takes time, at least with me it will.

"Hey," I hear a voice shouting from behind me. I turn and see Oliver jogging toward me. "You left this in class." He hands me my textbook. I didn't open it once in class. Not that I'm oozing with massive intelligence but the lesson Mr. Marshall was teaching was rudimentary. "You'd be surprised how often textbooks get stolen around here then you end up paying a butt load."

"Thanks," I say.

"So, where are you going? The cafeteria's that way." He nods at a few people and gives a high five to a guy who is dressed just like him only a Clemson Tigers hat is dangling from his belt loop. He becomes distracted by a redhead passing us by. "You're looking real nice today, Jessica." He turns his attention back to me after he watches her walk away.

"The library," I answer.

"The library," he scoffs. "You can't go in there."

"Why? I read. That's where the books are."

His expression is filled with alarm. He leans close to me and says with a serious expression, "Never eat in the library. That's one big losers table, and it's as bad as eating in the john, got it?" He gives me a confident nod like he's just saved me from impending death, or worse, social isolation. "You want a shitty senior year? Eat in the land of misfits." He rolls his shoulders, then reads my blank face, because I'm trying to understand how reading a book in the library can make me a misfit. "I'm just trying to help," he says. "Can't have you learnin' the hard way. You're comin' with me." He juts his chin in the direction of the cafeteria. I follow him like a duckling following its mother because what other choice do I have in this situation?

I see The Activist storming down the hallway being escorted by a man who's wearing a cheap suit and tie. How do I know it's cheap? The sheen on the fabric. It's polyester. Not that I'm some fashionista because I'm not. I'm more of a shorts and t-shirt type of guy. The prosthesis makes wearing jeans or any pants for that matter a real bitch. Anyway, I'm obsessed with natural fabrics and swore off polyester because it's synthetic.

"BB," she calls. "Get my assignments for me while I'm out, will you?"

"They suspended you? In summer school? I didn't think they did that," he says. "What'd you do this time?"

"One word: Katelyn!" she says. She looks over at me, then says to BB, "You making friends with the Pink Floyd fan?"

"Yeah," BB says. "His name is Trip."

"Some people here are friendly," I say, trying to emphasize that she, in fact, is not.

She laughs, then flips her braid off of her shoulder. "I'm not trying to win Miss Congeniality."

"Clearly," I say. "Or you'd live a life full of disappointment."

CHAPTER 4

Cafeteria food. You can't blame the lunchroom ladies because it's not their fault that the food is bad. It's probably ridden with ingredients strong enough to kill even the mightiest of humans. The government regulates what we eat. They seem to be the experts on nutrition. Ha. That's a laugh. I don't trust the government to fix our roads let alone tell me what to ingest.

I try not to twist my lips when the woman scoops a heap of slop-like gravy and mashed potatoes onto my plate.

"Want the steak, too?" she asks. A hair net covers her gray curly hair.

If that's steak then I'm Adam Levine. "No, thanks," I say. "Just the carrots."

She places a plethora of carrots on my plate and offers me a toothy smile. "They're good for you. Make your eyesight stronger."

She is actually correct with her statement: carrots are high in vitamin A, which is essential for good vision. But, given the butter and salt she added, I don't think these carrots are going to make my vision equivalent to Superman's.

I move my way down this line, feeling all eyes are on me or maybe I'm just being paranoid. They must not get many new students, or maybe it's because most of the students stick to eating the pizza or nachos and I'm eating from the hot food section.

I pay, then scan the cafeteria, searching for Oliver. He's standing up near the end of a long table, animatedly telling a story. He flings his arms in the air and the rest of his bunch laugh in unison. All of his friends look the same: ball cap attached to belt loop, denim jeans, t-shirt, and boots.

"Trip," he says with a smile. "You made it."

"I struggled at the moat, but I made it here unscathed," I say. He and his friends give me a clueless look, then something clicks because Oliver starts laughing.

"You're funny." He points at me. "Join us." He gestures to the empty seat beside him.

I have a seat and face the rest of the bunch, who all look like they belong in a John Deere catalog. They introduce themselves, and I won't remember their names because there are too many: Austin, Cody, Tommy, John, Logan. I can't remember the rest.

"So, where are you from?" one asks with a mouth full of cheesy pizza.

"Here," I say, which is mostly true. I wasn't born here but I've lived here for most of my life so that should make me an honorary native.

He gives me a skeptical look like I'm lying. "You ain't from around here. I've never seen you. And you talk funny."

Pot calling the kettle black.

"What are you doing here?" one of them asks me.

"He's taking statistics," Oliver answers before I can. "I deliver meat to his parents. They're the ones who train the dogs," he whispers loudly.

"Oh," they all say in unison. I guess the dogs are a hot topic of conversation amongst high school students.

"He doesn't have leprosy," BB says to them.

I guess they were pooling bets on my supposed illnesses.

"So, what ails you?" one of the Cody's asks.

"Too much tryptophan," I say.

A wrinkle forms across his forehead, but he doesn't ask me any other questions.

I lean close to BB and ask, "Why is everyone calling you 'BB'?"

"For Butterbean," he answers.

My brow furrows. This ought to be interesting. "Why Butterbean?"

"When I was in second grade, I brought a can of butter beans for lunch 'cause we were so poor. It was all we had in the pantry," he explains with a sad expression. "Ever since then it's stuck even though I don't eat butter beans no more."

"So, should I call you BB?" I ask.

"Might as well," he says and takes a bite of his peanut butter and jelly sandwich. Grape jelly oozes onto his fingers. He licks each grimy finger then chews. "I can't believe you're here. When I'd see you creeping from behind the curtains, I figured you had something wrong with you." He peers down at my leg. "What happened to you?"

Loaded question of the year. Short and to the point, too. I don't mind it, though. Most people skirt around my leg and act like they can't discuss it, but when it's the big fat elephant in the room they're better off announcing it's there. Or not there.

"Long story. I'll tell you some time," I say, evasively.

He gives me another nod. His lips curve upward, taking up half of his round face. It's the kind of smile mothers trust. The kind that could allow him to get anything he wanted if he tried. The kind that's harmless and unassuming.

"Why'd you come here?" he asks. This is his failed attempt at interrogation. I guess I don't blame him. If I saw some guy hiding in his house, then all of a sudden he came out to go to school, I'd wonder about him, too.

"The government would have been after my parents if I hadn't," I say.

He swallows. "Ha, ha. No, come on, what made you come here? To school?"

I shrug. "I was tired of being homeschooled."

His eyes light up. "I'd give anything to be homeschooled."

This surprises me. "Really? Why?"

He forms a mischievous grin. "I'd build my own creative curriculum: hunting and fishing class, for one."

"It doesn't really work that way," I say. "There are regulations."

He shrugs. "I'd find a way. I bet you took some creative liberties." He gives me a nudge.

"Nothing like hunting and fishing, but I took a snorkeling class once." One of the few "daring" things I've ever done. I wish there was more, like skydiving and swimming with sharks or other daredevil adventures, but I've got overprotective parents, and truth be told, although I want to be that guy, the one who does all of that stuff, I'm just a regular person underneath who isn't one for taking chances. Coming to this school is the biggest risk I've taken in a long time.

He leans in and whispers, "Wouldn't that be hard with that leg?" His eyes dart down to my left leg.

"It isn't easy, but it can be done."

He gives me a look of amazement.

I roll my shoulders because I'm not into this "You're amazing" type of look he's giving me right now because I'm not one to be marveled at.

I take a bite of my carrots, which taste like butter and mush. I know there is no such thing as tasting like mush, but that's the only word I can come up with to describe the wretchedness of this supposed vegetable.

"You shouldn't eat that. Your shit will glow in the dark," he says.

"I think I'll brown bag it tomorrow."

"Smart choice," he says with an approving nod.

"Hey, BB!" one of the Cody's or Austin's shouts. "Is it true Millicent cursed out Buckley?"

BB waves his hand down, dismissing him. "Nah. She shoved Katelyn."

"I don't blame her; Katelyn's mean," he responds, and the rest of the troop shake their heads in agreement.

So Millicent is The Activist's name. "Are you two dating?" I ask him. Why do I even care? Why do I even care!!!? Argh.

He makes a squeamish face and emits a gagging sound. "No way! Mellie's my cousin," he says. "She's alright lookin' I 'spose, but most of the guys around here don't like her so much since she's a bit opinionated. I think they're scared of her."

I'm not surprised to hear this.

"She has her causes. Last year, she was in a protest when the state cut teachers' retirements. Ain't no kids our age who care about that, but she does," he says. "She's really smart," he goes on, defending her. "She's probably going to be valedictorian." He makes a proud papa face. "That's why she's here in summer school: to get ahead. Meanwhile, I'm here out of necessity, like the majority of us." He points to his friends. "We took too many days off during huntin' season," he says. "You want me, to," and he leans close again and juts his chin, "you know, talk to Mellie for you?"

I read his meaning loud and clear. I shake my head vigorously and say emphatically, "No, thanks. I'm fine on my own."

He laughs. "Said a man who's sailing on the river of denial."

***

I stand outside the school with the other students who are waiting for their ride because they're either too young to get a driver's license or they don't have a car. I'm in the shade, trying to hide from the sun, but I'm still hot. Sweat pours down my entire body. My shirt is soaked through and through. I'll melt if my mother doesn't get here soon. The heat and I don't mix very well. Like oil and water or sugar and salt. Or whatever other bad combination you can drum up. It's my leg. When I get hot, my residual limb (the little part of me that's left) shrinks, which isn't good because then my socket can get loose. A prosthesis is meant to be tight fitting. One that isn't is a problem. A problem like tumbling to the ground because you can't walk. Been there, done that. Not hoping to repeat this one-act play today, but I just might.

I'm probably the only senior standing out here. Like me, most of them have that freshman-new-to-high-school look about them, except I have stubble on my face and hair on my chest and nethers. I am a good foot taller than some of them, too. I'd asked to drive myself to school, but Mom and Dad are sticklers about their cars. It's an act of Congress to even borrow theirs. I think it has more to do with fear from my mom's end. She's afraid I'll get into an accident.

The long line of cars fades away, and it's just me sweating my balls off and some short freshman who's drenched from standing right in the sun's path. He keeps his head down low, staring intently at his phone.

I text my mom. *Where R U???*

She takes five whole minutes to respond. *I'm so sorry. Someone is interested in Chumley. Be there as soon as I can.*

Chumley is one of their German shepherds. One that responds to commands in French and can fetch the newspaper and do other miraculous tricks that people get a kick out of. I'm not so easily duped by these balls of fur. Their brains are still half the size of a human's, and they shit where they eat.

I begin to text a response, which includes a whole bunch of exclamation points and all capital letters. That might not be such a good idea, so I delete it before I'm tempted to click "send."

"Hey, Trip," I hear him call me. He beeps the horn before I can even look up from my phone.

When I do, I see BB sitting in a light blue 1980s era Volkswagen Beetle. Not the car I pictured him driving. Not the music I imagined him listening to, either. It's rap. Old school rap.

I amble slowly toward him, feeling the difference in my stride. My leg feels unsteady. This isn't good.

I try not to think about it and lean down into the passenger side, palms flat against the hot door. Ouch. I bring them to my sides, hoping I'll keep steady. He turns down the volume on his radio. Now I can barely hear The Sugar Hill Gang.

"Whatcha doing out here standing around?"

"Losing weight."

He gives me a strange look, then catches my sarcasm. "You need a lift?"

"Ahh, that's okay."

"I don't mind. Your house isn't too far out of my way."

My phone vibrates in my pocket. It's another text from Mom. *It'll probably be another half hour. So sorry.*

Another half hour? By that time I'll be sopping wet. I text her back. *Don't worry about it. Found a ride.*

I pocket my phone, feeling it vibrate. I'm sure my mom texted me back all giddy because I am making friends.

"You know what? I'll take you up on your offer."

"Get in," he says.

CHAPTER 5

BB shouts over the blaring music. The bass thumps loudly from his speakers, which fill up the entire backseat bench and look brand spanking new, especially in comparison to the hunk of junk he's driving. I'm surprised he was able to get it to start. I think the car might be older than my mom. The engine sputters along as he speeds down the two-lane road. He bops his head to the music and taps one hand against the steering wheel. He's out of sync, but that doesn't seem to bother him.

"I got to stop at Mellie's house before I drop you off," he says.

He checks his phone and reads a text, swerving the car from one side of the road to the other. I grip the armrest, holding on for my dear life. He looks over my way and laughs.

"Relax. I ain't going to kill you."

Somehow I doubt that.

He peers down at his phone, reading his text; meanwhile, the car is drifting into the other lane. I assume his wheels need to be aligned.

"Car," I tell him, trying to keep my voice calm.

He glances up and jerks the steering wheel again, moving us back into the proper lane. He drops his phone into his lap.

"I should tell you..." he begins and sips on his bottle of Coke, "Mellie lives in a commune."

Commune? Who lives in a commune in this day and age? All I can picture is Woodstock, which leads me to imagine her sans shirt..., which leads me to think of the slogan, "Make love, not war."

"They're not the kind of hippies who dance around naked and

smoke weed, though."

I fight a frown.

"Just some peaceful folk that live off the land," he explains, interrupting my dirty thoughts. "They're out in the sticks, but it's a right nice piece of property if you ask me. A bunch of developers has been slithering around for years trying to get them to sell, but they'll die there before they do that."

He turns right onto a dirt road, flanked by overgrown trees. I bounce from the potholes and hit my head on the roof of the car.

"There's another thing..." he begins, and I wait for him to continue. "Mellie's got two moms. They're, uh," and he clears his throat, "together."

I shrug. "Okay."

He smiles. "I knew you was a good egg." He turns his attention to the road. "Some people got issues with that. But love is love if you ask me."

The music continues to drown out everything else, and as we continue down the isolated road, I begin to sense we're really not near anything. "You taking me out here to kill me?" I ask.

He laughs. "I told you they lived way out there."

He continues driving another mile before pulling up next to a maroon station wagon covered in grime and resting on four cinder blocks. It would take more than a thorough washing to make it look better. The back window is covered in dirt with the exception of the words "Wash Me."

A horseshoe of houses—all different and distinct from one another—face Spoonwood Lake. I'm sure that's why BB said developers want their property. It's vast, and the lake is beautiful – jade in color and large, must be one of the biggest in the state.

Actually, it might be the biggest. I'll search on Google later.

One of the homes is a red caboose; the one next to it seems fit for a garden gnome or Smurf. It's a mishmash of homes, if I ever saw any. A garden with a burlap scarecrow complete with denim overalls and a straw hat stands off to the left side of the eclectic housing units, and a timber frame structure towers over the tiny homes. Rows of sunflowers fill the horizon, with a assortment of wildflowers interspersed amongst them.

The Activist is tilling the garden and wearing a yellow bikini top and a pair of cut off denim shorts. I try not to gawk, and BB notices my poor attempt at avoidance. "Sure you don't want me to talk to her?" He waggles his bushy brows, moving his cap up and down along with them.

I decide it's best not to answer.

We get out of his car, and he turns toward the garden, shouting, "I have your book and assignments!"

"I see that!" she shouts back. Sunflowers surround her. If it didn't come across as creepy, I'd whip out my phone and take a snapshot.

"What do you want me to do with them?"

"That's a loaded question," she teases. "Put them in my room!"

"A please would suffice," he says.

A Rubenesque-shaped woman with wild salt and pepper hair wearing a Hawaiian printed mumu comes out to greet us. Her name is Maria, but she's called Mama Sauce, because, according to BB, "She makes the best damn spaghetti sauce in the whole wide world." She's all smiles and asks who I am.

"This here is Trip," BB tells her. "The one I thought had the leprosy."

She scrutinizes me. "Well, we can see he doesn't have leprosy." She turns her attention toward The Activist and says, "Mellie, get over here and quit being so rude!"

"I'm working," she says.

"Working," she scoffs. "As if that's ever stopped you. Get. Over. Here." She waves her hand vigorously. By the scowl on her face and another, "Get over here now," it's obvious another, "I'm working" won't suit her.

The Activist reluctantly comes our way. She's covered in dirt, and I'm making sure I don't stare so she doesn't call me out again. I look instead at everything else; there's a lot to distract me even if she's half-naked. Okay, honestly, it takes a lot of effort not to look at her. The homeschool association group I was in only had two females: one was quite a bit younger than me; the other had a dandruff problem. I can get past a lot of things, but when a person wears black and is adorned in white flakes like it's snowing outside, well, it's hard not to be repulsed.

"There's rumors going around about you," BB says to her.

"They're all true of course."

"Even the one about you standing over Katelyn and spitting on her."

Mama Sauce shoots her a disapproving look. "We didn't raise you to be this heartless," she says with a tsk-tsk - the kind only mothers can give.

"As if I'd waste my saliva on her." Millicent folds her arms against her chest. "I see you brought company," she says, looking at me. "Enjoying the scenery?" She's tongue in cheek, relishing in her quip. Mama Sauce shoots her a look catching onto her obvious meaning, which does little to rattle her.

I don't answer since her mom is here. But yes, Millicent in a bikini top is great scenery. Who needs Zion National Park?

"Y'all want to stay for dinner?" Mama Sauce asks us. "I made macaroni."

BB leans over to whisper to me and says, "She's a good cook. You don't want to turn her down."

"That's okay," I say, not wanting to impose.

BB shoots me a look. "You never turn down Mama Sauce's cooking," he says with a stern-you-better-agree kind of tone.

"Okay," I relent.

"Come on inside." She beams, waving us toward the timber frame building. Isn't this the way those horror films begin: some unsuspecting buffoon walks into a commune by invite only to find he is going to be slaughtered?

"What'd Katelyn do?" BB asks Millicent in a whisper.

"She said something derogatory about Mama Sauce and Mom. I just couldn't ignore it this time," she whispers back.

"That's what I figured," he lets out a disappointed sigh. "She's going around the school telling everyone you're mad 'cause she's dating Jake now."

She rolls her eyes at this. "Let them have each other."

I'm so busy eavesdropping and wondering who Jake is that I don't look down when I'm walking and plummet to the ground.

CHAPTER 6

I'm laying on the dirt, staring directly at the culprit: a rock. And I thought the summer heat would be the cause of my demise. Mama Sauce is hovering over me with a look of concern like I might die. BB offers me his hand, and I take it, holding tight, as I get myself off of the ground.

"Thanks," I tell him.

He slightly nods and doesn't fawn over me like Mama Sauce is.

"Are you okay?" Mama Sauce asks. She pats me on my shoulders.

"I'm fine." I brush the dirt off of me.

"You gave us a scare," she says.

I don't tell them all that this isn't my first rodeo. I've fallen plenty. So many times, in fact, I'm tempted to raise my hands up high in the air like gymnasts do when they land after doing a summersault. This one gets a seven. My ten was downtown Asheville. Hills and heat are my worst enemy.

"Come inside for something cool to drink. I'll get some bandages for those hands of yours," she says.

When I fall, I still make the mistake of landing hands first. You'd think that years of practice would make perfect, but I must be dense since I keep doing it. Even after all of this time. My wrists don't work too great now—thanks for a bad fall years ago—the ten I was talking about. That's the one that sealed the deal - the deal of doom. Dun, dun, dun. Anyway, sometimes my wrists get out of whack and crack too much the way senior citizens do only I'm not eligible for AARP.

I glance down at my hands, noticing a few scrapes and trickling blood.

"We'll get you cleaned up good," Mama Sauce says.

The room is a broad, airy space: wall-to-wall pine paneling and pine floors filled with all kinds of folk art. Red cabinets cover one wall, which seems to be the designated kitchen area. The countertops are made out of concrete, and an island constructed from bamboo faces the black stove and refrigerator.

A brown suede sofa sits off to one side of the room, facing a bookshelf filled with board games, folk art figurines, and face jugs. There's a glass coffee table sitting on top of a sisal rug, and a few beanbags and a leather chair and ottoman are across from the couch. There are also a few relics from the 1970s: a papasan chair and macrame plant holders.

Mama Sauce points for me to have a seat around their long rectangular dining table. The table is made of strips of wood nailed together. All of the wood appears to be from different types of trees because the grain and color aren't the same. A bouquet of wildflowers centers it in a ceramic vase, which looks homemade with its imperfections and overuse of bright colors—like an art project from elementary school.

I have a seat and let her have at it. She douses alcohol on my hands, then pours peroxide—because I guess she was aiming to kill me by fumes alone—then applies an ointment to them before wrapping me up in bandages.

"All better now," she says and wipes her hands together, forming a self-satisfied smile.

BB made himself at home and is sprawled on the couch. He's kicked off his boots and his bare feet dangle over the arm.

"Thanks," I say and hear snoring. "Is he asleep?" My eyes dart to BB.

"Probably so. Every time he comes over here he takes a nap. I think his parents work him too hard." I hear a slight tsk-tsk come from her thin, wrinkled lips.

Speaking of parents, I text my mom. *Eating dinner with hippies. See you later tonight.*

She texts me right back. *???*

I text back: *I'll explain later. Son fed and socializing. Be happy. Or be like ET: be good.*

She texts me back: *:)*

The word *emoji* comes from the Japanese because it has a picture and character in it. Regardless of its origin, the fact that people use these in their messages to one another is stupid, but Mom likes them.

I pocket my phone. Millicent is standing off in the corner, watching us. I raise a brow, looking at her, and she mimics my expression, then opens the refrigerator. She grabs a pop. I know they're called sodas, or, here in the South it's Coke even if it's (god forbid) a Pepsi, but my parents are from the midwest. Well, so am I, and the vernacular rubbed off on me.

"Trip, you want something to drink? Mellie can fix you something," Mama Sauce says.

I sit back with my arms folded across my chest, enjoying this little moment of servitude. I hear her breathing from where I sit, and that's a good twenty feet.

"Want something?" she asks without much enthusiasm.

"Sure," I say.

"Well…." she taps her fingers impatiently against the counter, holding the refrigerator door open.

"Strawberry milk," I say.

First of all, strawberry milk is not high on my favorites list, but I'm doing this just because it's a pain to make, and I noticed the box of Nestle Quick Strawberry on their shelf. I haven't had strawberry milk since I was a kid. Nostalgia and all that.

As I hear her grumble, an older woman and man join us at the table. Their black mutt of a dog rushes up to me, places his paws on my leg and begs for a pat on the head. I oblige, then face the rest of the aging troop of hippies.

"Hi," I say to them. They're staring at me curiously.

"This is Trip," Mama Sauce says to them. "Trip, this is Myrna and Snuff. They live here, too," she explains to me.

Myrna and Snuff look as if they've been around the block, maybe ridden the hard road and have come back again. Like hippie bikers, if there is such a thing. Snuff's wearing a leather vest over his Waffle House t-shirt with a pair of grimy jeans, and Myrna is sporting a tank top and short shorts, like short enough that Mr. Buckley would send her home for a wardrobe change. A paisley scarf covers most of her white hair. She gives me a toothy smile, and I see that cigarettes and a lot of coffee have left their permanent mark.

I ask Snuff how he got his name. He said he's had it so long he doesn't remember, so I leave it alone. He asks me about mine and concludes that Trip is a much more suitable name for me than Beckett.

"We had the best ride today," Snuff says, shaking his long gray shaggy hair. He's got a handlebar mustache that curls up every time his lips move. "You ride?" he asks me.

"On a horse?" I ask.

They all laugh.

"Motorcycle," he explains.

"No," I say. It'd be tough with the leg, and I'm not one for sitting on death traps. Motorcycles have a higher fatality rate than automobiles. And automobiles have a higher death rate than airplanes. If I were rich, I would travel by a private jet.

"You ought to try it some time. It's the most freeing feeling in the world," he says, looking off into the distance with a glint in his blue eyes. "Like pissing out in the woods or skinny dipping." He focuses back on me. "You Millicent's boyfriend? You seem nicer than the last one."

"No, Snuff," Millicent says like I'm the most repulsive human being ever to grace her presence. "He's BB's friend."

I glance over at her and watch her add a heap of strawberry Quick—more than needed, but beggars can't be choosers—then she pours in the milk. She clanks the spoon against the glass deliberately, then comes my way.

"Here you go," she says, glaring. "Would you like anything else? Maybe a neck massage?"

"A neck massage would be great!" I say and point to the left side of my neck, side glancing her. "I am kind of stiff."

She lets out a low grunt and heads toward the door. "I have to study," she huffs.

"Dinner will be ready in thirty minutes," Mama Sauce says. "Don't be late."

"You sure do know how to get her goat," Myrna says to me after Millicent leaves the room.

I shrug with indifference. The term "getting one's goat" comes from horse racing when goats were placed in horse stalls to calm the horse down before a big race. It's an odd expression and I'm surprised that people use it.

"Might want to take it easy on her; she's sensitive underneath all that pit bull exterior," Mama Sauce says. "So, how'd you and BB meet?"

I tell them about my first day of school. They listen intently, asking a lot of questions to keep the conversation going. Even though there's a big age gap between us, they're easy to talk to. I guess because they're good communicators, and I tend to communicate better with the silver foxes than people my own age because I'm an old soul - at least that is what I've been told.

"And after all of this time, you decided to immerse yourself back in public education?" Myrna asks. "How brave."

"I wanted... well, I wanted to see what I was missing."

She smiles, then Snuff, who I assume is her partner or husband, says, "We all wonder what we're missing, but rarely do we have the guts to see what that is."

***

Evidently, when Mama Sauce said macaroni, she meant pasta and she calls sauce, "gravy." We're eating baked ziti with meatballs. My stomach is begging for me to stop chowing down, but the rest of me says, "I want! I want!"

BB wasn't lying when he said she could cook. The smell alone makes my mouth water, but the taste, the taste is out-of-this-world-good. She could put Olive Garden out of business.

Millicent's biological mom, Anna, joined us. She's beautiful – an older spitting image of Millicent, who everyone calls Mellie. Anna strikes me as one of those tingsha clinking types who practices tai chi in the morning and only eats organic foods because everything else is filled with toxins. She's wearing white pants and a white tank top, and her graying dishwater blonde hair is tied up into a loose bun. She smiles a lot, but not in a creepy psycho way, more like a serene-genuine-i'm-truly-happy-way.

"I'm writing a letter to that Mr. Buckley to let him know my thoughts on his Puritan dress code policy. It's a sundress, not a bikini," Anna says to Mama Sauce.

"It won't do any good," Mama Sauce says.

"You have to start somewhere; I highly doubt Elizabeth Cady Stanton said the same, Maria."

"You had to throw ole Stanton in the mix, didn't you?"

"Yes," she says with a sly smile.

"Mom," Millicent interrupts. "He's dogmatic; I don't think your letter will all of a sudden change policy."

Anna places her hands on Millicent's shoulders and says, "Never, ever give up. You might have done wrong by shoving that mean-spirited girl, but your education should not be sacrificed because some skin is showing."

"Sometimes mean-spirited people deserve reciprocal action."

"Violence never solves anything."

"It made her shut up; I was doing society a favor," Millicent retorts.

I hear Anna breathe heavily but she says nothing in response. I fight a laugh because it is funny how much alike she and Millicent are: they both grunt when they're angry.

Anna turns to face me and says, "Tell us about yourself, Trip."

She asks me a lot of questions about myself. Actually, most of the hippies seem curious about me. Where I'm from. Where I've been. Where I'm going.

"Why did your parents choose to homeschool you for so long?"

Mama Sauce asks. Anna shoots her a warning look.

"It's okay," I say. "They have a crazy travel schedule, so they needed flexibility when it came to me." I don't mention the other reasons… the obvious reasons, at least to me but maybe not to the rest of the world. Some things are better kept as secrets.

"Did you enjoy it?" Anna asks. She leans forward, cupping a ceramic mug. They made hot tea for all of us after dinner even though it's a sauna outside and we're all stuffed, but I'm still sipping on it anyway.

"At times," I say. "It allowed for creativity in the curriculum. My music classes were taught by Josie Hobbs." I don't want to sound like a braggart and regret saying this the moment the words leave my mouth. Now I sound like a name dropper, and name droppers are never cool.

Anna gives me a knowing look and doesn't seem to be giving me the stink eye someone would give a bragging douche, so I guess I'm good.

"She was big back in my time. She ended up marrying her drummer."

"Chic," I add. "He's a good guy."

"Yes," she says. "He had quite a few hits, too."

"They're both really talented and still produce music, but they're busy running The Maple Tree Inn," I say. "She taught me how to play the piano."

Anna claps her hands together. "You have to play for us then!"

I get all bashful and wave my hand down. "That's okay."

"We insist," she says, and I see the rest of the aging hippies are shaking their heads in unison. "No one ever plays it. I bought it for Maria years ago, but she's more intent on honing her cooking skills."

She smiles at Mama Sauce who pats her belly. "The piano would be better for my health."

I get up from the table and amble to the piano. It's not a baby grand, and by the looks of the yellowing keys, it probably hasn't been tuned or played in a long while. I sit on the bench and look at up them. They're circled around me like we're in a pub and I'm about to be their main source for entertainment - even Millicent, who's peeking at me from the throng of patchouli-scented folk. Maybe I should grab a bowl from the cupboard to hint for tips.

I can read music well, but the playing part isn't my strength. I'm more of a writer than a player. Or a lover more than a fighter. Actually, I'll let you in on a little secret: I'm kind of a novice when it comes to the loving part, but I'm sure if I found someone to love, I'd be one hell of a lover.

I tap the G key, then hit B twice, then C, and they instantly know what I'm playing.

"Blister In The Sun!" Anna says with excitement. "I love this song!" My music teacher was a teen in the 1980s, so she made a point to teach me all of the music from that decade.

Anna starts humming, then the rest of them start singing the lyrics, even BB, who should never quit his day job, neither should Anna, but she's singing louder than them all like this is Carnegie Hall.

And before I'm finished with the song, they're all belting out the lyrics word-for-word, which makes me bob my head and really get into it. That's another secret I should let you in on: I look like a weirdo when I play. Like I'm having a seizure or something. That's usually why I stick to writing music.

When I finish, they clap and hoot and holler, like I've just made their week. Mama Sauce pats me on the back and tells me I've done a good job.

"You're good," BB says, but people say that when they have nothing to compare something to.

Josie, my piano teacher, told me in the most gentle and respectful way that my gift was at writing music, not playing. I was fine with that. Sometimes you have to accept the truth. It's easier that way.

I catch Millicent staring at me, and for the first time, she's not glaring at me. She offers me a silent gesture: both corners of her mouth are curved upward into a grin, a nice one at that.

CHAPTER 7

Mr. Marshall, our fearless math teacher, began class by cracking one of his lame jokes. This is his daily ritual. Today's joke was just as bad as the others. He proudly stood at the front of class with a piece of paper in his hand. "How many mathematicians does it take to change a light bulb?"

No one responded. Most of us had the same thought: Can't this be over with already?

"One: she gives it to three physicists, thus reducing it to a problem."

He laughed to himself because no one else in the class gets his humor. He then went on to tell us what the day's assignment was, which includes a group project.

"You will work in groups of two or three and create a survey question. This must be verified by me. You'll make three conjectures about this survey topic: for example, what you think you'll find. Then you'll survey at least thirty males and females. There must be an equal number of women and men. You'll analyze your data...."

He continues to discuss the project, and I hear a few groans and some low grumbling from irritated classmates who aren't too keen on working together. Marshall holds up his finger to shush us, and the class goes silent. It's not that he's scary, it's that he's one of those people you want to please. Actually, he's a cool guy. A little on the strange side, but still cool. Rumor is that he was once a Green Beret in the Army. I believe it. It's always the quiet ones. He did mention that he once traveled in a van around the country (guess the Army thing is hush, hush). He said he stayed at campsites and national parks, going from here to there without a care in the world, then decided he wanted to teach others to love math as much as he does. So, he sold the van and got a respectable suit, and the rest is history.

I flip through my copy of *Pride and Prejudice*. I haven't finished it yet. Mr. Finley, my former tutor, suggested I first read the likes of Vonnegut and Atwood, then move to the classics to help me prepare for AP Literature in the fall. So, here I am with Austen. Finley used to get excited when he talked about books, and truthfully, it was refreshing to talk literature with someone who is just as much of a geek about it.

Everyone is circling around the classroom like we're playing musical chairs. This is the hard part. It's magnifying the fact that I'm socially inept or don't have many friends in this school.

I get up, searching for a partner because BB gave me the shove off when some girl looked at him desperately. BB will do anything for a pair of boobs. I guess all male species will. Pathetic really.

I don't expect anyone to come up to me. Actually, most of the students have been avoiding me. With the exception of BB and Millicent, I'm a nonentity. I wanted this, yet, I don't want it. No one wants to be ignored.

Millicent is sitting in the front of the class, planted in her seat and reading *Pride and Prejudice*, snickering to herself. I take a seat next to her and don't say a word, then begin writing in my green notebook. Ideas. Thoughts. Quotes. I jot what comes to mind expecting to use it later in a song I write.

She looks up from her book and glances at me. "Can I help you with something?"

"Since no one wanted to pair with you, I figured I would come over here."

She shoots me a dirty look. "I didn't want anyone to pair with, so there is no need for your pity."

I laugh. "I'm not pitying, I'm empathizing. I'm the new guy, remember? And," I lean close to her, thankful my breath smells like spearmint, "people are scared of this." I point to my leg.

"They're idiots," she mumbles.

I lean back in the chair and crack my knuckles. "So, you're reading Austen?" I side-glance her book. "I'm reading her now, too. Isn't that a coinkydink?"

She snorts. "Did you just say 'coinkydink?'"

I sit up taller and say with confidence, "Yes, yes I did."

"Humph," she says. "I don't need a partner for this project. Why not pair with BB?"

"He's busy with the redhead." I nod toward the back of the room where BB and a ginger are chatting it up. "Anyways, Mr. Marshall says we need to work on a team. Don't make me be *that* guy."

"What guy?"

"The one who's picked last for kickball."

"This is hardly the same."

"It so is. Look around the room, Millicent, everyone else is paired up."

"Fine," she relents. "But it's not my choice."

I smile.

"Is something funny?" she says with frustration.

"We're not going on a date; we're just working on a statistics project together."

She forms a "no way in hell" expression at my mention of the word "date." I'm not chopped liver. I read her expression and lean close to her again, saying, "You're too high maintenance, so don't worry, I won't be asking you out."

"I am not high maintenance," she argues. "And, I wouldn't go out with you anyway."

"Whatever," I say, like I don't believe her, then stare at her for a moment. "Do you just hate me, or do you hate everyone?"

"I don't hate you; I don't even know you."

"You sure spend a lot of your energy being mad at me. Don't you ever get tired of it?"

She stays silent.

I laugh. "You've got circles under those blue eyes of yours, so it must be wearing you out to put so much effort into being mean to me. I'm wearing you out, aren't I?"

She scowls at me.

"First of all, the dark circles are a result of seasonal allergies. Look it up."

"Circles are also a result of lack of sleep, medication, and sleeping on your stomach," I add, then realize I sound like a big know-it-all, which is not sexy to any woman.

She gives me a surprised look. "Google much?" she says. "I don't hate you, Trip. The truth is I don't hate anyone."

"Please," I say. "We all vehemently dislike someone or some type of person. I'm not fond of the ignorant, racist types."

"Is anyone?"

"Racist, ignorant types are. Maybe if you stopped judging me for a second or being mad at me all of the time, you would get to know me. Then you could decide if you really wanted to hate me or not."

She closes her book. "Hate is a wasted emotion."

"I can't argue with you there, but I'm not buying your rhetoric.

You," I say with a smirk, "hate just to hate."

"Don't make assumptions about me when you don't even know me."

"Isn't that what you're doing? Making assumptions."

"You didn't give me much of a choice. All you've done since we met is make snarky comments."

"Says the girl who is the queen of them," I say and start writing in my notebook, showing her I'm done with the discussion, but I can tell she's still worked up because I hear her breathing and muttering under her breath like she's ready for a debate or for mud wrestling, which leads my mind to dirtier things, like her covered in mud and wearing nothing but a bikini. I glance up from my notebook and look into her sky blue eyes, "Millicent, you're not the first person to make an assumption about me, and you won't be the last."

Guilt flickers across her face, and she's about to say something, but Marshall starts talking before she has a chance to.

CHAPTER 8

I've been brown bagging my lunch ever since I researched the company in charge of food services at school, which, evidently, is also the same company that services the state prison. The food is ridden with preservatives and unnatural things that will probably cause all sorts of cancer. For example, the hamburgers are ninety-eight percent soy, which we all know isn't good for guys. Soy has been known to cause moobs.

I have a seat next to BB and his hunting bunch, who aren't much for stellar conversation but they're harmless enough and don't treat me differently. They usually give me a head nod, say, "what's up," then proceed to discuss girls, hunting, and football. I only like one of those three subjects. I'm sure it's obvious which one that might be.

Millicent is seated across from me, reading and paying them no attention. She has stealth concentration. I would never be able to read a book when she's around me.

"What are you reading?" I ask her. Desperate for conversation much, Trip.

She holds up her worn copy of *The Handmaid's Tale*, then lays it back down on the table, reading once more. I like that she can read more than one book at a time but don't tell her so.

An open Ziploc bag of carrots rests next to her book. Every now and again, she pulls a carrot out and bites into it and chews.

"Atwood," I say.

"Uh-hmm," she says, still glancing at the text. Crunch, crunch, crunch.

I open my lunch box and pull out my tray of sushi. Last night

I tried my hand at tuna rolls, which I have to say are quite good. Mom ate some; Dad abstained since he doesn't like raw fish.

Her eyes dart up from her book, and she makes a disgusted face, staring at my food choice.

"Fish is good for you."

She shakes her head and mutters something to herself.

"What?"

"You're an odd one."

"Because I don't eat crap." I dart my eyes to BB's lunch choices: Mountain Dew, a bologna sandwich and a huge bag of Ruffles potato chips. "So, he's the norm?"

She says nothing more, but I'm desperate for a conversation with her. I imagine I'm like those irritating boys in the sandbox who dump buckets of sand on a girl just so she'll pay attention. My flirting skills are probably equivalent to a five-year-old's.

"So, do you like that book?" I ask.

"Yeah. I'd like it even more if I could read it."

"I can read. Need me to teach you?"

She looks up at me, glaring.

"You know what I meant."

"You said you struggled to read. I can help."

She rolls her eyes and glances back down at the book.

I place my index finger on the text and say, "That word is 'the.'"

"I know lots of words," she says. "Like these." She pulls out her phone and types, then flashes the screen at me. The words "Shut up" show.

"That's good," I tell her. "But if that's the extent of your vocabulary you're going to struggle with that book."

She sighs in a dramatic way, then proceeds to read again. So much for my attempt to charm her. I look at BB for help, and he just shakes his head in pitying fashion.

"You've got no game," he whispers.

***

Millicent sits in the front of the class. I constantly stare at the back of her head, watching her flip her long braid from her left shoulder to her right. It's become a fascination of mine, which isn't healthy. She's distracting. Really, Marshall should make her sit in the back of the class away from me so I can stop paying attention to her. She chews on her left index finger a lot, too. That's the only one. When she's thinking hard and trying to solve a problem, she brings her finger up to her mouth, chews, then places it back in her lap when she's figured out whatever dilemma she's facing.

She's constantly raising her hand, answering his questions, participating in class - things we should all be doing, but half of the class is too immersed in Snapchat to care. The other half is clueless and can't add one plus one. It's an odd mix for sure, and a part of me feels some sympathy for Mr. Marshall for having to teach such a mishmash of students who don't all have the same learning styles. He has a hard job, yet he doesn't get compensated like he should. Teachers educate future brain surgeons and judges for the Supreme Court but are paid below the national average. Doesn't make a whole lot of sense to me.

Millicent is your quintessential teacher's pet, only I think she's probably not Marshall's favorite. I have a feeling Millicent wouldn't care if she was anyway. She doesn't strike me as the kind of girl who needs affirmation; maybe that's why I like her so much.

"I wish she'd just shut up," says Mattie, who has to be one of the most vacuous people I've ever met. I heard her once state she was going to college to meet her future husband. "She makes us look bad." Her friend agrees with a "Yeah."

I'm tempted to tell her that Millicent cannot make her look bad since she already had that going for her, but since I'm low on the social totem pole, I think I'll keep that thought to myself.

I've learned that Millicent isn't a favorite with anyone our age. BB might be one of her only friends. I guess I can relate. No one here has made a point to strike up a conversation with me except to ask me how I lost my leg and if I could feel anything with the prosthesis. Kind of personal questions, if you ask me. It's like going up to someone and asking them if they have a mole on their ass.

The rest of the day goes painfully slow, and the bell finally rings. I have a hard time sitting in this desk for hours at a time and wonder how the other students' butts haven't fallen asleep. I stand up; my leg buckles. I latch onto the desk and save myself from a near fall.

"You good, man?" BB whispers.

"Yep," I say. I feel the hardening stares from Mattie and her crew.

Millicent comes our way holding her textbook, a worn copy of *The Handmaid's Tale* and a calendar. The girl is obsessed with keeping lists and writing things down in her calendar. It's old school: keeping an actual calendar. I have no idea what she writes in it: *Glare at Trip. Drive Trip crazy. Roll eyes at Trip.* Check, check and check.

"What happened to you anyway?" Mattie asks me, staring down at my leg. One of her friends elbows her, then shoots her a look. I guess one of them might have some decency after all. Mattie has met my expectations, however.

"He's the world's first living organ donor," Millicent tells her.

Her mouth flies wide open.

"Better close your mouth, Mattie, or you'll swallow a fly," Millicent says.

"Shut up," she snaps, then turns back to me with an eager expression. "So, you donated your leg to someone?"

"Yeah," I lie, looking at Millicent who seems to have a twinkle in her eye, or maybe that's just me because the girl did just defend me. "It's a new concept."

"But it's your leg," she continues.

Really I'm starting to wonder how this girl made it to high school. I don't even know how to respond to such idiocy.

I hear Millicent sigh in exasperation. "It was sarcasm. If you had any brain cells, you'd know that."

Mattie turns to face her. "No one understands your weird hippie sarcasm."

"Coming from you, I take that as a compliment," Millicent says. "Are we going?" she asks BB.

"Yeah," he answers.

We leave the classroom, hearing the nonsensical chattering from Mattie and her friends.

"Thanks," I say to Millicent.

"For what?"

"For, you know, that."

"Some people have no boundaries," she says with obvious irritation. "I can't believe she asked you that."

"You'd be surprised by what I'm asked. Some people even go up and touch it."

She gasps, appalled.

"Anyway," I shrug my shoulders. "It was a clever response."

"I know."

"Confident much." I elbow her. The tip of her braid touches my skin, making me a woozy, which is pretty pathetic. At least I'm not boning up from it. "Well, anyway, thanks."

"Don't say 'thank you' for something a friend should do."

"So, we're friends, are we?" I smile too wide and sound too eager.

"I guess," she says nonchalantly, but when I look closer at her, I see a gleam in those pretty blue eyes of hers. Things are looking up.

CHAPTER 9

I'm waiting for BB to come get me. We're going to Millicent's house. No, she didn't all of a sudden get the urge to be friendly and invite me over for afternoon tea. Her family is hosting a barbecue and invited BB, who insisted I tag along for the occasion.

Mom places several brownies inside a sheet of red tissue paper, folds the ends of the paper together, then curls a red ribbon with the blade of her scissors. I've never been good at curling or making things look respectable. I can't even wrap a present that well. She's been giddy as a school girl all day, ecstatic that I'm hanging out with people my own age.

"Thanks," I say to her.

"So red means something good?" she asks.

I nod. I'd asked Mom to pick up some red tissue paper and ribbon on one of her errands. In Japanese custom, red is seen as a color of energy and longevity. Whereas, red and black mean sexuality. I made sure to tell her no matter what, don't buy black. I don't want to send the wrong message, even though I can't help but think about sex when I'm around Millicent, no matter how crazy she makes me.

I'm not Japanese, but I like the cultural custom of presenting a gift to someone when they're doing something as simple as inviting you to their house. I don't get invited to many people's houses (hardly ever - so few that I can count the times on my hands), so, I've been dying to try my hand at practicing this custom.

I hear BB driving up. His deafening music causes the dogs to bark, and some howl. "That must be Oliver," Mom says. She doesn't call him BB because she says it's silly to call someone Butterbean.

The irony of her calling me Trip is not lost on me.

He knocks on the door, and Mom goes to greet him since she's faster than I am. Let's face it, a turtle is faster than I am.

I hear him gushing about the size of the home and how nice it is. He's never been invited inside. When he drops off the meat, the transaction always takes place outside. I used to stare at him from my window, wondering what his world was like, but I never had the nerve to go outside and say a simple "Hi." Guys aren't like that I guess. And when you're my age, it looks kind of strange if you go up to some familiar stranger and try to establish a friendship. Had I known BB was like he is, I would've gone outside a long time ago, but that's the problem with me and taking chances. I think about doing stuff but I never take the leap. I've got a journal full of things I'm supposed to do before I die. Believe it or not, this was one of them. That's how lame I am. Writing "go to a party" is how pathetic my social life is— thus, the need for a list of things I'm supposed to do before I croak.

Mom and Dad are private people. I guess because they felt like they had to guard me all of this time, so, as a result, they became reclusive, and that has rubbed off on me. Big time. I'm great with the sarcasm, but delve a little deeper and you're trying to cross an electric fence.

BB enters the kitchen, wearing a wrinkled yellow t-shirt and pair of navy blue swim trunks. He looks around our kitchen and smiles. "This is like something on TV. Like one of those cooking shows Momma watches," he says, then takes a whiff. "Smells good in here, too."

"Would you like a brownie?" Mom asks.

"Yes ma'am," he says. She hands him one on a plate. He takes a big bite, a few crumbs fall to the floor. He chews, then swallows - all in one bite. "That's good."

"Trip made them," she says. Mom is all for my developing friendship with BB. If the Unabomber came over, she'd probably encourage a friendship with him, too, just because I had a friend.

"You're too introverted," she has said to me so many times that I've lost count.

Tell me how someone can be too introverted.

"You can cook and play the piano?" He gives me a look of awe like I have all of these hidden talents which aren't anything special but to him maybe they are.

Dad comes in for a break from the summer heat. His shirt is soaked, and his white hair is wet. "Hi, Oliver," he says.

"Hey, Mr. Wentworth," BB says smiling, showing remnants of chocolate on his crooked teeth.

"Where are you two headed?" Dad asks. I've told him. Mom's told him. But he's old, and when I say old, he qualifies for an AARP card. He is a good fifteen years older than my mom. The two met when Mom was a student at the University of Chicago. He was her professor (gasp). Yes, Dad used to teach French, and Mom, I guess, received extra tutoring sessions.

"To the commune," Mom whispers to him.

He nods reflectively. "That's right. Don't eat their brownies." He wags his brows. "They might be potent. I had a few brownies back in my day."

Mom playfully slaps him. "Beck," she admonishes. I'm sure he did. Dad was a "Make Love, Not War" type back in the 1970s.

"It's not that kind of commune," BB says.

"He was teasing," Mom says.

BB grins at her, then turns to look at me. "You ready?"

"Yeah," I say and clasp the red tissue brownie-filled present.

"Be careful," Mom says. She hands BB another brownie before we leave. He leaves a trail of crumbs from the kitchen to the front door.

We go outside. BB waits by his car as I slowly climb down the steps. He gets tired of waiting on this old geezer and walks over to the dogs, petting as many as he can with his two chocolate-covered hands. Shadow, who is my favorite, but that's not saying much since I'm not a big fan of the balls of fur, licks him on his cheek. BB grimaces. "They say dogs mouths are cleaner than a human's but I don't buy it. They lick their nuts and butts."

"It's a myth," I tell him. "They lick their wounds, so people naturally assume they have these potent tongues, but really their mouth is as dirty as ours—if not dirtier, since we don't lick our balls and buttholes."

"Every guy in America would lick his balls if he could, though." He snickers. "You're a walking Google. Got all this useless knowledge locked up in that head of yours."

I shrug. "I read a lot." I read too much, so much that Mom and Dad refused to support my spending habit and told me I had to take up another hobby. Little do they know that the public library is helping me with my addiction. They'd hoped I would choose a social hobby where I'd get out and mingle, but I chose cooking instead, which is as solitary as reading.

He pets the dogs again. "If I had all of these dogs, I'd be out here with 'em all the time." He coos at them in a sweet and saccharine tone.

"They're alright," I say.

***

Everyone has shed their clothes, replacing them with swimsuits. Myrna has on a skimpier bathing suit than Millicent. She's wearing a white string bikini and is dancing on the dock with a beer in one hand. Not the image I wanted to see. Like a strip of fabric wrapped around a wilted prune. Sorry, but there it is.

"You coming?" BB asks me, dripping wet.

"Nah, I'm good right here." This is a lie, but BB doesn't read people well. He's so non-judgemental he doesn't look for signs. Right now I'm waving a big banner; he's just oblivious to it.

"Okay," he says with some doubt. I don't blame him. I look like I'm baking in a sweat box. "I'm going back in," he says, rushing toward the water and leaving me to wilt.

The truth of the matter is, I'm self-conscious about my leg. If it was just me out here, I'd swim, but with strangers and… Millicent, I don't want to. I can't get my prosthesis wet. So, I have to take it off, and ole stumpy might be too much of an oddity even with this group. You know, I've never been swimming in this town since we moved here? The town was built around the lake, so you'd think I would've attempted to swim at least once, but we don't have the luxury of living on the lake like these hippies so that would've meant swimming at a public beach.

Millicent lags behind, stalling like she's trying to figure out which way to go. If she turns around, she'll catch me gawking. She's wearing a bikini, and bikinis are like bras and underwear, which is the gateway to all good things.

She spins on her heels and comes my way. "While you're here, we should discuss our project."

"Okay," I say. "Want to go inside?" Please say yes. I'm sweating my balls off (which would be a travesty if that could truly happen, but as it stands, one cannot sweat his nutsack off—thank goodness), and in case you didn't know, the liner I have to wear under my prosthesis makes this dreadful heat ten times worse.

"Okay." She shrugs noncommittally.

I heave myself up from the chair and follow her into the spacious common room. The cool wave of air hits me as I find my way inside. I collapse on the sofa. The Eagles play on the stereo. It's an actual console stereo from the olden days. She turns down the volume, all the while still traipsing around in that jade bikini of hers like it's no big deal.

She darts to the kitchen, opens the refrigerator and pops the lids on two cans of pop, then meanders to me. "Here," she says, handing me a can of Coke.

"Thanks," I say. "Is there a full moon out tonight?"

"Why?"

"Because you just offered me something. Is this a peace offering?" I smile at her, hoping I'm being charming and not annoying. "I don't have an olive branch in my pocket."

"Just a cease fire….for now."

She takes a t-shirt, which is draped on one of the chairs and pulls it over her head, covering that lovely bikini. She sits crossed-legged on the couch and faces me. *Pride and Prejudice* lays on her coffee table. She chews on a pen, then takes it out of her mouth to speak. And all I can think is, "I want to be that pen!"

"How'd you enjoy Austen?" I ask her. I finished it days ago and actually enjoyed it. Who cares that it's a girly book. Darcy kicks ass.

"I really liked it but it seems to me that these women had it rough back then."

"Rough how?" I scoff. "They sat at home all day, embroidered and tied ribbons around their hats, or played the harp or piano. Yeah," I say, "really rough."

"Spoken from a guy. Sexist much," she murmurs. There's this twitch Millicent has when she gets upset. It's the left side of her cheek close to her ear.

"Don't call me a sexist just because I'm being a realist," I argue.

"Actually, you're being close-minded. Women didn't have choices. They either had to be born into money or work for horrible pay under the most dreadful circumstances, and no matter what, they all had to marry because that was the expectation: that they'd marry and have children. They couldn't own property or vote."

"Okay, okay, I see your point. Things were bad."

She gives a confident nod. "I can be persuasive."

I shrug. "No, you were just being vague at first and once you said what you meant, I had to agree."

She gives me an incredulous look. "Of course you were going to agree with me."

I laugh at her need to get the last word in, then fall back against the couch cushions.

"I'm glad I didn't live back then," she says.

"You would have been thrown in prison or burned at the stake."

Her mouth gapes wide open. "Hey, that wasn't nice."

"It's true. Women were expected to be complacent, and you are far from complacency."

"Thankfully," she says. "Would you have liked to live back then?"

"As I am now?" I ask.

She glances down at my leg, and I hear her breath catch, then she shakes her head. "I didn't mean…"

I laugh again. "It's okay. You're one of the few people who treats me like you don't even notice it, you know?"

"I didn't at first," she says.

"I don't believe you. It's kind of like a big fat boil festering, waiting to be popped."

"Really, I didn't. I noticed your t-shirt, because Pink Floyd is one of Mom's favorites, and no one from that school wears anything remotely cool."

"Oh, so I dress cool, huh?" I grin.

"Don't get an ego," she says. "I'm just saying, I didn't know until you came over here that day and…" her voice fades.

"Fell," I answer for her. "It's okay. I do it all of the time," I say. "Anyway, this is a first: most people see the leg first, then see me, maybe."

It's quiet, and there's this awkwardness between us. It could be the Coke I'm drinking, but my heart is pumping double-time and my insides are all haywire. Somehow I think caffeine is not the problem.

"To answer your question, no, I wouldn't have wanted to live back then. Not like this anyway. Prosthetics were pretty barbaric back then, and I wouldn't have enjoyed living like that." I don't tell her that it's hard enough as it is. Not to gripe or complain because really I don't have it bad. I've met others who have it worse than me. People without both legs or no arms. But, yeah, sometimes, I'd just like to wake up and have my leg back. Just one day.

She's about to say something, but the phone rings. I'm taken aback by the sound because it's a landline phone and most people don't have these relics. She jumps off the couch to answer it.

"Hello," she says, then grows silent when the person on the other end begins talking.

"Can I tell her who is calling?" she asks. "Oh, okay. Hold on for a second," she says with a worried frown. She lays the phone down on the counter and heads outside. A minute later she and Mama Sauce come into the room. Mama Sauce picks up the phone.

"Hello," she says, heavily breathing. "Yes, this is Maria Moretti."

I stare at Millicent as she watches Mama Sauce with a curious expression. She tilts her head to the side and mouths, "Everything okay?"

Mama Sauce doesn't answer her.

The person on the other end continues to talk. Mama Sauce's expression changes dramatically. Her tanned face becomes pale, and her eyes widen in horror.

"No!" she screams.

CHAPTER 10

I never know what to do in those type of situations. I'm not one for consoling, and there's not anything I can say to make it better anyhow. Death is expected when we're old, but from my understanding, Luca wasn't much older than me, twelve years older. Hardly a life lived. (Says the guy who's one to talk.)

BB said Luca was like a son to Mama Sauce even though he was her younger brother. She basically raised him when their parents died. That's probably why it hit her so hard. But losing anyone you care about hurts, and I'm sure the type of relationship it was doesn't matter. If you love them and they're gone, it's going to be heartbreaking.

He was skydiving and chose to try swooping, which is when you jump from a plane at five thousand feet instead of the typical thirteen thousand foot elevation. He was going too fast and collided with a tree. He died in an instant.

BB cried. Everyone cried, except Millicent, who sat away from them all in silence, taking it all in, handling it like a champ, but even champs have their breaking points. Everyone handles tragedy differently. I remember my mother's reaction versus my father's after I lost my leg. Mom wears her emotions on her sleeve. She's a crier. Tears well up when she sees Hallmark commercials and sappy movie trailers. Dad, on the other hand, is stoic. I've never seen him cry. He didn't shed one tear after my surgery, but I know he feels sad because the eyes are always a giveaway, windows into the soul. Millicent is like my dad - she hides behind a mask, but her pale blue eyes tell a story. There are times when I catch my dad looking at me, thinking I don't see him watching me, but I do. I know he is staring and thinking, thinking about the "what ifs," which is unhealthy because things can't be changed. I gave up on that notion years ago.

My mom had to come get me at the commune. BB's car wouldn't start, and he was too shaken up to take me home anyway. Mom pried, and I just shrugged, telling her, "Someone died." She didn't ask me any other questions. No one ever wants to talk about death except for funeral directors. They make their living off of people's sadness. Not a good way to live if you ask me, but I'm not meant to be a funeral director.

I'm lying in my bed, thinking too much, tossing and turning, hating that I have to get up to go pee because that means grabbing my crutches then making the trek to the bathroom. It's never quick. The process I mean. Showering, peeing, getting dressed - they're all acts that take longer than the average time.

I do my business, then amble back to my bedroom, falling back on my bed from the exertion. Like I said before, it's a process, and I expel more energy than someone who has two legs.

As I lie here in the quiet of the night, I hear something tapping against my window. I sit up and see a shadow. I suck in a lungful of air like a wimp, but I watched *Saw* earlier this week and am still feeling the residual effects like those soldiers with PTSD. Not sure why I subjected myself to such a movie, but I do stupid things from time to time.

"Trip," he says. "Psst. Trip."

It's BB.

I flip the light switch, then hop over to him, trying to balance on one foot. I'm strong (I work out, but not in a compulsive-I-look-like-I'm-on- the-roids-kind-of-way) but I'm not that strong. Even the most fit person would have difficulty balancing on one foot for any length of time.

"What are you doing here?" I say in a breathy voice through the glass panel.

"Open," breath, "up." He takes another breath. He points to the window. His face is flushed.

"Can't. Alarm."

He inhales once more. "What do they need an alarm for if they got all them dogs?" He pouts in a frustrated way.

Speaking of dogs..."Why aren't they barking?"

"I tossed them some meat. Should keep 'em occupied for a while." He gives me a sly grin. "Come on and let me in."

"Give me a minute," I say.

Putting on a prosthesis is an act: an act that takes a while. First I have to take off my shrinker sock, then the nylon sheath, only to put on a liner liner, yes that's what it's called, and then the silicone liner before slipping into my leg. It's like those girls who are in beauty pageants caking their faces with makeup and spraying their hair - a ritual. This ritual usually takes five entire minutes (I've clocked it), and I'm sure the dogs aren't going to be quiet much longer, so I grab my crutches, then walk down the hallway, hoping I'm not going to wake my parents. Dad is a heavy sleeper, but Mom could wake up at any given moment. I tap the code into the alarm then make my way back to my room.

I head to the window, unlock it and BB climbs inside.

"'Bout time. I nearly pissed my pants," he says a little too loudly.

"Shhh... you'll wake the units."

"Sorry," he shouts again.

I gesture for him to quiet down.

"Sorry," he says again, this time quieter.

"What brings you here? I'm sure it's not to tuck me in."

"No." He lets out a nervous giggle, then frowns, growing serious. "I need to ask you a favor."

"Okay," I say. I didn't think we were that good of friends yet, but what do I know about friendship or friendship protocol? Maybe this is the way things work. Bartering and all that. He was nice to me, now I do him a favor. I don't know.

"If you want to say no I understand, but you're our only option."

"Thanks. That gives me a lot of reassurance."

There are signs of sweat on his green t-shirt and khaki shorts. He finds a seat and rests his hands on his thighs. He looks down at his hands, pondering for a moment, searching for words, then looks up at me and says, "As you know, my car ain't working right."

I nod.

"Millicent and me need to go to Wyoming, and we were wondering if you'd be willing to drive us there."

"Wyoming? For what? And why me?"

"Yellowstone. To get Luca," he says. He doesn't answer the *why me* part yet. "We need to get him so he can be buried here."

"They usually ship bodies, don't they?" I try to ask in the most gentle way possible, but it still comes out all wrong. I wish I was one of those adept communicators who knew how to phrase things eloquently but, alas, I suffer from inept social skills.

He takes a deep breath, hearing the word "bodies," then goes on to say, "They can't afford it. Millicent overheard her moms talking about it, how they can't pay to ship him back home. Mama Sauce and Aunt Anna were so upset 'cause they can't say a proper goodbye.

He has to be buried here. He already died alone; he can't lay to rest out there by himself."

"There has to be someone that can loan you money to get him here."

He shakes his head with a rueful expression. "No one's going to lend them money. They ain't on everyone's Christmas list. Still some close-minded people who don't want to associate with them 'cause they love each other. And, my family is too poor to give them any money. We barely survive as it is. We can't help 'em pay even though we sure would if we had the money," he says.

I give him a sympathetic look, knowing that's true. BB would probably donate one of his organs if they needed it. No questions asked.

"Most of my friends don't have cars, and those who do are in the same situation I'm in," he goes on.

I sit on the edge of my bed, trying to wrap my mind around what he's just asked me. "So.... you want me to help you steal a body?" Wrinkles form on my forehead. It's one thing to ask for money, but to ask something of this enormity is beyond the requirements of a new friendship.

"It's not really stealing," he argues, sounding like those people who say, "I wasn't really lying when I omitted that one comment," but it's still a lie. "It's more like we're moving him out of Wyoming and back home where he belongs. Mama Sauce is really superstitious and says he has to be buried here or his spirit will wander the earth forever. I believe her."

When I spilled salt on the table during dinner, Mama Sauce immediately grabbed a small handful and pinched it together between her fingers. She tossed it over her left shoulder and said a prayer, then looked at us as if this was normal.

"I'd like to help you..." I start.

"But what?" he interrupts.

"It's not legal to steal a body, and I don't want to get arrested."

"This is hardly a crime," he scoffs. "We're bringing him back here so we can have a proper burial for him. We're just not paying the funeral vultures their fees."

"I'm sorry, BB. There's nothing I can do."

"Yeah, there is." He stands up, and his hands are balled into fists. His lips are all puckered, and he's glaring at me. "You could help us. We don't have any other way of going. I asked everyone I know. You're our last option."

"I can't; I'm sorry. Maybe someone else..." my voice drifts into the air.

"There ain't no one else. Why do you think I'm here in the middle of the night asking you? Because I'm desperate. Hell, I rode my bike over here just so I could talk to you man-to-man, square in the eye."

"You've got the wrong guy. I'm sorry."

"Yeah, you are sorry," he snaps. "Staying holed up in the house all these years only to finally reveal yourself to be a real wussy," he says with disgust. "A real wimp," he adds.

I glare at him and feel my heart thumping hard. "That's a cheap shot. What the hell! I don't deserve this!" I shout.

"I call it as I see it." He folds his arms across his chest. "All that time I thought you were dying or had some illness 'cause you were holed up inside this house. Felt really sorry for you, too. 'Cause I thought you were sick and that's why you shut yourself out from the world. The truth of the matter is you're just a guy with one leg who's afraid to take any risks." He shoots me a look full of pity. "Good luck." He moves to the window. "You're going to live a lonely life full of boredom."

He begins climbing out of my window. I'm fuming. Angry. Seeing red. Hating him for what he said because, because... I know it's the truth. The truth always hurts. No one ever rejoices from hearing it because it's unkind, unfiltered, and harsh. It's what I know deep down to be my reality, only I can't bear to hear it because I don't want to face it. I don't want to admit to myself that my life is a joke. That I'm a joke. If I died, my imprint would fade as quickly as the rains came, washing my existence away because I've done nothing worth remembering. I've never taken a risk, and without taking risks, there is no life lived.

Without even thinking, I blurt, "BB. Wait."

CHAPTER 11

One of the convenient things about Mom and Dad's work is the travel requirement, and it just so happens they're traveling the week I decide to rebel against them. This makes it easier for me since I didn't want to outright lie to them. At least this way when Mom checks in with a text, I can answer vaguely, with a "Fine. How are you?" Change the subject. I read once, that when you want people to lay off your case and get out of your business, you have to turn the subject back on them or on something else entirely. Compliment them. Start a new conversation.

They left early this morning for Pennsylvania with Toby, one of the German Shepherd's, because some couple is paying them too much money for a dog that answers to commands in Dutch. BB hid in my closet while Mom said her goodbyes, and I'll never admit it to him, but I felt guilty when Mom was telling me how she'd made my favorite dish: manicotti, and had placed several servings in the freezer for me to eat while she and Dad are gone. At that point, I was ready to confess to her that I was taking their car and traveling across the country on a fool's mission, but something kept me from doing it. That little voice again. The one that told me I needed to jump without looking.

Thankfully, I don't have to worry about the dogs while they're gone. They pay this man, Clyde, to feed them and keep an eye on them when they're not around, which makes my covert mission even more convenient. The last thing I need to worry about is feeding a bunch of bilingual German Shepherds who eat too much.

BB and I are standing in the garage, looking at our transportation options. Mom and Dad love their cars, like

Cameron's father from *Ferris Bueller's Day Off* who was so obsessed with his Ferrari that Cameron nearly had a breakdown when it flew from the second story garage. Dad drives a Ford F150. He has the thing professionally cleaned each month, waxed, vacuumed and everything. It's his baby, and I think if Mom wasn't in the picture, he'd have a full lot of these beastly vehicles, which do nothing but ruin the environment and suck up gas.

Mom drives an Audi S6, silver and sleek, low to the ground, which is not so great for the leg – neither is Dad's truck, since it's a little high off of the ground. I can't win. Getting in and out of a vehicle isn't fun.

I assess both cars, thinking about who is more likely to have a conniption that their precious is in the hands of their now irresponsible son. If the Outback was here, I'd take that one. It's their work car: the one they cart the dogs around in when they have to go to the vet or groomer. It's in fine condition, but to car snobs like Mom and Dad, it's a Yugo.

"Let's take this one," I say.

BB's eyeing Dad's F150 like a stripper at a gentlemen's club. Not that I would know. They call them gentlemen's clubs, which is ironic since the term means a man of good or courteous conduct and something tells me a lot of the men who frequent the joints might not be on their best behavior around a bunch of naked women.

"It'll be easier to take Luca in. We won't be able to fit him in that trunk," I say, which sounds strange to say out loud, and I realize I've crossed some line where I can't redeem myself.

I'm sure I'll face a fate worse than spending time in a Turkish prison once I return from my travel, yet I still feel compelled to press on.

"It's nice," he says, trailing his fingers against the shiny coat of paint – just waxed, mind you. I toss my duffle bag into the truck bed, heave myself up to have a seat then turn the ignition.

BB climbs in the passenger seat, runs his fingers against the polished leather and takes a whiff. "Smells good, too."

As I drive off, I glance in the rearview mirror at my home, my safety net, then face forward to the unknown.

***

BB's parents aren't home by the time we make it to his house. They work the third shift, so we are free to be as noisy as we want. BB packs up a cooler filled with a bunch of sugary crap that's sure to make us all crash: Coke, Snickers, and deer jerky (homemade he said). He tosses some wadded clothes into a camouflage bag—one that he pulled from a shed which stank like something had died. BB turned the bag upside down and mud daubers and other creepy crawlies made their way to the ground.

"This'll do," he says, brushing it off as if one sweep from his hand cleaned it.

He scribbles a note to his parents, telling them he's camping for a few days, then grabs his charger for his flip phone (he says he can't afford a smartphone) before we head to the truck.

"Won't they worry that you're camping when you're supposed to be in summer school?"

"Nah. They're too busy working all the time, and they don't pay attention to my schooling."

He doesn't seem bothered he's lying to them or by the fact that they wouldn't notice his lengthy absence or care about his education. I'm not sure which is worse – his lying or the fact that they don't care.

"We're picking up Mellie at the turnoff to the road to her house," he says.

He calls her Mellie, but to me, she's a Millicent. Someone like her shouldn't be reduced to a nickname. Nicknames are for pets. She deserves to be called by her full name, which is unique, just like her. Alright, now I sound like some douche canoe from an Austen novel. I need to start reading war novels or things are going to continue to go downhill for me. I'll be the guy that girls think is sweet but never want to date.

"Okay," I say, whispering, still thinking we're in the midst of a covert CIA operation. I've never been one to sneak around all *Mission Impossible* style. With the leg, it's next to impossible, and even before the incident, I wasn't much for disobeying or doing anything that felt sneaky. My parents are experts in the art of inducing guilt even when I'm not doing something bad. So you can imagine the guilt I'm filled with right now. There's this pit in my stomach that's aching, making me feel like I've just committed a major crime. It's the good guy, the one who stays on my shoulder at all times. Only, I think he's barely hanging on, because that other guy, the devil, he's shouting at me: "Quit being a pansy and lighten up!" I'm turning a deaf ear to one and have turned up the volume on the other.

He laughs. "We don't have to whisper, you know?"

I shrug him off. "I know."

He fiddles with the radio station and hums along to the song. I join along. I'm surprised wild dogs and stray cats haven't circled us and whine and howl from our ruckus.

And I'm having fun, thinking, "I can do this; I can do this." So, we keep on belting out the tunes and drive on to pick up Millicent. All worries about impending prison sentences and parents' anger are pushed to the side. For now.

We reach the turnoff to Millicent's, and I see her alone sitting on her duffle bag, pensive and stoic looking. She jumps up when we drive up and lugs the bag behind her. BB gets out and takes the bag from her, then tosses it in the truck bed.

"What you got in there, Mel? Bricks?" BB asks as they both slip into the truck.

"Sustenance and clothes," she says, buckling her seatbelt.

I glance at her in the rearview mirror, and she stares into my eyes. "You surprised me, Trip Wentworth, and people rarely surprise me anymore."

CHAPTER 12

My leg is killing me. I get phantom pains. You know that feeling you have when your limb has fallen asleep? Well, this is one thousand times worse. It's like someone is piercing my skin with long, sharp needles. You wouldn't think I'd feel pain, but I've felt it since my leg was cut off. It's as if it's still there, saying to me, "Hey, don't forget I was once attached to you!" How could I ever forget? Every time I look down, I see what's missing.

I punch my thigh and then knead it like dough. It brings some relief, but I can't keep driving for hours on end. Sitting cooped up in a truck without much leg room isn't ideal, either. Really, it'd be best if I sprawled myself out in the backseat and took off my prosthetic because my leg needs to breathe, but as I've said, I'm self-conscious.

I've never driven longer than an hour at a time. When I glance at the clock, I see it's been more than a few hours. Woot! World record breaker right here.

BB is snoring - the guy could sleep anywhere at anytime. We're in Tennessee, and the landscape is starting to change. The mountains are disappearing, and we're entering the foothills.

"Get off at the next exit. I need to use the restroom," Millicent says.

I do as she says and pull off at the next exit. I get out of the truck and feel my leg buckling, then grasp the door handle. Millicent sees my potential fall but says nothing.

She nudges BB, and he wakes up, then rubs his belly while wearing a soft smile. "I'm hungry."

"You're always hungry," she says with annoyance and dashes to the bathroom.

We walk into the gas station store and browse the food options. BB grabs more junk food even though he has a cooler stocked full of sugary sustenance. Millicent meets up with us and shakes her head disapprovingly at BB.

"We have food," she says to him when she sees him stocking up.

"I want this," he says, shaking the bag of Combos and Lays Sour Cream and Chives potato chips. Great. Now his breath will reek. BB is a human garbage disposal. He should go on one of those reality TV shows where the contestants have to eat a live snail or some other slithery creature for a chance at ten thousand dollars. He'd win, hands down.

"It's junk," she scoffs, then darts to the coolers, taking a couple of Faygo RedPops from the shelves.

She comes my way, trying to balance three Faygo RedPops and a pack of gum.

"You know that's junk, too, right?" I raise a brow and offer her a sly smile.

She refuses to make eye contact and heads to the cashier.

I walk outside, finding Millicent sitting in the driver's seat. A bottle of pop sits in the drink console. I lean down and look at her, giving her a questioning look.

"You can't do all of the driving," she says.

"Are you a safe driver?" is all I can think to ask. I have no moves. No technique. I am the opposite of all things suave.

She laughs, leaning her head back against the headrest, which gives me a good view of her chin and neck, of her chest. She's taken off the gray hoodie she had on earlier and is wearing a turquoise tank top which is a nice color on her.

"I don't drive like you, Grandpa, but I did score highest in Driver's Ed."

"Grandpa?"

"You grip both hands on the wheel and talk to yourself every time there's a semi charging your way."

I didn't think she was even paying attention to me. "They're... intimidating," I say, which I immediately regret since she's laughing at me again. It's nice to hear her laugh. It's a pleasing sound, like raindrops tapping against a tin roof or birds chirping early in the morning. Oh man, I need to get a life. I really need to stop reading literature from the Romantic period and stick to horror or thrillers.

"Anyway, I'd like to drive. You know, pay my fair share and all," she adds. "I'll pay you for what I can."

I shrug. "Okay." I never thought about the money. About who would pay for what. I was so focused on taking the risk, I didn't think about the logistics of the matter which probably isn't good since it looks like BB is intent on spending all of his money on junk food. We'll need money to pay for gas, to eat, to sleep. He said we'd camp when we stay anywhere overnight since it's cheaper.

I make my way to the passenger side and stand there, waiting for BB to come out. He's carrying a brown paper bag and a cup of coffee. "I call shotgun," I tell him, feeling my inner child come out and wearing a smirk I'm sure he's annoyed by.

He frowns at me, then reluctantly slides into the backseat without much of an argument.

"With all that coffee, you'll have to pee in less than an hour," Millicent says. "And we don't have time to stop."

"I'll aim out the window and promise not to hit your head. Maybe." He smiles, sipping on his coffee.

BB is snoring again, like a tractor tilling the fields on a warm summer's day. His sounds fill the truck, drowning out the music playing on the radio. Every now and again I can hear the steady beat of drums or a guitar strumming, but BB's so loud, it's difficult.

"He sleeps all of the time," she says to me with a worried frown.

"You think?"

"Mom thought he was on drugs because he fell asleep during a party one time. Right on the living room rug while we danced and sang, too. I've told him he needs to see a doctor, but he won't go," she says.

"Do you want to be a doctor?" I ask.

Her lips curl up a grin. "Nah. I just read too much WebMD because Mama Sauce is a hypochondriac. Actually, I want to be a lawyer. I like to argue."

I laugh. "Well, we know you're good at that."

She turns to look at me briefly before glancing back at the road. "You want to study music, right?" She opens her Faygo RedPop and gulps it, then wipes the residue off of her upper lip.

"I want to write and produce it, not perform. I'm not much for having the spotlight on me." I performed in a concert a few times. Played the piano, sang, the whole shebang, but the whole time, I kept wondering if the people were clapping because I'm good or because of the leg. It's awful, but when you all of a sudden have people treading lightly around you who once didn't, it's all you can wonder if an audience is doing the same. Josie, my music teacher, is one of the few who tells it like it is. She's the one who encouraged me to look into the production aspect because I write and read music well.

"Most producers don't know anything about music. You've already got that going for you," she said. "And you're really good." She's not one to mince words, either. So I must be halfway decent.

So, now it's all I can think about doing. I've spent countless hours in my studio making music, but no one has heard it yet but Josie and my mom. Mom doesn't count because she will tell me I'm great even when I'm not. It's part of the Mom Code of Ethics written in the scribes, which are locked in the arc of the covenant that only mothers are privy to. Anyway, Josie keeps telling me to play my music for people. That I can't keep creating only for myself.

"Where will you go after high school?"

"Maybe UNC. Maybe Elon," I say with a shrug. "Maybe the Peace Corps," I tease, which she is smart enough to catch my sarcasm. Mosquitos and I don't agree on things so the Peace Corps is out since they typically send you to countries ridden with them. Plus, I like indoor plumbing.

"I'm going up north," she says with confidence. "I'm applying early admission to Boston University."

"I had a friend from Boston. His mom would say, "Paul, get in the cah." I laugh, thinking of her lack of Rs.

"Maybe I'll develop an accent," she says.

I give her a peculiar look.

"A Northern one, I mean."

"It'll happen. Your environment shapes who you are despite your fight against it."

"You don't have a Southern accent."

"I haven't been around enough people to have that influence." I don't tell her the other reasons. What happened after the leg. How it changed me in all sorts of ways. "Maybe that will change this year. Just the other day I caught myself exaggerating my I's."

She laughs. "Just don't call Mama Sauce I-talian." She grimaces. "She hates that."

"And she should. It's not I-taly"

"Exactly." She nods in agreement.

"How long has she been a part of your family?"

"Since I was six-years-old. She treats me like I'm her own daughter. She's a bit bossy sometimes if you haven't noticed?" She laughs then grows serious, biting the corner of her bottom lip. "I hate that she lost Luca. Because of their age difference, he was like a son to her, you know? That's why it's so important to have him near her. So she can feel his presence," she says. "He was like an older brother to me, too." She turns her head slightly and looks at me. "He taught me to bait a worm on a hook and how to dance. He didn't live with us long because he went off to college, but the time he spent with us was memorable. And every time he'd come home to visit, it was like Christmas all over again. He was this enormous presence in our little community. Everyone loved him. To know him, well, it was to love him."

"He sounds amazing."

"Amazing doesn't do people like him justice. He was grit. He was all heart, you know?" She inhales and brings her finger up to her mouth. "I wish...well, I wish we would've had more time with him, but I guess everyone says that when they experience loss. They wish for time, which is unrealistic. You can't wish for things that won't come true." She rolls her shoulders. "Anyway, that's why I'm doing this. Because I want Mama Sauce to have him near her. It'll help her feel closure."

I open the bag of Sour Patch Kids I bought at the gas station and offer her some. I pour a handful into her palm, and she drops them into her mouth. She chews, then swallows them. "I love this candy."

"I know," I say. I saw her eating a bag at lunchtime once. It's why I bought them today. I'm not that much of a sugar addict. I also made a bag of homemade trail mix and brought a box of granola bars, but Millicent doesn't strike me as the type to appreciate more earthy foods even though she lives in a commune. Maybe I should be the one living with the hippies?

"I guess that was an easy guess," she says. "I ate an entire bag at lunch that one time." She laughs, which is a pleasant sound. "I haven't figured out your favorite yet."

You, I want to say but don't.

"Maybe sushi. Maybe some other weird food like that trail mix I saw you snacking on earlier. Whatever it is, I'm sure it's not common."

"I'll never tell," I say, raising my brows up and down.

She grows quiet, and rain begins to pour. The windshield wipers swoosh across the glass, creating a repetitive sound. "We're crossing over the Mississippi," she says.

I glance out the window, seeing a valley of endless water. "The world was new to me, and I had never seen anything like this at home," I say, quoting Mark Twain.

"*Life On The Mississippi*," she says.

"I read it years ago. Now that I've seen it with my own eyes, it makes what he wrote more powerful."

"Who are you?" she asks in a disbelieving tone. "You read Austen and Twain and can carry on a conversation. You do have a staring problem, but other than that, you're not like other guys I know."

"I'm just a guy who reads."

"I think there's more to you than you let on."

"Ditto." I smile at her.

"I'm as boring as they come," she says. "And, by the way, I hate the word 'ditto.'"

"It's a simple word and matter of fact. How can you hate it?" I ask. "There's nothing boring about you," I murmur.

She looks up at the dark clouds in the sky. "Camping in the rain sucks."

"I wouldn't know," I say. "I've never been."

She glances at me for a split second with a surprised look, then stares back at the slick road. "Not once?"

I shake my head ruefully.

"Well, now you will be able to say you have," she says.

CHAPTER 13

We slip a twenty dollar bill into an envelope and claim our spot in the campground. "And they just trust that you paid?" I ask when I see there isn't a soul around to collect the funds. Not that I imagine some bookie is going around with a baseball bat wrapped in barbed wire threatening campers, but still, someone should at least make sure payments have been made.

"Usually there's some old geezers who live on the campground who double-checks to make sure everyone's paid up," BB explains. "I wouldn't mind their job when I get older. It's cake if you ask me."

Our site is close to the bathroom, which was Millicent's request. It's not like it was a struggle to find a site since the campground is nearly empty. Probably because it's raining buckets outside and the ground is a big puddle of mud. Perfect for me and the leg.

It's not good for me to get my prosthesis wet. Plus, water seeping into my liner isn't ideal. It can lead to infection and other problems. That's something I have to constantly worry about: infection. I had one once. On my fourteenth birthday. Spent time in the hospital. I don't want to relive that time. There's so much from my past I don't want to repeat. I guess that's good. At least I'm not constantly looking back, trying to rekindle fond memories.

I struggle as we put up the three man tent. My shoe is caked in mud and I have a hard time moving because I'm stuck. Millicent and BB both tell me to park my butt in the truck. There's nothing worse than being the weak man on the team.

"I can help," I say.

"No way," Millicent says. "We don't want your help."

"Really," I protest. "I'm good."

"No. Not even listening," she says and proceeds to talk to BB like I'm not even here.

So, I make my way to the truck, and I feel like a jerk for staying all nice and dry while they're getting soaked putting up the tent. The tent is a questionable structure. Given how wet the ground is, I'm doubtful the stakes are going to help it stay put, but BB swears by it. "I've taken it with me when I go huntin'. It's good. Trust me."

After they finish setting up the tent, BB and Millicent rush to the truck, swing the doors wide open, letting the rain in, then have a seat. Water drips all over the floor of the truck and onto the seats. This will add to Dad's anger when I return. I will never see daylight again.

"Who's hungry?" BB asks.

"I could eat," Millicent says. Droplets of water drip down her entire body and her tank top is soaked, suctioning against her wet skin, which leads me to stare at her, imagining things that I probably shouldn't be thinking.

She shoots me a look. "Admiring something pretty again?"

I shoot her a foul look in return, then smile when I see she's teasing me. I'll never hear the end of it. Somehow I don't mind.

"I've got jerky and candy," BB says.

"I need real sustenance," she says. "Not crap."

"I think I saw a restaurant down the road from here," I say.

"Then we'll go there," she says. "Drive on, Mr. Wentworth."

I crank up the engine and back away from our tent site. An elderly woman wearing a red raincoat waves us down as we pass her. I bring the truck to a halt, and Millicent rolls the window half-way down.

"Y'all staying at number 18?" the lady asks.

"Yes," Millicent says.

She glances up at the sky with a frown, then stares back at Millicent. "Weatherman's calling for bad weather. Might want to stay at a motel instead."

"We've camped in worse," BB chimes in.

Millicent looks at the two of us, catching my look of concern. "If it gets bad, we'll stay somewhere else."

The lady shrugs. "Suit yourself. Make sure you're back here before ten o'clock. I lock the gate."

"We will. Thanks," Millicent says and rolls up the window.

I drive on toward the restaurant, which is called "Dina's Diner." Only it doesn't look like a diner. It's basically a square-shaped concrete structure with two big windows in the front. There's no landscaping surrounding it, and it's painted an insipid color. It's the kind of building you'd miss because it just doesn't stand out. There's nothing remarkable about it, which makes me wonder if the food is going to be just as unimpressive.

We enter, then make our way to a booth. There's a smattering of customers, but not so many that I'm feeling optimistic about the place.

The waitress hands us the menus. After perusing the one-page choice of items, BB rubs his hands together and says, "I'm having the fajitas."

"You can't get fajitas from a place like this."

"Why not?"

"Because we're out in the middle of nowhere, BB," Millicent says with exasperation. "I highly doubt they specialize in Mexican cuisine."

I decide this is not the best time to correct her. Fajitas are actually Tex Mex and do not originate from Mexico.

"It's a fajita. How can they screw it up?"

Famous last words.

He orders them anyway. I stick with a turkey sandwich, which I figure to be a safe bet, and Millicent orders tomato soup and a grilled cheese. We drink our Cokes and feel everyone's eyes on us as we wait for our food.

"Where are we anyway?" BB finally asks. "I was sleeping."

"Speaking of your nocturnal habits...you're driving the first leg tomorrow. Fair is fair," Millicent says. "We're on the border of Kansas and Missouri."

"Ah, darn. I wanted to see the arch," he says with a frown.

"This isn't a sightseeing trip, BB."

"I didn't say it was, but it's kinda silly to miss out on things like that if we're out here. Not like I'm going to get out to Missouri ever again."

"You might," I say. "I mean, you're young, so it's not like you won't have the opportunity."

"Things cost money, and money I ain't got. I highly doubt my job at the mill is going to pay me a big enough wage to take off on a trip out west," he says.

"You could save up..." I offer, and he rolls his eyes at such a suggestion. It's the first time I've seen him so pessimistic, but I've never had to worry about money. We all have our woes, I guess, and this is his.

"We have to stay focused," Millicent says, then pulls out her phone and points to a map. "We leave first thing tomorrow morning and take this route. There are about seventeen hours left on the trip."

"Seventeen hours?" BB says with alarm.

"What'd you think, this was a quick stroll?" she asks.

"I didn't think it was this long of a drive."

I try not to let the look of worry show on my face, but sitting in the truck for seventeen hours with a prosthesis isn't my idea of a good time.

***

BB's been farting non-stop since he ate the plateful of fajitas. It's like eating sushi from a gas station or seafood in a mountain town. You just don't do it, and he crossed that line. You get my point.

The truck reeks. We can't roll the windows down because it's still raining buckets outside. Millicent has plugged her nose, and I have my t-shirt covering my nose (shirts up for safety), but the strong scent is still permeating. BB's sitting in the back seat oblivious to his wretched stench.

"You're sleeping in the truck tonight. We're not smelling that all night in the tent," Millicent blurts, without even thinking of what that means: No BB means it'll just be her and me in the tent. Not that it matters. She's just a person like me. But if truth be told, I've never been alone with a girl like this.

"Fine. It's cozier in here anyhow," he says, unbothered by her request. "I'll sleep like a baby while y'all are roughing it in the tent."

We drive through the campground. A light flickers from the old lady's RV. It looks all warm and cozy in there, and I'm tempted to tap on her door and ask to be let in so we can have a cup of hot cocoa and get all snug as a bug in a handmade quilt.

I drive to our tent. It's still standing, but all of the water falling from the sky is sure to help it float away. I loathe the idea of sleeping in it on a night like this. A warm motel would be much better, but I know how limited my cash flow is and we've already paid for the site.

Millicent hops out of the truck and runs to the tent, then unzips it and lets herself inside. I follow behind, moving slowly. She takes one look at me and climbs out of the tent, meeting me halfway.

"You'll get soaked."

"I won't melt," she shouts over the pouring rain.

I nearly tumble, and she grabs my hand. I grip tight and cling to her. "One could argue that I'm doing this for a chance to hold your hand."

"That would mean you're clever, and somehow I doubt that."

"Or maybe you're not clever for suspecting my suave moves."

We walk to the tent, then let ourselves inside. I flip the switch for our lantern. The soft glow illuminates the space. Although the tent is tall enough for her, it's not for me. I have to stoop lower since I'm a good foot taller.

There isn't much space between us. Just two sleeping bags rolled up in their bags and one worn blanket, which belongs to BB. I'm sure he dug it out of a hamper or from a pile of dirty clothes.

The bottom of the tent is damp from condensation and rain, and I worry that it's sprung a leak. That's all we need. But I don't see a puddle, and I don't feel droplets hitting my head, so for now, I think we're safe.

She unrolls her sleeping bag, and I try to keep steady on my feet but it's hard when the ground is rocky and wet.

"I'll do that," she offers, referring to my sleeping bag.

I lay my hand on her shoulder. "No, please don't be like that. I like it better when you're mean to me."

"I'm not mean to you."

"Okay, you're not mean, but I wouldn't call you a welcome wagon, either," I say with a sincere smile, hoping it makes it hard for her to be mad at me since I just called her mean. But I like mean people, evidently.

I unroll my sleeping bag. Millicent slides down into hers and squirms around like a worm. I slowly, and with much effort, ease myself to the ground.

"You alright over there?" I ask.

"Just trying to take off," grunt, "these wet shorts." Another grunt.

My mind is overloaded with the imagery. Too much sensory overload. "Could you change the subject? Maybe discuss something boring like baseball or CSPAN."

"Baseball is boring," she agrees, then says no more about stripping wet clothes off of her body. Thankfully.

I turn off the lantern, and it's pitch black inside the tent. I grunt and take off my leg giving ole stubby a chance to breathe.

"Just my leg," I assure her.

"Oh," she says it like a question.

"Don't worry. It doesn't bite... but I do."

"I have repellant with me," she retorts.

"I'm immune to it," I say, then pause for a moment. "When we get up in the morning, I'll make sure I put it on when you're not around. Some people... well, some people get freaked out about seeing ole stubby."

"I'm not some people."

"True," I say and slide into my sleeping bag.

"Why did you agree to come?" she asks.

"I didn't have anything better to do," I say, yawning. Turkey makes me tired, and yawning seems like a safe bet since I'm in no mood to have a deep discussion about my reasons for breaking the law with her.

"So, driving across the country and stealing a body sounded like entertainment?" she presses. She will make a great attorney, only she has ethics. What's that joke about a bunch of attorney's being on the bottom of the ocean?

"It was something BB said to me," I confess.

She rolls on her side, facing me even though she knows I can't see her and she can't see me. "BB said something profound?"

"It was the crux of his statements to me more or less. I…" I struggle for words, "I don't take risks."

"Well, you sure picked a fine time to start."

"If I don't start somewhere, I'll never begin."

"I'm thankful to you," she says. "For agreeing to come. It was nice of you."

"Well, isn't this a sugary sweet moment for you?" I say and hear her sigh through her nose. "Thanks for the kind words, but I'm not doing it out of gratitude. It's more for selfish reasons. Proving to myself that I can. I've been tempted to turn around a million times already."

"Good thing I've been driving then," she says. "You're okay sitting in the truck a long time, right?"

I turn over on my side, regretting the moment I do. I can hear her breathing, and having her so close in the dark, sleeping with next to nothing on, well, it's…. let's just leave it at that. So, I flip on my other side with my back facing her. It does nothing to calm my nerves since my heart is racing and my stomach is doing gymnastic style summersaults. I inhale, taking a deep breath because all of the yoginis tell their yoga students to do this to find their inner peace. I'm sure a yogini never taught a class to Millicent Huxley in the middle of the night wearing next-to-nothing. I try to get my mind on other things like taxes and economics class. It's helping. Anytime I picture Wall Street moguls, I tend to feel too queasy to have pleasant thoughts.

"It's no different than you, only that ole stubby gets hot because of the liners and such," I say. "Your concern for me is sweet."

"As if," she scoffs.

"I think a little part of you likes me." At least I hope. A guy can only hope.

"That's your big ego talking again."

"Sure it is."

"I'm not the one who stares too long," she says, which is a weak comeback.

"I already explained that to you. Maybe if you had some warts or frowned all of the time I wouldn't, but as it is, you're like one of those Michelangelo paintings."

I hear her take a deep breath, which makes me wonder if my compliment has that kind of effect on her, and if it does, I'll keep dishing them out. "He went blind."

"Actually, he didn't. His eyesight deteriorated because he ate nothing but stale bread and lied in awkward positions for a long time when he was painting the Sistine Chapel. It's a sad ending to the man's life."

"Why do you know such things?"

"I read."

"I read, too, but you're a walking encyclopedia."

"They don't make those things anymore," I say wistfully. "It's sad. Like typewriters and VCRs. An obsolete thing from the past never to come back."

"I'm sure no one misses VCRs."

"I was just discussing things that won't ever make a comeback."

"Like Luca…" her voice fades into oblivion.

"You had to go and be a Debbie downer, didn't you?"

She jabs me with her elbow and ends up hitting me in my bicep, which, I'm glad, is somewhat built. I fake like I'm hurt, a little too dramatically, complete with a few oohs and awws like she has super power strength.

"You can't hit a gimp. There's a law against that," I whine.

"You're not helpless. Just mouthy, and not very sensitive."

"Says the one who has no filter, and," I pause, "I don't know what else to say. Death can be uncomfortable, and when I feel uncomfortable or nervous, I tend to make jokes to lighten the mood." Why am I telling her this?

"So, I must make you very uncomfortable then?" she says it in a haughty, I'm-more- superior-than-you tone.

"Nope. Not at all." Biggest lie ever.

"Yeah, right," she says. "Try not to feel threatened by me, Trip," she teases.

I sigh.

"Silence says everything," she rattles on.

I don't say anything. What can I say? Yeah, you're right. You make me crazy! No. Not going to do it. Not confessing. I'll never hear the end of it then. I do have some restraint.

I hear her let out a yawn. "I'm going to sleep."

"Okay. You want me to tuck you in? Read a bedtime story?

Braid your hair?"

And he's back! Take that, you over-confident woman! She rolls on her side, facing the opposite direction.

"Goodnight, Millicent. Sleep tight. Don't let the bedbugs bite."

"You're the only one in here who I have to worry about getting bites from."

CHAPTER 14

The sun is setting, and there's perfect lighting, the kind you get in the best photographs. The ones where even ugly people look good. I see Millicent in the distance. She's wearing a blue string (quite revealing) bikini and is walking into the ocean. The waves crash against her and she laughs, saying my name in a coquettish way.

I look at her greedily, then move in haste to her. I look down at the sand as I walk, and see two feet, both mine.

"Look!" I tell her, pointing to my legs.

"Come on!" she says waving at me, her voice growing louder. She doesn't seem to care about the sudden appearance of my other leg, but I do. I run wild, leaping into the air like those Riverdance dancers and kick them back and forth like a kid celebrating. "Look!" I shout. I point to my leg again before I rush to her.

The waves hit me as I pick her up. I twirl her around. "Did you see? My leg grew back. It's back!" I kick high in the air.

She jumps onto me, laces her fingers in my hair, then wraps her legs around my waist. And I think she's about to kiss me because she leans close to me with parted lips and there's a look of wanting in her eyes, but then her lips form into a frown and her eyes widen. Water suddenly rises and inches its way up to her neck.

"We need to get out!" she shouts. The water is rising. Higher and higher.

I try to move but I'm stuck. I look down and see my leg is missing, then find myself teetering, trying to stand on one foot against the rushing water.

"It's gone!"

She screams in horror. At first, I think it's my leg that has scared her but then I see what she's pointing to: a giant wave is coming our way and once it hits us we will surely die.

She pulls on me but I can't move, and the harder she tries, the more out of breath she becomes. "We need to get out now!"

My body shakes violently, and I feel her grip growing tighter and tighter. She yanks on my hair. The pain burns and the now bald spot on my scalp stings.

I wake up, grimacing. She's sitting on top of me. I widen my eyes, feeling her close presence and offer her a dreamy smile.

"This is a pleasant surprise," I say, but then I notice the look of frenzy on her face. When I peer down, I see why: water is seeping into the tent. Our lantern and my prosthetic are floating.

She shakes me again. "We have to get out!"

I touch my hurting head. "Why'd you pull my hair?"

"Because you wouldn't wake up, Rumplestiltskin."

She rolls off of me and stands up, hovering over me with her hands on her hips. I reach over for my leg, and she briefly stares down at what's missing on my body. My shorts are long enough to cover ole stubby, but it's plain as day that there's no leg. I wish it wasn't like this. I feel ashamed, embarrassed, things I don't want to feel because the look on my face is reflecting these feelings. I know I shouldn't feel this way, but I do.

Her eyes meet mine. It's not often I have a beautiful girl (well, any girl for that matter) sharing a tent with me, and boy does it suck that this is how things turned out tonight.

I cough from nerves and have trouble putting my leg on because I can feel her watching me.

"Maybe if you looked the other way," I say.

She lets out an exasperated sigh. "A leg is a leg is a leg. Who cares about such things? Now hurry it up before we drown."

I slip into my prosthesis and get my bearings, then go through the process. It takes so long that when I stand, the water is up to my ankles. She's waiting patiently and hasn't said a word but I know she's looking at me because when I look up I catch her staring at my face. Not at my leg but at me. Like she's appreciating artwork at a museum.

"Caught you looking," I tease, and you know what? She blushes. If I had enough guts and was manly like Brawny the paper towel guy, I'd grab hold of her and kiss her. But as it is, I am not a manly man and have no cool moves. And, it's probably not so cool to just grab a girl and kiss her when you're not so sure if she's repelled by you or not.

"To the truck," she barks.

The campground is flooded. We're trekking as best as we can, fighting the mud and the rain.

When I get to Dad's truck, I pull on the handle. It's locked. I tap on the window, trying to wake BB, but he's sound asleep.

We bang on the windows, trying to shout over the pouring rain, "BB! Wake up!" but he's out cold and can't hear our pleas. I look to Millicent for a suggestion of what the next course of action should be.

"The old lady," she says.

I give her a simple nod, understanding the meaning behind her vague statement. We walk in the rain to the old woman's RV. A light is on, and we hear Elvis playing. Millicent taps on her door, and the old lady looks out her window, then opens the door.

"We're locked out of our truck, and our tent is flooded,"

Millicent explains.

"Y'all come on in and get out of this nasty weather," the old lady says.

Millicent climbs up into her RV first, then I follow behind. When we step inside, we're immediately greeted by a plume of smoke (peculiar scent) and the color red or various shades of it: red curtains, red silk roses in a red vase, framed prints of red apples and strawberries, and a red lampshade. A red velvet couch sits against one side of the narrow RV. There are two red velvet chairs sit on the opposite side of the couch next to a Formica countertop, which has a stainless sink and one burner stove. Up front is the driver's seat. And toward the back is one twin bed (covered in a red quilt) and a closet-sized bathroom. I bet if I take a peek, there's probably a padded red toilet seat.

The cramped space smells like skunk weed. Millicent nods to the culprit: a red ceramic bong sits on a side table.

"Are y'all hungry?" the old lady asks.

I am sure she is.

"No, thanks," we both say.

"Sorry it smells like a skunk died then got beat with a broom in here," she says. "I had to take my medicine. You'll forgive me if I'm a bit hazy." She chuckles quietly. "I have tea and Coke. Two things every good hostess should have just in case company comes around. And voila, look what I have: company."

"Tea would be great. Thanks," Millicent says.

"You, too?" she asks me.

"Yeah. Thank you."

She searches through her cabinet and pulls out a box of Lipton, takes out two tea bags, then pours water from the faucet into her tea kettle. "Gonna be a moment." She gets two cups out of her cabinet. "Sugar? Milk?"

We both nod, and she adds a heap to both. If I lived with her I'd be stoned, fat, and possibly have to take migraine medication from the exposure to the color red.

Minutes later, the tea kettle whistles and she pours the boiling water into two red mugs and brings them to us.

"Where are y'all from?"

"North Carolina," Millicent answers.

"Indiana originally," I say. "But I live in North Carolina now."

"I'm from the panhandle, or as some like to call it, 'The redneck riviera.' Are y'all here to see the exciting sites of the fine state of Missouri?" she asks with an incredulous expression."So much to see and do."

"Something like that," Millicent answers.

She gives Millicent a knowing look like she is onto us but doesn't seem to care. Maybe she's desperate for the company or feels sorry for us. Or maybe she's just humoring herself. There's a glint in her hazy brown eyes telling me she knows we're full of crap and can't handle a wet night in the woods. "Do you have names or are y'all pronouns?"

"I'm Millicent and this is Trip."

She smiles at us. "I'm Helen," she says. She doesn't offer to shake our hands and continues to watch us like we're good entertainment.

She reaches for a glass bottle of Coke and takes a swig, then sets it down on the coffee table. "Aren't y'all a pair? Right cute, too."

"We're just friends," Millicent says.

"No one your age is 'just friends' if you look like you two. And if you are honey, you might want to get your eyes checked." I smile confidently at Helen's compliment and turn, holding my eyes with Millicent's, shooting her a smug look. She rolls her eyes at me in response.

Helen reaches for a bowl of popcorn and takes a handful of popped kernels, tossing them into her mouth. "You want some?" She gestures to the buttery concoction. "It's movie theatre kind, but I like to add extra butter because you can never have enough butter."

We both decline. I blow into my cup, hoping to cool the steaming cup of tea, then take a sip. It's nothing but sugar and cream with a little bit of tea added, but it's comforting on this dreary night.

Helen looks at me and says, "I have a hair dryer if you want to dry off your liner. It's not good to keep it wet."

I give her a surprised look because most people don't understand the logistics of prosthetics and liners.

She pulls up her pants leg and reveals a prosthetic leg. "We must be related; we've got the same leg."

***

"Bone cancer," she explains. "It took my leg. My good one, too. I thought I was through with the big C, but it's come back again, and this time it's worse. A lot worse," she says without much emotion but her eyes tell a different story. "Really, I feel finer than frog hair split four ways and sanded twice."

Millicent and I form clueless expressions.

"Frog hair is so fine you can't see it," she explains. "My doctor says I'm not going to make it this go around. I figure this old gray mare has a few more kicks left in her, though."

"I'm sorry," I offer, which sounds trite when someone basically just told you that she's dying.

"No reason to be. I've lived a full life and have loved and been loved. You can't ask for more. Maybe a new car or a pot of gold, but," she shrugs her shoulders, "love is enough, isn't it?"

We nod in agreement.

"I'm ready to be with my soulmate again, anyhow," she says wistfully. "And I can't wait to haunt the people who've been mean to me," she says with a mischievous grin. "I got a list, and if they're still alive, they better watch out." She chuckles again. "The pot helps with my lack of appetite if you're wondering. I'm not a pothead. It's kind of ironic that I never smoked it until now since I did grow up in the 1960s. The chemo makes me nauseated. But you probably know that, don't you?" She looks at me and waits for me to answer.

I don't say anything, but I see Millicent side-glance me when she asks.

Helen leans back into her chair and folds her hands in her lap. "So, what's your story?"

I point to my chest and give her a perplexed look.

"The leg," she says.

I don't answer her. My eyes dart over to Millicent, who has an eager look on her face. I'm sure she's dying to know how stumpy came to be. Most people are. People enjoy a good scar tale.

Helen picks up on my body language, and says, "My husband always said I could be awfully nosy." She shrugs, then coughs. Her chest rattles; she chokes, then clears her throat. She pounds on her chest, then makes eye contact with us both, offering a faint smile. "I don't get much company these days and don't have good social skills, but they can't be that bad if you haven't run out screaming yet."

"It's okay," I tell her. Truth be told, if it was just Helen and me in this RV, I'd tell her. She has that kind of face, and since she and I are in the lost limb club, I feel a connection. But I'm not ready to share my tales of woe with Millicent. "Most people ask."

"But you have the power in deciding if you want to tell them or not," she says. "You kids up for a game of gin rummy?"

"Sure," I say with a shrug, and Millicent nods.

"Great." She claps her hands together and smiles. "Maybe I can get the real reason why you're out camping in the middle of nowhere."

CHAPTER 15

The weather never cooperates, and we end up staying in Helen's RV. The sounds of hard rain hammering Helen's precarious roof are keeping me awake. Any moment now, rain could gush through that flimsy roof, drowning us.

I'm sitting across from Millicent in Helen's red recliner. She's laying on Helen's couch and has tossed and turned many times throughout the night. Her eyes slowly open, and I avert my gaze.

"Quit staring," she murmurs.

"I'm not," I lie.

She sits up, running her fingers through her tousled golden hair. "You were. I could feel your eyes on me."

"I can't sleep," I admit.

She yawns and stretches her arms above her head. "I would have thought the whiff of Helen's special potion would have had residual effects on you."

I let out a low laugh, trying not to wake Helen who is sound asleep in the other room.

"I'm having a hard time sleeping, too."

I lean forward.

"I miss Luca," she says with a frown. "And my heart breaks for Mama Sauce. For everyone," she admits. "And," she adds with a sigh, "I'm hurting my moms right now, which I don't want to, but I can't turn back now."

"We can if you think we should," I say.

"No," she shakes her head resolutely. "No. We need to do this; I need to do this."

"People cope with grief in their own way," I say. "This venture is helping you, I suppose."

"It's distracting me, which I need. Have you ever lost someone you love?"

"Yes, and it hurt, but in time, I got through it."

"I've experienced loss more than once in my short seventeen years of life. I know I'll heal in time," she says somberly. "I hate the lingering effects of it. Why can't it all be good all of the time?"

"Then you wouldn't be grateful for anything. Like seeing a rainbow in the sky every day. You'd appreciate it at first, then start to ignore it because it's always there."

"Sometimes I wonder if it's even worth having relationships with people if, in the long run, they're going to leave."

Something about this statement angers me. It's pessimistic, but there's more to it. I don't want her to shut me out just because she's afraid. I need her to take a chance on me. I need her friendship. "If you think that way, you might as well ask yourself if it's worth getting out of bed," I snap.

She flinches. "Ouch."

"Sorry, but it irks me when people ask what the point is of everything? What's the point in working if you're going to retire? What's the point in getting out of bed if you're going to end up there again anyway? The answer is life. You can't live a life without connections. Just ask a guy who doesn't have a lot of friends and realizes he can't keep going on without having them."

"I don't have a lot of friends, either," she says, peering downward.

"You have a commune of friends."

She looks up. Her brows perch together. "True, but in school, it's just BB… and… you," she confesses.

"That's more than some people," I say. "And I'd say the two friends you have at school are loyal and good friends to you even if you do choose to be a tad snarky with one of them." I form a crooked smile.

"One of my friends deserves a little snark sometimes."

She yawns again.

"You should go to sleep," I say.

She lays back down, facing me. "Don't be embarrassed about your leg. BB and I don't define you by it. We see you." She closes her eyes and murmurs something else, but I can't catch what she says.

***

I wake to the sound of Helen rummaging through her cabinet, humming some unknown tune (ineptly) and searching for food. She pulls out a packet of oatmeal and adds it to a cup of boiling water, then stirs the contents with a spoon, clinking it against the ceramic mug. She catches me watching her and says, "Want some roughage?"

"No, thank you." I feel like we've infringed on her good will long enough.

She waves her hand down and huffs. "You can't start your morning without eating breakfast. I have Little Debbie cakes, too." She pulls a box out of her cabinet and empties it, then tosses one to me.

"Thanks," I say.

Last night, Millicent and I didn't confess our plans to her, and after a few minutes of hard pressing, she decided to give up and told stories of her life in campgrounds. She's been an overseer of sorts since her husband died because she wanted adventure and thought it'd be less lonely than staying cooped up in her home.

"Did you sleep well last night?" she asks me.

"Yes," I lie. I didn't sleep well at all, but I don't want to tell her that since she did save us from floating away.

"There's something about sleeping out in nature. Makes you get a better night's rest," she says.

"With your health concerns, shouldn't you considering living in a more stable place?" I ask her.

"Why? So I can shrivel up and die either from loneliness or boredom? At least this way, the only thing that can get me is the SOB cancer, a bear, or maybe a crazy serial killer. I'm betting on the bear," she says.

I look at Millicent and see she's finally opening her eyes and waking up. She shoots me a soft smile and says a pleasant "Good morning" to Helen and me.

"Want some roughage?" Helen asks her.

"Probably not a good idea for a long drive," she says.

"Little Debbie it is." She tosses one to Millicent, who catches it with one hand.

I search for my prosthetic leg, which is leaning against the paneled wall. I feel Millicent watching me. This is usually a private act, but after last night, I guess that kind of modesty needs to be tossed out the window.

I lean forward and reach for it, let out a low grunt, then begin the process of putting it on.

"It's like being constipated," Helen says, and she gestures to me as I slip into my prosthesis. "You try and try, then finally after taking forever, something happens."

I laugh. "I've never thought to compare it to my bowel habits."

"Everything relates to poop." She eyes my prosthesis. "That's a nice one. When'd you get it?"

"A year ago."

"I've only had this one." She taps on her leg. "And it's not the luxury model like yours."

"I guess I have better insurance."

And I think it must strike Millicent as odd that we can laugh at such things, but if you don't laugh, you cry.

"Probably so," she says. "Medicare is the pits. The old and the young are treated horribly in this country."

"That's true," I say. "And the disabled and mentally ill."

"Yeah," Helen says with a wistful sigh.

"We should probably get going," Millicent says. She taps on her phone screen, pointing to the clock, and I notice she has several notifications for unread text messages.

"You kids were good for my blood pressure," Helen says. "Thanks for letting an old lady tell tales."

"We enjoyed it," I say. "You have lived an interesting life."

"That I have," Helen says reflectively. "Make sure someone else can say the same about you when you're as old as I am."

I nod, agreeing with her. I don't want my tombstone to read, "Here lies Beckett Wentworth the Third, a man who did nothing and made no impact on this planet. He existed; he never lived."

We move toward the door. Helen opens her arms and pulls us into a hug. And for a moment, I just let her because hugging her feels like being outside on a sunny day. She releases us from her embrace and offers us another smile. I push the door open and step outside.

The sky is clear, and the sun is shining. The ground is still wet.

Helen stands inside with her front door open watching as we amble to Dad's truck. "You kids be careful!"

We turn and glance at her, waving another goodbye.

"I want to be her when I grow up," I say to Millicent.

"Really? Why?"

"She's lived. Really lived. And she's so at peace with death."

"She's old. They are more in terms with the inevitable."

"It's more than that…" my voice trails off. "Like she knew she lived, so death isn't so scary."

Millicent shrugs. "I guess if you're happy with the way you lived, you're not so scared of death."

"We all end up in the same place; our way of getting there is the only thing that is different."

"So deep for early in the morning," she says. "You might stare too much, but you sure are good for conversation."

"All of the best gawkers are."

We find BB standing outside of the truck. He jogs toward us with pursed lips, waving his hands up in the air and shouting, "I thought something happened to y'all!"

"Your tent is a piece of crap!" Millicent says to him.

"There ain't nothing wrong with that tent. It was fine last time I used it," he says.

"It doesn't hold up in the rain, BB." She shakes her head in frustration. "We were flooded out."

He half shrugs like it's not a big deal. "Where'd you sleep?"

"Helen's RV."

He squints like he's thinking. "Who is Helen?"

"The old lady who runs the campground."

"I bet she had warm cookies and hot chocolate, too," he says with a sigh.

"She wasn't your average grandmother," I say.

Millicent laughs, and we look at each other, sharing a private joke, which irritates BB. "Great. Now I'm out of the loop on y'all's inside joke."

"Maybe if you didn't eat fajitas and have farts that smell like a sewage plant then you would be in the know," she says. "I've got to brush my teeth and use the bathroom before we go. You guys should do the same."

"Okay, Mom," we say in unison.

"Jinks," I say to BB.

"Aww, man," BB grumbles like I'm holding some power over his ability to speak.

"No one says 'jinks' anymore, Trip," Millicent says.

"I just did."

"It was cool when we were in first grade."

"It's still cool. Look at him." I point to BB. "He can't speak until I unlock his jinks spell."

She rolls her eyes and fights a laugh because I'm smiling and wagging my brows, and BB is begging me to unlock the spell of the jinks, which we all know doesn't even exist. "I'll be back."

"Okay, Arnie," I shout.

BB and I walk toward the bathroom, which is filled with cobwebs and creepy crawlies. BB shudders when he sees a spider crawling along the sink.

"It won't get you," I say. I try not to laugh, but it's ironic that the guy will go hunting, which means hanging out in the woods with bears, but he can't stand the sight of a harmless spider.

"Sorry y'all got flooded out," he says, applying my toothpaste to his finger. He didn't pack a toothbrush or toothpaste. At this point, I wonder if he packed anything other than junk food.

"It's not a big deal, but I don't think we'll be camping anymore on this trip," I mumble with a mouth full of toothpaste. I brush my teeth, then spit and rinse.

He runs water from the faucet all over his toothpaste covered finger, then shuts it off. "Yeah," he says with sadness. "I don't know what I'm going to do come huntin' season."

"You can always sleep outside."

"No way."

I push the door open and start my way toward Dad's truck. "You mean to tell me you're afraid of the dark."

"Just of bears and bobcats," he says.

"There aren't any bobcats," I argue.

"Sure there are. I saw one once. Thought I was hallucinating, but the thing just sat there and stared at me then went on its way."

Somehow I doubt he saw a bobcat. It was probably a fox or an obese domestic cat that was fed way too much Friskies.

"Wonder who she's texting," I say, referring to Millicent, who's standing off to the side away from everyone and being all conspicuous.

"Probably her mom. They're real tight, and I'm sure she's probably feeling bad about worrying her."

I think of my own mom but don't say anything. As a guy, rule number one is not to appear soft, which is stupid because who said we had to be these macho tough unfeeling jerks? We're human, too. We feel, too.

I click the remote on the truck, unlocking it. We climb in. I sit in the back; BB takes the driver's seat.

Millicent squints in our direction, then comes marching up to us and taps on my window. "Get out. I'm not sitting up front."

"Why?"

"I don't want to smell BB," she says, but I sense she's lying because no one is ever dying to sit in the back of a truck. It's fit for a little person or a small child, not anyone who is tall enough to ride a rollercoaster at an amusement park.

"I don't smell," BB defends.

I sigh, but secretly I'm relieved. There isn't much room back here (my legs are pressing against the seat). It's cramped and uncomfortable, but I was trying to be chivalrous and maybe a small part of me is like Mr. Darcy.

I get out and act like I'm bothered that she's asked me to move, then climb up into the front passenger seat. BB turns the key in the ignition and starts driving toward the campground exit.

"Beep the horn," Millicent says as we pass by Helen's RV. We see her wave at us from her window.

I pull out my notebook and jot down a few notes.

"Whatcha writing?" BB asks me.

"Thoughts," I murmur. When I'm inspired, I write.

"It's probably a good thing I don't write down all my thoughts," BB says, smiling. "Might get me in trouble."

"That's true," Millicent and I both say.

"Jinks," I say to her. "I know you said that you thought that was for first graders, but I never did." I smirk from the passenger side mirror. "Don't worry. I'll unlock the jinx spell soon. It won't be a pleasurable drive if we don't get to hear your voice."

CHAPTER 16

The general consensus (at least among the three of us) is that Kansas is the most boring, flattest state we've ever visited. I've seen the same scenery since we entered the state over five hours ago. I'm hungry and craving pancakes. Gee, I wonder why.

Millicent flips through her magazine and twirls her hair around her finger over and over. I hear her chewing the gum BB bought, who swears that it is the best chewing gum out there, but all I got from it was a dull taste of leather after a few chews. He smacks his gum and bobs his head to the old tunes playing on the radio. He's proof that you never can judge a book by its cover. When I first met him, I swore he'd be a country music fan.

"What's that magazine telling you? How to apply mascara or get bigger boobies," BB says with a snicker to Millicent. He's the only guy my age who likes to say, "boobies."

"Noooo," Millicent answers him with annoyance. "I'm reading an article."

"About?"

"Six degrees of separation," she says. "How we're all connected by a separation of six people."

"So, you're saying I'm connected to Taylor Swift?" he asks with an upbeat tone. The guy is in love with her.

"According to this article, you are. You know someone who knows someone who knows someone who knows a person who knows her."

He grins wide and says, "Hot damn! When we get back home, I'm quizzing everyone I know to see how me and Taylor are connected, 'cause when I meet her there's bound to be some love added to that connection."

I turn my head, looking over my shoulder at Millicent. "Do you agree with the theory?"

Her forehead wrinkles, and she twists her lips to the side, pondering. "I don't know. The world is a small place. We're bound to all be connected somehow."

"Like me and you, Trip," BB says. "We were connected before he even came to school."

"How's that?" Millicent asks.

"His parents buy meat from Mr. Tedder, and I deliver it to them."

"That's hardly a connection. Half the town buys meat from Tedder," she says.

"Still. We knew each other," he defends. "Ain't that right?" He looks at me.

"We didn't know each other, but, yeah, there was that," I say.

"A connection," he adds.

"If that's what you want to call it," I say.

"It is what I'm calling it. If you think about it, that means you were connected to Mellie, too."

"At this rate, we'll find out I have a connection to Kevin Bacon," I say.

"You just might," BB says.

It grows quiet, and music is all we hear. Dad has satellite radio, and BB has kept it on the 1970s and 80s station the entire drive through the incredibly flat state of Kansas. I know I'm beating a dead horse about its flatness. Same music; same scenery. Just blah.

I hear a familiar tune play and let out a groan. "Not this one again!" I reach to change the station, but BB swats my hand away.

I give him a dirty look, and he shakes his head while smiling, then reaches to turn the knob, pumping up the volume.

"This song is awesome!" he shouts over the music. He moves his head in beat to the 1970s tune and joins the chorus, singing, "Sexy Eyes."

And like a magnet for trash or bad things, I can't help but join along. BB and I are singing from the top of our lungs. I start to get into it and sway with rhythm to the beat of the music. BB gives me a look of approval, which encourages me to continue my buffoonery.

I don't realize they've grown quiet until the song ends and Millicent says, "You have a nice voice."

"Thanks." I shrug. I'm not Pavarotti, but I can carry a tune. I'd forgotten she was in the truck, which is strange because I'm always aware of her presence. Maybe I'm growing less self-conscious around her.

BB cups his hand over the side of his mouth and whispers loudly, "She can't sing."

She playfully hits him on his arm, and he moans. "I'm not that bad."

"Babies weep when you belt out a tune," he says.

I let out a soft chuckle, and she flicks me hard on my arm. "Ow," I whine. I rub the now sore spot on my arm. "What did you do that for?"

"You laughed," she says.

"I'm going to have a bruise," I joke.

We continue driving along and enter the state of Colorado, still seeing nothing but flat land.

BB frowns. "I thought there were mountains in this state. Where are they?"

"Further west," I answer.

"How much longer 'till we see 'em?" he asks.

"I'm not sure," I say. "Maybe another hour or so."

***

We stop to refuel and stretch our legs. BB tosses me the keys and tells me it's my turn to take the wheel. Millicent is halfway to the restroom before we even make our way inside the convenience store. I feel my phone vibrate and pull it out of my pocket, seeing I have a new message from Mom.

We've decided to stay here a couple of days. We're taking a mini-vacation. Will you be okay?

I type her back a response: *Not sure. Being left alone for so long could be too tempting. Might throw a party. Isn't that what the teens do when their parents leave?*

My phone vibrates again. *Haha. Just make sure to hide the crystal.*

I text her back. *I will. Bye.*

Simple, sarcastic texts keep her from suspecting anything. It's almost as if the gods are looking out for me. *A mini-vacation.* That gives me a little more time. Enough time to do what I came here to do and possibly get back home without them ever knowing. Of course, Dad might notice the thousands of miles we've put on his truck. So, there's that.

I purchase an ice cream sandwich and head outside, then stand in the shade while I eat it. A woman and her son walk past me. He stops, pulls on her hand and points to me.

"Look. He's a superhero," he says. His small index finger is aimed at my leg.

"Don't be rude," she admonishes him. A flush of embarrassment sweeps across her face.

"It's okay," I assure her. This kind of thing happens more often than you would think. A lot of kids come up and touch me, which doesn't bother me because they're kids. What do they know? It's the adults who know better but still try to cross boundaries who bother me.

"Can you fly?" he asks me.

"No, but I wish I could," I say.

"I do, too," he says. "I wish I had a leg like that."

"Your legs look perfect to me," I say.

"No, they're not cool like yours," he says, and his mother thanks me with a slight grin before walking away. He peers over his shoulder, waves at me, then hops along, following her.

Millicent comes out, searching for me, then spots me leaning against the brick wall, watching people.

She stands with her hands on her hips and gives me a look. "You didn't get one for me?"

"Nope." I eat the rest and pat my belly, smiling.

"Humph," she mumbles.

"Isn't that something a couple would do?" I move towards her. "We're not a couple, unless you want to change that." I wink at her and notice a blush creep up on her cheeks.

"In your dreams."

"Or maybe a nightmare in my case," I say with a smile.

I unlock the truck, then climb inside and sit down, feeling the summertime heat from Dad's black leather seats. Why black, Dad? Why black? My skin sticks to the seat from sweat.

I turn the ignition but nothing happens. I turn it again and hear a clicking sound.

"What the?"

I try again, but the truck doesn't respond. Millicent shoots me a look of concern, and I shrug at her. I try once more and have the same result.

"Maybe you should look under the hood," she offers.

"And look for what?" I say in annoyance. Why do girls assume all guys are walking mechanics? Like all of a sudden, I'm going to diagnose the problem just by one look under the hood.

"For the corncob that's stuck up your butt," she quips.

Touché.

BB climbs into the truck. "It's hot as hell in here. Turn on the air," he barks.

"We're seeing what a Native American sweat lodge feels like," I say with annoyance and see he hasn't caught on to my sarcasm. "The truck won't start."

"What do you mean? It's brand spanking new."

"It won't start." I demonstrate by turning the ignition.

"Battery's dead," he says.

I slam my palms against the steering wheel, inadvertently beeping the obnoxious horn, and startle a woman walking by. I give her an apologetic look, but she still glares at me.

"We're going to need a jump," BB says.

CHAPTER 17

We found someone with jumper cables. BB and I wanted Millicent to do the asking, but she told us in no uncertain terms that she would not be used as a sex object. "I'm not the kind of girl who hikes up her skirt and whistles at men just so I can get something," she said.

"Fine. I'll use this then," I said, tapping on my leg.

"That's not right, either."

"You can't have it both ways. People are people, and you get a lot more attention if you look like you or you have something like this."

It didn't take us long to find someone to help us. A few minutes at the most. A veteran named Willie—who assumed I had been injured in the war—says he'd be happy to help. "I always help my fellow brethren. Semper Fi."

I know the Marine Corps hymn on the piano, so if it came down to it, I'd sing him the song just to show my solidarity. Desperation is desperation, and we're low on funds.

"Amen," I say to him.

"It's not right," Millicent whispers to me.

"I didn't say anything but an 'amen.'"

"But you're leading him to believe you are something you're not," she argues.

"Like all people. We're all performers in one way or another. You do your argumentative, I want justice," and I wave my hand up in the air, "kind of thing."

"It's not a thing. It's who I am."

I smirk. "Everything pisses you off."

"No, just you."

I laugh, which I know irritates her. "You're angry at the world, and for what? From where I stand, you have a family who loves you and you're wicked smart."

"You just said, 'wicked.'"

I become flustered. "Yeah," I say, "So."

"So, it's a term people from the 1980s in Boston used."

"Mr. Finley, my former tutor, said it a lot."

"That doesn't mean you should, too."

"I thought we were discussing you."

"I changed the subject." She flashes me a sardonic smile. "And saying 'wicked' makes you stranger than you already are."

I nudge her arm with my elbow. "Ahh, but who wants normal, right?"

Willie, who tells us he was named after the singer Willie Nelson, drives one of those monster trucks that competes in rallies. It's dirty and is too big for someone his size (he's the height of Tom Cruise). His brown hair is cut in a pseudo-mullet, and tattoos adorn his arms and frighteningly pale legs.

He starts up his engine, and it drowns out all background noise. He gives me the signal to turn the ignition. The truck runs but only for a moment. Within seconds the lights dim, the gages flicker, and it shuts down again.

Willie turns off his truck and hops out, moving toward us. "It's not the battery. It's the alternator."

I rub my hand across my face, flickering worry. "Those aren't cheap to replace, are they?"

"I got a buddy who's a mechanic," he offers. "He won't steer you wrong."

"We'll have to have this towed," I say with uneasiness. "That's not cheap, either."

"I'll call him up," Willie offers. "I bet he'd put the alternator in right here for you."

A woman wearing the gas station logo on a greasy button down top marches our way. "You can't leave that parked here!"

"It won't move," I say to her.

"You'll have to push it then. You're keeping the customers out." She folds her arms across her chest and waits for us to get a move on.

I hand Millicent the keys. "Put it in neutral."

"Why me?"

"Because you're not Chuck Norris and you won't be able to push this thing."

"Who says?"

"Why are you arguing with me about this?" I groan in frustration. "Could you for once just listen to me?"

She leans close to me and whispers, "Can you push the truck?"

I shoot her a strange look. "Do I look frail to you?"

She sighs heavily. "I was trying... well, I was trying to help. I thought," and her eyes dart down to my leg, "I thought it would be hard to do..."

I roll my eyes and mutter under my breath. "Don't. Please don't."

"I..." her voice fades.

I grow serious. "We can't be friends if you're going to make concessions."

She doesn't say anything more and climbs into the truck, then puts the gear in neutral while BB, Willie and I push it to the closest parking spot. She hands me back my keys, and I don't make eye contact with her because I'm trying to catch my breath and my leg is killing me.

Willie checks his phone. "He says for us to come by his shop and buy the alternator, then he'll come here and put it in after he gets off work."

"That works," I say, and BB nods in agreement.

"I'll drive you guys," Willie says.

"That would be great. Thanks," I say.

Willie holds the passenger door open for Millicent and says, "Climb on in, little lady."

I snigger, knowing it's probably killing her to hold her tongue at Willie's comment.

BB and I climb into the back seat, and we drive off to Willie's friend's auto shop. It's a good fifteen miles up the road. Willie doesn't strike me as the type, but a dream catcher hangs from his rearview mirror and spa music plays on his radio.

"My doctor said I needed to learn how to relax so I bought this CD," he explains. "I figure that thing will catch all my nightmares." He gestures toward the dream catcher.

There's a strong scent of freshly cut grass and empty bottles of highly caffeinated products clutter the floor. I swiftly kick one out of the way and hold on for dear life as Willie speeds down the road. We feel every bump and pothole. Willie has no problem cursing everyone out who drives too slow or gets in his way. He likes to give people the bird, too. For someone who is supposed to be practicing inner chi, he's a truculent guy, aching for a fight.

"Damn roads are awful here," he says. "Fucking government types take our taxes but don't spend it to keep up our roads. They legalize pot, saying the money will fix the roads. Ha!" he scoffs. "Look at this." He takes one hand off of the wheel, pointing to the cracked asphalt. "It's in fucking disarray."

He rattles on about his problems with the government, expressing what sounds like conspiracy theories—which makes me wonder if he has a doomsday shelter somewhere—then discusses his issues with the VA. "You know how it is," he says to me, looking at me in the rearview mirror. "You're lucky you've even got that prosthetic. It's the world's worst care. We fight for our country but can't get decent medical care."

I don't say anything, but Millicent makes sure to. "You sure are lucky, Trip," she says, raising a brow.

We pull into the auto shop parking lot. The garage door is open, and oscillating fans are blowing at full speed. Men are working on cars and don't stop what they're doing even though we're standing outside the garage staring at them, waiting for some assistance.

"Yo! Jorge!" Willie shouts over the heavy metal music.

A man who has to be Jorge rolls out from under a car and stands up, then walks our way. He wipes his dirty hands on his blue grimy pants. He offers us a tight smile and says nothing. He's a big man—the type who could crush you with his pinkie finger. I make a mental note not to piss him off since I like the idea of breathing.

"This is the fellow Marine I told you about," Willie tells him in reference to me.

He offers me a head nod. "How you doing, boss?"

"As good as I can be," I say.

"I feel you."

"So, he needs an alternator," Willie goes on.

Jorge shuffles toward glass doors—which lead to an office—and he opens them, gesturing for us to step inside. There are a few chairs and a stack of magazines on the nearby table. When I get a closer look, I see they're from 2013. That's probably how old the coffee in the coffee pot is, given its consistency: Mississippi River brown. It reeks of gasoline in here.

He flips through a book, then looks up at us. "It'll be $170 for the alternator. I'll waive the labor fee since you're one of us."

"We have to pay you for your time," I say.

Jorge holds up his hand. "It's on me. I was in the service, too, and had plenty of buddies who got hurt."

Millicent looks at me like I'm supposed to all of a sudden confess, but I ignore her and don't argue with Jorge any further.

"I don't get off here until five," Jorge says.

"That's fine," I say. I turn to look at Willie. "Can you drop us back off at the gas station?"

"What will you do there for the next few hours?" Willie asks.

I shrug. "We'll think of something."

"There's a decent pub nearby. How about we go there and kill some time?"

I look at them, and BB says, "Sounds good; I'm hungry."

I wait for Millicent to answer. "It doesn't matter," she says with a clipped tone.

I read her voice loud and clear. "To the pub, it is," is all I say.

CHAPTER 18

Classic country music plays on the jukebox, and a smattering of people fill the pub. Most are drinking shots of whiskey or drowning their sorrows in pints of beer. The air is smoky and stale, and all bloodshot eyes watch us as we are seated in a corner booth. Willie wanders off to talk to the bartender and comes back to our table with a pitcher of beer and a stack of glasses. No one thought to ask us for our IDs. It's a teen's dream, just not this particular teen.

BB helps himself to a full glass like a greedy dog. I pour myself a glass and have a sip. I've never tried warm piss, but this beer is giving me an idea of what it tastes like. I try not to let Willie see my sour expression.

There's a bowl of nuts on the table. BB scoops a handful and tosses them in his mouth.

"You shouldn't eat those," I say.

"Why not?"

"They're covered in germs." People don't wash their hands, then proceed to touch the nuts, and places like these don't empty out the bowls. They refill them with whatever is left.

"We're all germs," BB says and grabs another handful.

"You were in the Corp. What's a bowl of nuts gonna do to you?" Willie says.

I choose not to respond for obvious reasons. What am I going to say? Hoorah! Semper Fi! Grab a gun and go!

Millicent asks the waitress for a glass of water as we drink (well, I'm faking) the beer and talk about nothing of importance: sports, speculation about sports, and more sports. The conversation is mostly two-sided, with BB and Willie doing most of the talking.

I'm not a sports kind of guy. Then Willie starts talking of his woes from the war. Uh oh. Millicent gives me an "I told you so" type of look.

"Bootcamp doesn't even prepare you for war," Willie says. "How long were you in?" he asks me.

"Long enough," I answer, purposely being vague. I feel bad for lying to him, but at this point, I'm in the thick of this fable. "What made you move here?"

Millicent catches on to the obvious subject change, but Willie doesn't. He goes on to say how he is from Colorado and couldn't imagine moving anywhere but back home. Most people like talking about themselves, and Willie is one of them.

The pub is nothing spectacular. At best, it's a watered down version of what I imagine pubs are like in the UK. Only this one is in need of a refurbishing and the customers aren't as lively or interesting - at least not like the ones they show in the movies. There's nothing but a bunch of people desperate for cheap drinks and bland food.

We all order hamburgers and french fries, and the waitress refills the pitcher with more beer. I give BB a warning look, but he ignores me and indulges in more like a rebellious child. "Fine. Drink up," I say, giving him permission to get inebriated. I'm still on my first glass and have since asked for a Coke.

There's a baseball game playing on the television, and a few cheers are heard when the Rockies score a home run. I catch Willie staring at Millicent

"What's your story, little lady?" he asks her.

"The name is Millicent," she says.

He smiles like she's being funny. "What's your story, *Millicent*?"

"There isn't one."

"I doubt that. You look like you've got a lot to say."

"Not really," she says with an irritated tone. I wish she could feign some kindness just until we get the new alternator.

"I'm good at making people talk," he says with an air of cockiness. "I bet I can get you talking."

"Only if it will shut you up," she says. I shoot her a look, but she's unfazed.

He laughs with uncertainty - like he's not sure if he should be insulted or not. "Feisty. I had a girlfriend who was feisty, just like a palomino horse. I tamed her, though. Bet I could tame you."

I reach down and squeeze her hand, hoping it will not, in fact, let the floodgates open. She jerks her hand free from mine.

"So women are like horses to you? That's such a compliment," she says with sarcasm. "I bet that works like a charm when you're on a date."

He drinks the rest of his beer and sets the glass down on the table, then wipes his lips with his the back of his hand. "It's worked here and there. I like you," he says. "How about you come live with me in my trailer for a couple of years? We'll get to know each other better."

"Why a couple of years?" I ask him.

Willie shrugs. "We'll see how it goes."

I unconsciously scoot closer to her. I proceed to wrap my arm around her and give her a gentle squeeze. I notice Willie is watching me getting cozy with her. If it were any other time, I'm confident she'd move my arm, but since Willie all but invited her to shack up with him, I get to play protective boyfriend today. I feel a swift kick to my prosthetic (when it moves, what's left of my leg feels it), but it doesn't hurt because of the lack of feeling (no foot=no nerves). I smile because Millicent is gloating.

I lean in and whisper to her, "You're kicking my left foot."

"I know," she says with a smug expression.

"There aren't any nerves down there," I whisper, mirroring the smug look she just gave me.

She scowls at me before rising from the tattered pleather ('cause it's not leather) seat. "I have to use the restroom."

Willie watches her walk away; his eyes zoom in on her butt. "She's good looking."

"She's a pain in the ass," BB slurs. "But I still love her."

"You two together?" he asks me.

"Yeah," I lie.

"Since when did you and Mellie hook up?" BB asks.

I swiftly kick him under the table, hoping he'll take the hint but it doesn't even faze him. "A while ago. We didn't want to tell you because we knew you'd be mad."

His face lightens up. "Mad? That's the best news I've heard all week!"

I feel bad, knowing I'll rain on his parade later, but this isn't the time to say, "Ha! Got you!"

Willie gives me a skeptical look but doesn't say anything else about Millicent. We watch the game, which is as boring as watching paint dry, but the two of them are really into it. So is the rest of the bar. Something tells me that even if curling were on the television right now, they'd be enthralled. Most are so drunk they don't even know what they're watching.

At first, I think it's the television, but when the game cuts to commercial, there's a brief moment of silence and I hear Millicent shouting. "Let me go!"

I jump up without even thinking. "That's Millicent!"

BB takes a while to respond, and I shove him hard in his shoulder. "Did you hear her? She's in trouble!"

He stands up, but I don't wait for him to follow me. I rush (as best as I can). When you have a prosthetic, it's hard as hell to run. Try running with one leg that won't bend and see how well you do, then you'll know what I'm talking about. They make special prosthetics for running, but obviously, I didn't pack that one with me. Not that I run often anyway. I'm one of those being- chased-will-make-me-run type of guys.

I reach the hallway leading to the bathrooms and see two drunk men hovering around Millicent, trapping her. One has his hands all over her. The other is standing off to the side, laughing like this is a good television show.

"What's your problem?" he asks her, then trails a finger down her arm. She jerks his hand away from her, and he laughs. "Spunky, aren't you?" He clamps his hand on her shoulder again.

"Millicent, are you ready to go?" I ask, coming from behind him. Willie and BB are standing behind me, although I'm not sure how much help BB will be since he's unsteady on his feet. And, given our physiques and these two brutes, I'd say we're not very intimidating.

"She's busy," one answers.

"I wasn't talking to you," I say.

"So, this isn't none," (yes, he used a double negative, which is annoying) "of your damn business," he says.

"I've made it my damn business," I say. "Now let her by."

He drops both of his arms to his side, then balls one of his hands into a fist, bringing it up to my face. "You shouldn't get involved in things that don't matter to you." His breath smells of beer, and he reeks of sweat and piss and all other things that have putrid scents about them. Pig pens smell better than he does.

"She matters to me," I say. "Are you going to keep being a dick?"

His jaw clenches, and his lips snarl. Uh oh. I'm in serious trouble.

His friend lays his hand on his shoulder and says, "He's crippled."

His eyes dart down to my leg, then back to my face. "I'm not fighting a man with one leg. So, take a hike."

"I've still got two fists, so I'd say we're even," I say, then deck him right in the face. Sucker punch! I didn't know I had it in me.

He's taken by surprise and brings his hand up to his cheek, then like a switch, something in him changes. "I don't care if you are a cripple," he says, (by the way, I hate being called a "cripple") and he's about to hit me, but Millicent kicks him right in his nuts before he can. He grovels, then tries to catch his breath and clutches his groin, groaning in agony.

"We better get out of here," Willie says to us.

We start hauling ass with one of the guys following right behind us, cursing loud enough for the whole pub to hear. He's drunk as a skunk. So is the other one. That's the problem with places like this. The people who come here want to get drunk, and the bartenders let them. Then they do stupid things like these two guys just did.

The bartender stands in his way (now he comes, how convenient) and tells Willie and the rest of us to get lost. We make it to the door, and as I stand outside, I see Millicent panting. She's bent over and has her hands on her knees. I'm not sure if she's going to hurl; even so, I go over to her and gently lay my hand on her shoulder, hoping she won't flinch from my touch.

"Are you okay?" I ask quietly, but the tempo of my voice is faster than normal. My adrenaline is at full speed. I feel like I've drunk a couple of bottles of Red Bull.

"I could've handled them."

"I didn't want you to have to take that risk."

"I don't need your protection," she says.

"I know you don't. But maybe I need to feel like I'm protecting someone."

CHAPTER 19

Well, the appreciation for my heroism was short-lived. Now my knuckles are bloody, and my hand is sure to be bruised. I don't know what I was thinking getting into a fight. This is my first, by the way. I don't think a shoving match with Ryan Belcher counts. It seems like I'm having a lot of firsts this week.

All I know is, something in me clicked when I heard Millicent shouting like a damsel in distress. It was like all reason ceased since I stormed over there like I was Vin Diesel in an action film ready to go all gung-ho and kick some ass! That guy could have killed me. I guess I should be kissing the asphalt with gratitude that I got out of there relatively unscathed.

She hasn't said a simple "thanks" or anything to me. Just, "I could've handled it." Maybe she's right. She did kick the guy in the nuts. That'll stop any guy unless he is wearing a brass plated jock strap, but even then there's bound to be some residual effect on the precious jewels.

We're back at the gas station, and the diagnosis was correct: the alternator is shot. Jorge works on it for almost an hour. Willie tries making small talk with Millicent, but his game is worse than mine, and he finally decides it's futile.

I start up Dad's truck. Willie looks like he's going to cry since we have to part ways. I'm feeling a little guilty for taking advantage of him and Jorge, but I'm not feeling the urge to suddenly confess.

"To Wyoming, we go," I say, trying to corral the troops, but BB is still half-drunk and Millicent isn't joining in my enthusiasm.

Willie gives us all a tight hug goodbye; Jorge gives us a head nod with a simple, "Bye."

"Look me up on Instagram," Willie says to us. "I'm @ theterminator31."

"Like in Arnold?"

"No, that's my truck's name and my number for the monster truck rallies," he explains. "It helps with the aggression. If you're as pissed off as I am half the time, you need some sort of outlet."

We say our goodbyes, then head north toward the fine state of Wyoming. The roads are definitely better than they were in Colorado, and the speed limit is a whopping eighty miles per hour, which is great since I'm one of the few drivers on the road. So I've got the truck on cruise control and am sitting back and looking ahead. Secretly I'm kind of glad to be driving. I need something to do, and the silence (from Millicent) is killing me.

The scenery begins to change (thankfully). Mountains are in view, but everything is still brown with a touch of green here and there. I've never seen so much brown in my life: burnt sienna, chocolate, doo doo brown. Call it whatever you want, we're in the desert. The air is dry, so my curls are almost nonexistent, which isn't the best look for me since my hair isn't cut into much of a style, to begin with.

Millicent has been quiet for the past hour. I nudge her but get no reaction. I don't speak rare species, so I don't say or attempt to do anything else.

BB's humming to the music and slurring his words. He drank too much beer and is still buzzed.

"We'll stop soon," I say.

No response.

"Okay, Trip, that sounds like a good idea," I say.

I hear her sigh. Dramatically. I reach to turn the volume down and ask, "What'd I do?"

"Hey! I like that song," BB whines. "Why'd you turn it down?"

"You shouldn't even have to ask," Millicent says to me, ignoring BB's pleas.

"Obviously, I had to, since I have no idea why you're giving me the stink eye."

"What you did wasn't right."

"Punching that guy?" I say in disbelief. "He had his hands all over you. I think he deserved to be hit."

"I would've hit him too, Mellie," BB says. "Men shouldn't grope women unless it's a mutual decision."

"You're right, BB, and I'm thankful for Trip for helping me. But he shouldn't have made Willie and Jorge think he was injured in the war," she says. "You played on their sympathy, Trip."

So, this is why I'm getting the silent treatment. "If I told them the truth, the real truth of how I lost my leg, they'd feel even more sorry for me. At least this way, I was a part of something. At least this way, I'd lost it in honor," I say. "I think a part of them knew I was lying, but they wanted to be a part of something again."

She looks down at her lap and doesn't say anything else. I turn up the volume, hearing more disco tunes from the early 1980s.

***

We stop at a roadside motel aptly named The Bull Rider Motel, complete with a cowboy riding a bull in the bright neon sign. The sign also boasts "Colored TV and phone in every room." Not sure what decade we stepped into.

We're in the town of Casper, one of Wyoming's biggest and most populated towns, but it still feels small in comparison to cities like Denver or Nashville. I use the credit card Mom gave me "for emergencies only." I'd say this is an emergency since we need a place to lay our heads tonight and don't have any other way of paying. BB has spent most of his money on junk, and we're going to need the cash we have to buy gas and food. Thanks to BB's unreliable, now balled-up-into-a-bear-proof-dumpster-tent, we're reliant on cheap, roadside motels like this one.

Mom will see the bill in a few days. She checks her statements online all the time - like in an obsessive-someone-is-trying-to-steal-my-identity-type-of-way. The shit will hit the fan regardless of the splurge tonight. I know I should care, but I don't. I can't tell if this is apathy or if I'm so focused on the goal that I'm not considering all of the ramifications of my choices. It's kind of refreshing not worrying for once. Like I'm living my own life without any restraint.

"Here's your key," the old man in an Amish style beard says. Gray whiskers cover most of his pinkish face. A woman adjacent to him is sitting on a motorized scooter and is wearing a red hat and white lace gloves. She glances up at us with a toothy smile.

"You kids taking a road trip?" she asks. I hear a slight Irish accent. I imagine she observes tea time and likes a good glass of whiskey when it's cold outside.

"Yes," I answer since Millicent is still on a vow of silence and BB is recovering from too much alcohol.

"I went on one when I was your age. That was years ago, though. I'm eighty-four, you know," she says. Old people are apt to give you their age and tell you what they did when they were your age - like it's some sort of pissing match.

"She looks younger, doesn't she?" Amish beard man asks.

"Yes," I lie. What do I know about age and how someone eighty-four looks?

"I met her online," he adds. "We're still newlyweds." He gives her a mischievous grin like a horny teenager, and she giggles, playfully swatting him.

"I told him I liked cowboys and didn't sleep in pajamas," she says, adding a wink.

"That was all I needed to know," he says. "I used to be a cowboy until I bought this place, and I love a woman who doesn't like pajamas."

TMI.

"Why waste your time at our age? Just get to the point and say what you mean to say. We knew we wanted to have sex with each other," she says, and I hear BB choke. I fight hard to keep my face straight and expressionless, but when old people are talking frankly about sexual intercourse it's hard not to cringe or make some kind of disgusted face. Millicent is staring outside, not even paying attention to these frisky old farts. It's too bad, too, because you just can't make this stuff up. "Might as well make it known early on in the relationship."

Amish beard man pats her on her thigh and leaves his hand resting there.

"You kids be good, but not too good." She winks at us as we leave their office. Something tells me they're going to have a quickie as soon as we leave.

"That was..." BB starts.

"It's good to know you don't stop loving even when you're old."

"But I don't want to hear about it."

"That's the thing when you get old, you just don't care what people think. It's refreshing, really, but still gross."

"I threw up a little in my mouth," BB says.

"That's probably the beer and not the horny old people."

It's a little after ten o'clock and the sun set only an hour ago. Amish beard man told us there's a diner up the road, which, according to him, serves decent food. We pass by a pool and a jacuzzi on our way to our room. Not that I'll be getting in either. Since Casper is in the desert, the temperatures will drop tonight, and swimming isn't such a smart idea in cold weather. And hot tubs are dangerous cesspools, especially for a guy with one leg.

We open the door to our room and are greeted by iceberg cold air blowing from the old window unit. There's a scent of potpourri. Both beds have floral bedspreads and there is a table with two chairs near the picture window. The bathroom tiles are pink and green, like something from the 1960s, but they, too, are clean.

"This will do," Millicent says with her hands on her hips, appraising the room.

Not like we have any other choices.

BB's pressing his fingers against his temples and lays down on one of the beds. "I hurt," he moans.

"You deserve it," she says.

He rolls over and moans once more.

She unzips her purse and tosses him a bottle of Midol. "Take one."

"That's for PMS." He grimaces and tosses it back to her.

She catches the bottle with one hand, then proceeds to pop the lid open and turn the bottle over. A tiny white pill falls to the palm of her hand. She walks over to him and shoves it in his face. "It's basically a pain reliever, and it's all I have."

He pushes her hand out of his face. "I'm not taking a girl pill."

She brings her hand back to his face. "And I'm not hearing you complain all night."

He relents when he sees she's not budging. He squints at the pill and hesitates before he places it inside of his mouth, then swallows. "Don't say nothing about this to anyone."

"We won't say anything," Millicent replies correcting BB's grammar.

"Watch out. You might grow a pair of boobs," I say, teasing.

He grabs hold of his chest and looks at me with alarm. "What?"

Millicent and I both laugh, which BB doesn't find amusing.

"It's not a birth control pill, you dimwit," Millicent says.

"Y'all are mean," BB pouts.

"Shall we eat?" I say.

They readily agree, and we head out of the room.

***

We walk into the diner and see a few men wearing cowboy hats huddled at the counter. The waitress tells us to sit wherever we like but then adds that she has plantars feet and the closer to the bar the better. We take the hint and sit in a booth near the cowboy-filled-bar.

"I'll have the chicken nachos," BB says.

"No he won't," Millicent says to the waitress.

He glowers at Millicent.

"I'm not taking another day of your gas," she says.

"Fine. I'll have a hamburger," he says with reluctance.

We order our food, sticking to hamburgers because we're in cattle country and know that the meat they're serving actually comes from old Bessie and her pals, and not from a midwestern soybean field. Most of the fast food hamburgers are a conglomeration of soy and beef. Another factoid: every time a cow farts, it hurts the ozone layer. The same could be said for BB.

BB slurps on his chocolate milkshake, which he ordered to come before his meal, stating that dessert was better that way. "Brain freeze," he says. Chocolate ice cream covers the corners of his lips.

"It can't freeze if there's nothing there," Millicent jokes.

"Ha. Ha." He drinks the last of the milkshake, then slides the empty glass off to the side of the table. He belches, then pats his belly. The guy is a human garbage disposal.

Our food arrives shortly after, and we eat in peace, too hungry and too tired to talk. When the bill arrives, I slide my hand into my pocket and pull out my wallet ready to pay my share. I peer down and see that—with the exception of my license, credit card, and a few receipts—it's empty inside. I search again but still find the same result.

"What's wrong?" Millicent asks, noticing my worried frown.

"There's no cash in my wallet," I say, whispering. There's a big, black lettered sign on the wall stating, *"No credit cards! Cash or checks only!"* The exclamation points are to get their point across, I guess. And why would they accept a check but not a credit card? What kind of business is this?

She leans forward, glancing from side to side before saying, "You don't have any money on you?"

I shake my head ruefully, pathetically, somberly. You name it; I'm feeling it right about now.

A wrinkle forms at the bridge of her nose. "I only have a ten. I left the rest of my stash in my suitcase." She looks at BB. "What about you?"

He points to himself. "I thought you were covering me. I only got a few dollars."

"Because you spent it all on crap!" she raises her voice, which causes the flock of cowboys to look our way. "One of us needs to go back to the hotel room and get the money," she says, lowering her voice.

"I'll go," I say.

"I'll order another cup of coffee so they don't think anything is up," she says.

"They're going to suspect something when I walk outside."

"I'll think of something," she says. "Just go."

CHAPTER 20

It's not a reassuring feeling when you see that the door to your motel room is wide open. Nor is it comforting when your suitcases are missing. It's even worse when you see all of your money is gone and in the hands of unscrupulous thieves who are probably partying like it's 1999.

I think back to when we were going to the diner and remember that BB was the last of us to leave the room. He probably forgot to lock the door, or maybe he didn't think to lock it at all. Who would think we'd be robbed in the middle of hospitality country? It's Wyoming. It seems friendly enough.

After I search every nook and cranny in the room for our things, which are all long gone, I head out and lock the door. I laugh at the thought and effort. If someone wants to get in, what else could they possibly steal? The potpourri. There's nothing of ours left. They even took our deodorant. Who steals deodorant? A thief who struggles with body odor, I guess.

I walk to the front office to tell the horny old couple we've been burglarized, but the lights are off and no one is home, or in this case, they're making sweet love with no worries, dreaming of sugarplums and games of shuffleboard. I hate them right about now.

So I drive back to the diner, dreading the inevitable. When I walk inside, I see the cowboys are still sitting at the counter and our waitress with plantars feet is making them another pot of coffee. Nothing has changed yet everything has.

Millicent's holding a cup and her hand is shaking - probably from too much caffeine.

"You done with your important phone call?" The waitress asks me, but I can clearly hear the sarcasm in her tone.

"Yeah," I answer, then have a seat across from Millicent.

"I told her you had to make a phone call and were coming back. She asked," Millicent explains.

I nudge BB, then whisper to them both, "Brace yourself."

That wrinkle forms across the bridge of her nose again. Sometimes I want to get her to worry just so I can see her cute little nose bunch up like that.

"I don't like you starting a sentence with 'brace yourself,'" she says.

"Our room was broken into," I say, keeping my voice down so the eavesdroppers won't hear.

"What?" Millicent says. BB mirrors her shocked expression.

"And all of our stuff was stolen," I add, keeping my voice relatively calm considering we're canoeing our way up shit creek. "My cash is gone. So is yours," I tell Millicent. "We just have the good old credit card, which, by the way, they don't accept." I exhale, and feel a sense of relief from getting all of that out in one short sentence, although it felt more like a paragraph.

"Shit," BB says with a frown.

"This isn't good," she whispers.

BB rubs his hand across his face, and Millicent winds her hair around her index finger, staring off into space, thinking. Hopefully, she's coming up with something good because I'm all out of plans.

The waitress comes our way after saying something to one of the cowboys. Two of them stand up, slap a bill on the counter, then leave. I unconsciously check to see if there are spurs on the heels of their boots, and guess what? There are.

"You kids ready to pay?" In other words, her shift is coming to an end and she wants us out. She's tapping one foot impatiently against the tiled floor.

"Well," I cough (bad habit). "Our room was broken into and almost all of our money was stolen."

She raises one of her painted brows and gives me a "you're shitting me" kind of look. "Almost all of it you say." Her tone tells me she thinks I'm full of it.

I nod too vigorously, like I'm hyped up on caffeine, which Millicent is, because she's emphatically shaking her head, too. "I have a credit card, but you don't accept them," I'm trying to say it in a friendly manner, but really, no credit card? "We have most of the money to cover the bill but we're still ten dollars short."

She smacks her chewing gum. "Sounds like you're in a pickle."

We all fake a laugh. "You could say that."

She slaps her palms against the table and leans down, scowling at us. "You think this is funny? Guess who has to pay the difference? Me." She points to herself. "Guess who doesn't have a tree that grows money?" She waits for us to answer.

"You," we say in unison, although BB is late to the punch, and we hear his voice trail after ours.

"You got it," the angry bad-footed waitress says.

"We're really sorry," Millicent says. "Like Trip said, it's not our fault…"

She holds up her hand to stop Millicent from continuing. "I don't want to hear it. You think I haven't been through this song and dance routine of yours before? Plenty of times. Don't think 'cause I'm working in this joint that I'm two barrels short of an oil change." She stands there, staring at us for a moment. Her eyes move left to right, then move in the opposite direction, and finally lock with ours. "Tell you what you're going to do so I don't sick those cowboys over here to clean your clocks." Her eyes dart in the direction of the two towering gunslingers.

She's got quite the vocabulary on her. I'm tempted to break out my notebook and jot down her creative sayings, but that might not help things.

"Since I have to pay the difference, and we all know you ain't leaving me a tip even though I did serve you dinner and refill your drinks, you're gonna clean up while I rest my feet 'cause I'm dog tired."

"We can clean," Millicent says with a nod, almost panting like an eager puppy. I side glance BB, and he's doing the same. So am I for that matter. We're desperate.

"Anyone can clean unless they ain't got no legs or arms," she says, then flinches when she realizes she might have offended me. She makes eye contact with me for a brief moment before blathering on. "The floor's gotta be mopped, and the tables need to be wiped off. The ketchup needs to be refilled, too." She brings her arms up to her chest, folding them. "Well, what are you waiting for? Get moving!"

We shoot up and march behind her while she barks more orders at us. The two cowboys laugh, then make snide comments waving their fists in the air like they're teamsters at a union meeting. "Way to boss 'em, Roxie."

Her name is Roxie. What sixty-year-old woman is named Roxie? This one. Roxie is what you call a dog or name a porn star. Not a haggard waitress with plantars feet.

She slaps a wet, dirty rag in my hands and tells me to start wiping. BB is assigned the mopping job, and Millicent is responsible for refilling the ketchup bottles. BB is obviously the worst choice for mopping. He keeps sloshing the dirty water around all over the floor.

I finish cleaning the last booth, then amble to Roxie and the two ruffians who have finally finished their coffee but are staying put for a chit-chat. She's laughing at something one of them has said. I didn't even think Roxie had it in her - to smile I mean.

"You got 'em all?" she asks, still beaming.

"Yeah," I say.

The two cowboys glance down at me, noticing the leg. "You in the service?" one asks.

"No," I answer.

He frowns, thinking the worst, then says to Roxie, "You shouldn't be making these kids do your dirty work."

"I didn't mind," I say. "Besides, we owed her money."

He smacks his lips. His mouth must be dry because it sounds like he's chewing on cotton balls. "It ain't right, Roxie. Look at him."

I try not to let his last comment bother me, but sometimes I can't take it. And this is one of those times. "Look at me; Look at you. I've at least got all of my hair," I scoff, then regret my big stinkin' mouth the moment I let those words roll off the tip of my tongue. This man could kill me with his gigantic bare hand.

I wince. Inwardly. Outwardly. Here it comes. My face is about to suffer the consequences.

He stands up, towering over me. I'm over six feet tall, mind you, but he, he's a giant. Like *James and The Giant Peach* tall. One side of his mouth twitches, and I wonder if this is some sort of tic he gets when he's angry. When he's about to fight. But then the other side of his mouth starts to move upward, and before I know it, he's grinning from ear to ear.

I breathe a sigh of relief, and I'm sure it shows all over my face because he laughs, then he slaps a fifty dollar bill down on the counter. "That'll cover what you didn't get from these kids," he says.

I fumble for words and try to say "thanks," but he's out the door before I can.

Roxie slips the fifty inside her bra, which I didn't need to see because some things you can't get out of your mind, no matter how hard you try. Millicent and BB walk up to me, asking what that was all about, and I just shrug because I can't explain people. People are people are people.

We're feeling optimistic, which doesn't make sense considering we're dead broke and sleeping in a sketchy motel room. Maybe it's all the chances we're being given. Second chances.

We leave Roxie, who barely uttered a goodbye to us, and slip inside the truck. I'm in the driver's seat and crank up the engine, ready to drive us back to the motel. As I put the car in reverse, BB screams.

CHAPTER 21

I slam on the breaks. We're all breathing hard and heavy from the surprise halt. I turn and look at BB. He isn't wearing his ball cap and is holding up a stack of bills wrapped in a familiar money clip.

"I forgot," he simply says.

"Forgot what? That you had my money!" I shout.

Millicent lays her hand on mine, trying to quiet me, but it doesn't make a dent. I'm too angry. "We just spent an hour cleaning because we thought we were broke," I go on, still shouting at him.

"I, I," he stammers, "I saw it on the table in the motel and grabbed it 'cause I figured you'd forgotten it. Guess I forgot I had it when I put on top of my head." He laughs, but no one joins him. "My hair's thick, you know? Can't feel a thing up there." His eyes dart upward, then meet mine. When he sees I'm not finding humor in this situation, he offers me a slight, apologetic smile.

"Let me see if I can wrap my mind around what you just told me: you had my money on top of your head, but didn't know it," I say incredulously, angrily, harshly - the way a parent talks to a naughty child.

He cowers. "Yeah," he says quietly, then hands my cash to me.

I yank it from his hands, probably a little too aggressively, then slip it into my front pocket. Millicent shoots me a disapproving look, but I'm too annoyed to care. A million words are running through my head. Most of them mean, callous, hurtful. Then, without thinking, I blurt, "How could you be so stupid?"

"'Cause I am," he says softly, matter-of-fact as if this is the truth, his truth.

There are those moments in your life when you feel like you

might, in fact, be the biggest dick on the planet. This is one of those times for me. Because all I want to do right now is find a way to turn back time and never utter those words to him. I'm filled with regret, and I've let everyone down. I'm that guy right now.

***

We arrive at the motel after a painfully quiet ride. BB and Millicent get out of the truck and walk ahead of me like I don't exist. Or, maybe I'm too busy feeling sorry for myself. For being a jerk. Maybe I deserve the shunning. I take my time, walking, thinking, wondering how I can make things right. You can't right a wrong no matter how hard you try.

I make it to the room, and BB has already collapsed on the bed. He has his hands behind his head and his feet are bare. The television is on, and *SpongeBob SquarePants* is playing. Millicent is in the bathroom.

"I don't think you're stupid," I say, trying to apologize.

"Doesn't matter if you do or not."

"But I didn't mean…"

"It was stupid of me, but sometimes I can't help it." He sits up in bed like he's ready to tell me something, and I move closer, having a seat across from him in a chair. He's quiet for a moment, which is unusual for him.

"I played football from the time I was old enough to walk up until last year," he begins. "It's like I was born with the ball in my hands—I loved the sport so much. But during a state championship game, I got hit real hard by this linebacker who had about one hundred pounds on me, and I blacked out." He squints his eyes in thought. "They said I was out cold for five minutes. When I finally woke up, they told me I'd suffered a level three concussion.

I'd been hit before and had plenty of minor concussions, so I didn't think it was that big of a deal. But this one was bad enough I wasn't allowed back on the field. You can imagine how hard that was for me to stop playing," he says with a frown. "But when the doc is saying to me that if I play and get hit again, I'll die, I choose life. I'll always choose life…" his voice trails off. "Doc says I've got some permanent damage. The kind that can't be reversed. I can't remember as good as I used to. I guess that's obvious to you now." He shrugs.

"I'm a dick," I murmur.

He chuckles. "Quit beating yourself up. If the tables were turned, I'd be pissed, too. Cleaning that place wasn't that bad, though. Well, the mopping did kinda suck."

"But I shouldn't have said what I did."

"Whatever," he says, blowing off my attempt at an apology. I'm not so good at these type of things. "You're human, so am I. I've said worse to people, I'm sure you have, too." I guess this is his way of letting me know this rift is over. "Just don't go pitying me."

"You don't have to worry about me pitying you just 'cause you're damaged goods," I try to tease. I mean, we're in this together, aren't we? Society both determines that there is something wrong with us. But maybe society is messed up for judging us.

His lips turn upward. "You're alright. I don't care what they say about you."

"Who are *they* anyway?"

He half-shrugs. "Not sure, but whoever they are, they sure are opinionated." He lays back down, fluffs his pillows and crosses one leg over the other. "It's scary not remembering," he says so quietly I wonder if he's talking to me. "I have to write a lot of things down now like my grandma does, and I'm only seventeen years old. I don't know what I'm going to do when I'm middle-aged."

"By that time, you'll have one of those robot servants like they do in Japan, and it can remember everything for you."

"Maybe, but I probably won't even remember I got one, and what's that going to do for me?" He laughs again, because in situations like these, sometimes all you can do is have a sense of humor about it. If you don't, you'll become bitter. "Things look really bleak, you know. Like there ain't many choices for me. I ain't smart like you and Mellie. I'm not good at a lot of things. I wish I could just get paid to hunt and eat. Those things I'm good at."

"You have choices. You're good at a lot of things, and people like you."

"Yeah, sure," he says, but he doesn't sound like he believes it. "Anyway, quit being hard on yourself. You're not so bad, and let's stop this hippie love fest before I puke. I ain't into this complimenting each other thing."

"Me, neither...besides, it was a struggle to come up with something nice to say about you," I kid.

We're both laughing, and Millicent comes out of the bathroom wearing nothing but a towel wrapped around her waist and the tank top she had on earlier. "I'm going in the hot tub," she says.

"At this time?" I say.

"Yeah, Dad." She looks at BB, ignoring me. "You coming?"

"Nah." He yawns. "I'm tired, and *SpongeBob SquarePants* is on."

"I'll come," I say, too eagerly.

"I didn't ask you to."

"I didn't know I needed you to; it's open to the public."

She rolls her eyes at me, then opens the door and closes it on my face.

I look at BB, and he raises both brows. "She's mad at you."

"You think?"

"Better go find out what's ailing her or this trip will be a long one."

"Guess so…" I head out the door, leaving BB to his cartoons and me filled with dread as I head toward what feels like a battleground. I hear Imagine Dragon's "Battle Cry" song in my head. Why am I so afraid of this girl? I want to be near her but run from her at the same time. She's going to drive me insane.

There's a full moon out tonight—no surprise there since it's been one strange occurrence after another. I haven't had this much action since… Well, I think you can deduce when that might be.

I amble to the pool and open the creaky gate. Millicent looks up at me, then goes back to staring at the desolate road. There isn't a car in site. But that's how Wyoming is - unpopulated. Where are all the people? The state is huge, but there's hardly a soul living here.

She's sitting on the edge of the jacuzzi with her feet dangling in the water. I sit in a chair near her but say nothing. No sense in stirring that pot. The water is already boiling. I don't know what to say to her anyway. She's mad at me. Or, she thinks she's mad at me. Anything I say at this moment might piss her off even more.

She glances at me over her shoulder, then unwraps the towel from around her waist before stepping into the jacuzzi. She looks in my direction. "Did you come out here to stare at me?"

"No," I lie. Of course, I did.

She shoots me an incredulous look. "Either get in or leave."

I fold my arms across my chest and slouch into the chair, making myself right at home. "You're not the boss of me." Real mature, I know. "I can do as I like."

She splashes water at me. A few sprinkles of (filthy) chlorinated water touch my skin. Little factoid about jacuzzi water: it's been known to cause legionnaires disease. Actually, it does feel good despite the fact that it's ridden with bacteria. It's warm. And even though it was hot out today, there's a nip in the air now. And when I say hot, I mean the sun is closer here - so close I could touch it. Exaggeration of course, but you get my point. Anyway, I wouldn't choose to live in a desert. I want consistency with my weather.

"Hey!" I shout, feigning annoyance. I don't care that she's splashing me. Well, a little part of me does since the water could be ridden with germs. "What'd you do that for?"

"Either get in or leave. You can't keep sitting out here watching me."

"Who says I'm watching you? And, last time I checked, we are in a federal republic, and the constitution grants me the right to rest my ass wherever I choose fit."

"I'll splash you again," she threatens.

"I'll just move. It's not like I'll melt or anything." I stand up and drag the plastic chair with me as I back away from her. Far enough away that she can't douse me with over-chlorinated water again. I sit back down and give her a smug look.

She steps out of the jacuzzi, then marches my way with a look of fury on her beautiful face. Like she wants to kill me. And I have to tell you, I'm too busy gawking at her because she's soaked and is wearing nothing but a tank top and underwear - no bra, either. No bra! I'm getting a pretty good idea of what the rest of her looks like, which makes my horny mind wander onto other things.

She stands in front of me with her feet wide apart and her hands on her hips. I keep telling myself to look at her face, but the temptation is too great. I can't help but stare directly ahead, which is right at her chest. Bad move, I know, but it's like putting Krispy Kreme doughnuts in front of diabetics. They know they shouldn't eat it, but the sugar is too hard to resist. I'm the worst of the worst.

She flicks me hard on my shoulder and places her palm under my chin, then forces it to move upward. And I let her, like an obedient dog because she's touching me. "Quit staring at my chest."

I shift my eyes to the right, "I'm not."

"You are." Like an idiot, my eyes shift to the target zone once again. I'm an idiot.

"You did it again," she says with an added, "humph."

She releases her grip on my chin and collapses in the chair beside me like she's surrendering. "I don't stare at your leg because it's rude. You shouldn't stare at me."

"I… I don't."

"You just did."

"Because you're sopping wet and wearing next to nothing. Any man who isn't blind would do the same."

She thinks for a moment, twirling a few strands of her wet hair around her finger. "I'm not a sex object. Show some respect."

"I know," I say quietly. "I do respect you…"

I feel her hardening stare. So, I turn my head and look into her eyes, garnering enough courage to say what I need to say. Why not? What have I got to lose? I take a deep breath (like that's supposed to help me) but really it's a stalling tactic. Finally, I blurt, "You're beautiful and smart, and you just, you just drive me crazy most of the time because I can't decide if I want to arm wrestle you or grab you and kiss you."

Here comes the epic rejection. Being a guy is tough. Girls don't have to lay their hearts out on the line like we do.

She's not saying anything. I can't tell what she's thinking, but I can definitely see she's thinking since the twitch in her jaw is evident.

"I'm not into arm wrestling. So, maybe you should just kiss me then."

CHAPTER 22

I'm so taken by surprise that my mouth actually gapes wide open.

"You might as well," she says, like she's talking about something trivial. Like we're discussing which laundry detergent to use to get some stain out.

I'm still looking at her with uncertainty. Did she just give me an open invite to lock lips?

"You better do it soon before I change my mind," she adds, impatiently drumming her fingers against the arm of the chair.

"Are you messing with me? Am I secretly being filmed?" I search the sky for a hidden camera.

She sighs. "You are a big dummy. I give you the chance to kiss me, and all you can do is run your mouth. And you better do it soon because I'm getting cold, and we all know you're too much of a wimp to get in that hot tub."

A chance is a chance, and if she's offering, I'm taking. She actually wants to do this. Of course, she'll never come out and say it, but she might as well have handed me a sealed envelope with an invite asking me to suck face with her.

"So, should we stand or sit?" Who discusses such things before they kiss? Why do I sound like an idiot? Why do I sound like a novice? Because I am. I am!

"Get up," she commands.

I stand of course. If she told me to sit back down, I'd do that, too. Pathetic.

She gets up and stands across from me, looking up at me, appraising me. She squints her eyes and reaches to lace her fingers together behind my neck. "You're tall."

"Maybe you're just short," I say, trying to keep my breath even, but it's a challenge when I have her so close and touching me. She's touching me!

"This is the part when you wrap your arms around my waist," she adds.

My heart is thumping so hard, I'm sure she can hear it. "Are you always this bossy with guys you're about to kiss?" My voice is stupid and shaky.

"I've aged ten years since we started this discussion," she says with exasperation.

I place my hands on her hips. I feel her wet tank top and underwear against my (now) clammy fingers. She has a natural curve, and I can't help but let my fingers brush against her perfection. That sounded cheesy, but how else can you describe someone as beautiful as Millicent Huxley? She is perfection.

I notice a few goosebumps appear on her arms and start feeling confident because I'm having that kind of effect on her. I am doing this. Me! That's right. I am.

"You're taking," she inhales, breathing, "your time."

She's a basket of nerves. Yes! And the gold medal goes to me!

I pull her toward me, gently (but firmly enough that I seem manly to her), and wrap my arms around her waist. Her chest presses against mine, and I feel it rise, then deflate with each shallow breath she takes. I bring one hand to the back of her neck, feeling the tickling sensation from her baby hairs. I keep my other hand on her hips and lean forward, placing my lips against hers.

If you asked me what my best feelings in the world were, I'd tell you three things: eating an ice cream sundae any given day because ice cream sundaes are a gift to the world; when I got my prosthesis and finally got to walk on two legs again after several months of walking with one leg and nothing but a pair of crutches, and this, this right here. Because the girl can kiss. Like, knock your socks off good.

I start to get into it (any fool in my shoes would), and let my hands roam freely - not down to forbidden zones because I've got some class, but enough that I can feel how curvy her body is. Mind you, I'm not groping her, but gosh— I sure want to. Her skin is so soft. She smells so good. What's the scent? Chlorine with a hint of jasmine.

Her body feels good against mine because we're molded together like we're two pieces that fit. She's doing the same—touching me all over—and when I pull away (I don't want to seem too pushy or eager because we are making out right in the front of the motel for everyone to see, after all) she grabs me by my shirt and kisses me again. This time with more ferocity. If we keep this up, we'll have to get a room. Count me in!

She wants me. Me! This guy right here.

We finally stop (because she pulled away), and I guess we have some restraint and decency. I see she's flustered. Her face is ruddy; mine is too. We're both breathing like we just ran a lap around this place.

I give her a confident look and smile. "That was one of your better ideas."

She bends over to pick up her towel, then wraps it around her waist and sits in one of the white plastic chairs. I sit beside her and offer her my hand. "Trip Wentworth, at your service."

She swats my hand away and rolls her eyes. "Don't get cocky. It was just a kiss."

"If it was," and I air quote, "*just a kiss*, why is your face red, and why are you breathing heavy?"

"Because it's hot out here," she lies, fanning herself.

"I have four words for you: you kissed me back." I lean back in the chair and bring my hands up behind my head, feeling more confident than the President of the United States at the State of Union. Give me a defcon five situation, I can handle it right now.

"You're being smug, which is a big turn off, you know?"

"Admit it." I lean into her, laying my head on her shoulder, and looking up at her dreamily. "You enjoyed it as much as I did."

She jerks her shoulder, so I sit up.

"I'll admit no such thing."

"Keep living in denial then," I say.

"Did you apologize to BB?"

"Guess you don't want to discuss kissing me anymore, do you?"

She gives me a look.

"Yeah," I answer. "I did."

"It was a jerky thing to say. I expect better of you."

"Maybe you shouldn't have such high expectations of me, because I'm bound to disappoint you all of the time," I say.

"My expectations of you aren't unrealistic. You're a good soul, so you should know better than to insult good people like BB."

"I was mad. It was a human moment. You've had plenty of those I'm sure," I say. "He and I are good now." I pause for a moment. "He told me what happened to him."

"That's why it made me so irate. He can't help it."

"I didn't know that at the time. It's like someone getting mad at me for walking slow and not knowing about this." I tap on my leg.

"Well, please don't do it again."

I fake a salute. "Yes, ma'am. You sure are bossy," I say. "You're very protective of him."

"He's family. You're supposed to protect the ones you love."

"He's lucky then. Most people aren't so loyal."

"Well, I am loyal to a fault. It's a weakness I guess."

"Depends on how you look at it." Enough with this talk of BB. I thought we were talking about kissing. "So….do you want to kiss again?" One-track mind. I have a one-track mind. Kiss Millicent. Eat. Sleep. Kiss Millicent. Eat. Sleep. Kiss Millicent. Maybe eat. Maybe sleep. Kiss Millicent again. "You do." I smile. "I knew it."

She reaches forward and flicks me on my knee.

"Ow," I say. "Aggressive, too."

"You're obsessed."

"I can't deny that."

"We barely know anything about each other. I'm not going spend the rest of the night making out with you just because we enjoyed it."

"You do realize you just admitted to enjoying the act of kissing… with me, right?" I lift my head up high and smile at her again.

"It was a Freudian slip," she says.

"Which means it's been buried deep in your subconscious."

"You frustrate me," she growls.

"Ditto." I wrap one arm around her shoulder and give her a gentle squeeze. "It's because we're so attracted to each other."

"Ha," she scoffs.

"So, you normally go around kissing guys you're not attracted to?"

"I….I…" she fumbles for words. "I'm not spending the rest of the night making out with you. So, give it up. That ship has sailed."

"Fine," I say, sounding like a defiant child.

"Fine," she huffs.

Silence. Excruciating silence.

"Fine," I sigh. "Go ahead and ask me what you've been dying to since we met."

CHAPTER 23

"I…I," she stutters, and I see she's shivering.

"If we're going to have this deep conversation, let's get you some dry clothes or you're going to freeze."

"I'm…I'm fine," she lies.

"Sure you are." I get up and head back to our room, hearing her shout my name, but I ignore her. Sometimes I just want to be chivalrous. BB is sound asleep, snoring, and the TV is blaring. I turn the TV off and open the closet, pulling out a blanket, then carry it with me to the pool.

I hand it to her, and she wraps her petite body inside of it.

"Thank you."

I don't say "you're welcome" because I've never understood the point of that statement. We really should be saying, "Of course. You'd pay me the same service or you'd do the same for me," but we don't. It's like that handshaking sentiment. It's always been done so why change it?

"You read me all wrong earlier. I don't need to know."

"It's okay," I assure her. "Everyone wants to know the same thing: how."

"You don't have to tell me," she says softly. It's the first time I've ever heard her sound so gentle, so full of vulnerability. "It's not who you are. It doesn't define you." She reaches over and touches my chest. "This does. This is what makes you you."

I wrap my hand around hers, wanting so badly to tell her I'd do anything for her. Anything. Like go across the country and steal a body with her.

"As BB would say, 'you're good people, Millicent Huxley.'"

"You're not so shabby yourself," she says, still allowing me to hold her hand. "We can work on your staring problem."

"Sorry," I shake my head. "It's always going to be a problem as long as you're within my line of sight."

"You're handsome, too, but I don't stare at you."

My lips turn upward. "So, I'm handsome, am I?"

She rolls her eyes. "You know you are."

"I had hoped, but people tend to be a bit skewed when it comes to themselves."

"Yes, Trip, you're good looking."

"You like my face, don't you?" I give her a hopeful look.

"When you're not staring or being smug, you have a very pleasant face. Your eyes are my favorite," she admits. "But looks aren't everything. They fade away, and all you have left is what is inside, and you've got a good heart, so I think you'll be okay."

"That's a relief."

"When I said I wanted us to talk…" her voice fades, and I notice her cheeks are bright red. She's embarrassed. "Well, I thought it was a good strategy to get us to stop kissing because…." She takes a deep breath. "Well, obviously, I didn't want to, but I know we needed to. I'm not ready for that next step yet."

I try to hide my look of surprise, but did I hear her right? Was she hinting that this could go further? I'm just happy to be holding her hand, which I still am, by the way.

I give her a confident grin and wink.

She glares at me, releasing her hand from mine. "Quit being smug."

"Just feeling good is all. It's not every day I have a beautiful woman telling me she didn't want to stop kissing me."

"I never should have told you." She shakes her head remorsefully.

"It's okay to drop that guard of yours every now and again."

"I don't have a guard."

"Please," I scoff. "You've got a coat of armor thicker than bulletproof glass. We both know we like each other. It's okay to admit it."

"Fine," she relents. "I like you. Are you happy?"

"Very much so." I grin wide from ear to ear. "Ask me anything, and I'll tell you."

She chews on her one finger, thinking, then lets it slip from her mouth to her lap. "What is your middle name?"

"Random and lame question. But okay, if that's what you're asking, it's Johnson."

She scrunches her face. "That's a last name."

"It's my mother's last name. They wanted to keep it in the family," I answer. "What about you?"

"Harmony," she answers with a twist of the lips.

I laugh out loud.

"It's not that funny."

"It is, given your penchant for arguing."

She smiles despite herself.

"What's your favorite memory?" she asks.

"Five minutes ago," I say.

She folds her arms across her chest and skeptically looks at me.

"Okay, I'm still holding to *that*, and when I walked again. I'm talking about when I got this." I tap on my prosthetic leg. "It was the most amazing, freeing experience." I pause, thinking of that time when Mom and I held hands as we walked around the

PT room, while Dad cheered me on. "What about your favorite memory?"

"That's easy," she says. Her face brightens from the memory. "When my dad took me to the carnival. We rode the merry go round and ate caramel apples. We had so much fun," she says with giddiness, like a small child.

"I've never been to a carnival," I admit.

"That's sad, Trip."

"Well, there are a lot of firsts I'm experiencing on this odd little expedition of ours."

"I'm glad," she says. "Because you always remember your firsts."

"So, that's all you wanted to ask me?" I ask her. I decide not to tell her she's my first kiss. That I'll always remember that moment. Even when I'm old and gray and slightly delirious, the memory will still be clear as the bright blue sky because it's one of my favorites.

"I'm not going to ask you about your leg because it's personal and none of my business."

"But we just exchanged spit, so I'd say, we're past formalities and politeness."

She scowls at me, but I can sense from the twinkle in her blue eyes she isn't mad. She's easier to read now, or maybe I'm just better at paying attention to her. Maybe I can finally speak Millicent Huxley's language.

"It's true," I defend.

"I want to know things about you that you're willing to share."

I shrug. "This is one of them. It's a big part of who I am today, so don't you think it's important for me to share?"

"Yes, but…."

I get up and scoot the chair so that I'm facing her, then sit back down. What I'm about to tell her isn't the type of conversation you have just shooting the breeze and sitting back in lawn chairs, facing a jacuzzi while watching cars pass by in the dead of night. I could tell her in ten seconds - the how I mean. I could leave out all of the details and tell her exactly what happened, then leave it at that. But that won't be enough. She wants more, and I want to tell her everything - from start to finish. I owe her that.

Only a few people have ever heard my side of the story— aside from the obvious, like my parents and my doctor, the police, and all of the therapists. Oh, the therapists. They like to probe, those therapists do, and if you aren't telling, they keep asking. Insisting. Until they get what they want - which is you, all exposed and needing an anchor so you don't drift away. Anyway, this is not something I go around sharing with people unless I feel close to them, and it's not like I've been close to a lot of people in my lifetime.

"It wasn't cancer," I say, clearing the air because I'm sure that's what she thought it was. I see her breathe a sigh of relief. I guess because she thought I'd had it, and when people hear the C word they assume the worst, but I know plenty of fighters who've beaten the big C. "Everyone thinks it is. They just assume. But you... you and BB didn't think twice about it, and," I shrug, "it was nice." She's just looking at me, listening intently.

"Why would we?"

"You're an anomaly," I say. "You're quick to judge others for doing something wrong but fail to judge someone based on their appearances."

"Why judge someone based on their outside shell? It's the inside that counts."

"I knew I liked you for a reason," I say. "It wasn't just the good kissing." I grin too wide. There goes the game I thought I had.

"It…" she fidgets. "It was a nice kiss," she admits.

"See. That wasn't so hard, was it?"

"Quit messing around," she says.

"Okay," I relent. "Did you know my parents train German shepherds in a variety of languages: Dutch, French, German?"

She shakes her head, indicating she didn't. "BB just said, and I quote, 'That your parents were loaded and had a bunch of spoiled dogs.' He also said 'you had leprosy,' so, I wasn't sure what to believe."

"I used to watch him from my bedroom window, wondering what it was like to be him. He'll never know this, but I envied him for his carefree attitude. You can tell a lot about a person by their gait. His is nonchalant. You get what you get. There are few souls like him," I say.

"That's why I count myself as lucky to have him as a friend. He'll always be loyal and honest."

"He might argue that he's lucky to have you as a friend," I say.

"He's a much better friend to me than I am to him."

"Don't sell yourself short. You are the epitome of loyalty in a friend."

"Thanks," she says, smiling. "That means a lot."

"My pleasure. I have plenty of nice things to say to you if you just let me," I tell her.

"One step at a time," she says.

I nod in agreement. "Slow, baby steps," I say. "Where was I?" I think for a moment. "My parents have a niche, and it's not like there's much competition out there. How many people want to train dogs for a living? You'd be surprised how many people want a dog that can respond to commands in another language," I explain.

"People with money are peculiar. They forget about simplicity and spend on elaborate things."

"Like smart German Shepherds, but I can't judge my parents too much for their choice in occupation. It's a major part of my stellar education," I say. "My parents were able to buy fifty acres of land thanks to those dogs. But it's a waste since it's fertile land that isn't being used for a better purpose like agriculture. They once used it for farming … before this," I tell her, glancing down at my leg. "They grew soybeans, corn, tomatoes…" my voice trails off. "But there wasn't much profit in it, and really, farming is hard work."

"Like us," she says, referring to the commune.

"They were in it for a profit. Not like you peace-loving hippies," I say.

"No, we're not supposed to like capitalism, yet they keep pushing me to go to college and become something."

"That's not the same as capitalism. Maybe they just want you to have a chance at life, and by having a chance, you need to earn an education. An education is something no one can ever take away from you."

"Maybe so, but the irony is I'll probably end up working for The Man once I get my law degree."

"You don't have to. You could work in non-profit or for the Innocence Project. You could be a defense lawyer fighting for all of the wrongly accused poor people who can't buy their way out of a prison sentence. You're in control of your own destiny."

She smirks. "You say some profound stuff sometimes, Trip. But I have to agree with you: nothing is happenstance. Everything is connected in some way. We're all part of the same universe."

"Do you think everything happens for a reason?"

"I'm not sure. I think a wise person will look beyond the circumstance and see what they can learn from them. Most people accept that things happen for a reason because it's simpler that way, because they think it makes difficult things easier to bear. But what about Luca's tragic death? What reasoning can there be behind it?"

"I'm not sure. His death brought me on this trip, and without this trip, I would have never seen everything that I have in the last two days. I've never lived so much until now."

"At the expense of a loss." She forms a wry face. "But with loss comes living, right?"

"I guess," I say. "Look who's talking about saying profound stuff," I add, trying to lighten the mood. "Guess my wisdom is rubbing off on you."

"Or maybe I'm rubbing off on you," she counters. "But, I'll admit, you are smart."

I hold my head high. "I am, am I?"

"Don't act like I'm telling you something you didn't already know. I have a feeling we'll be competing for valedictorian."

"I was held back in first grade, and I don't know if my grades are as good as yours. Mr. Finley was an unforgiving tutor."

Her brows arch, and her mouth subtly opens, probably surprised by the fact that I admitted to being held back.

"The accident caused me to fall behind in school, and my parents thought it'd be best to have me repeat first grade. So, as it stands, I will be the oldest graduate this year."

"Who cares about age? Age is age is age."

I smile at her, then grow quiet, thinking. She waits for me to continue, saying nothing. "I wish my parents still farmed. There was something about growing food for others to eat. Something altruistic about it," I go on. "Plus, farmland is perfect for playing. I used to run through our corn fields—barefoot with my arms out wide—touching each and every corn stalk, and dashing about the field like I was an airplane soaring in the sky."

I laugh at the memory now, but it used to pain me when I was younger—when the loss of my limb was not a distant memory. Those kinds of memories used to haunt me. Taunt me almost. Like I could almost feel my leg was still there. Then the harsh reality of knowing it wasn't set in. It took years to get over, even though I should have been thankful to just be alive, but a kid doesn't think that way. A kid wants what he can't have.

"That's something I miss more than anything: running. In my dreams, I run." I peer down at my hands, noticing my thumbs are moving in endless circles, and I'm feeling like I've just confessed some deep dark secret to her. It's hard to put yourself out there - to be so vulnerable.

"In my dreams, my father is alive," she confesses.

"I didn't know he passed," I say.

"It's not something I usually talk about."

"Neither is this, but this is harder to hide." I glance down at my leg.

"He died when I was young... but it still hurts - even after all of this time."

"I'm sorry," I say. "I can imagine it's a pain you never overcome. They say a child's worst fear is a parent dying." I don't ask her how he died. I always hear people ask this when someone dies. They want to know how, but what does it matter? Death is death is death, and the reason doesn't matter since the end result is inevitable for us all.

"It's the worst thing I've ever gone through in my life. Even though I was young when he died, it aged me - made me grow up and question the reasoning behind it. Why did it happen? Why was my soul ripped to shreds? How could I go on with my life without him guiding me? Selfish thoughts because I only thought of me, but I couldn't figure out how I was going to move on. He was taken from me too soon. I have issues with time and with Death. He creeps into our lives at the most inopportune moments, and once He does his dastardly deed, all that is left are shattered memories."

"I think anyone else in your shoes has felt the same."

"I had a family surrounding me, more so than most people have in their lives. I shouldn't have been so selfish. Some people don't get any time with their father. I, at least, had five years."

"But he was your dad and you only have one."

"When it happened, I questioned the reasoning because I took offense that something so tragic could happen to me even though everyone on this planet is on a limited amount of time. I was angry for a long time. I never got to say goodbye to him, even at the funeral. The casket was closed because the car accident had torn him up so badly," she says. "I know for some people they don't need that, but I would have liked to have one last glance at him before he became part of the earth." She grows silent for a moment. "There's a hole that formed in my heart when I lost him. Like a piece of me will always be missing no matter how hard I search for it. It's gone forever. I know this is what Mama Sauce feels for losing Luca. I hate that we will grow closer because of our bond with death."

"It has to be tough—growing up without him."

"It is... at times. Like when I see a daughter and father out together, I miss what I don't have. Sometimes I get mad at those people, and I know I shouldn't. I shouldn't be angry because they have something I covet, but I do." She shrugs. "Sometimes I weep from hearing his favorite song. Sometimes I cry when I see a movie I know he loved. The pain lingers," she says. "My mom tells me stories about him from time to time, which helps keep him alive to me. They were really good friends. He wanted more from her, but she couldn't give it to him. She just didn't love him that way."

"What do you remember about him?"

Her face lights up. "He used to pick me up and place me on top of his shoulders and spin around. I felt like I was on top of the world, and he seemed so gigantic to me," she says, then pauses for a moment to catch her breath. "He was a voracious reader, too. I inherited his massive book collection. Somehow I feel connected to him when I read the books that he loved. His favorite book was *Catcher In The Rye*. I read it and imagine him laughing and crying at the same parts I do. Like our hearts are connected to it somehow." She stares off, thinking, and looks back at me. "It's nice discussing him with you. I don't talk about him as much anymore, and when I do, it feels good. Thank you." She reaches to touch my hand and gives me a gentle squeeze. I lace my fingers with hers and hold her hand for that brief moment.

"I was six when it happened," I tell her, and she leans forward, giving me her full attention.

CHAPTER 24

"I was playing hide and seek with Chuck. He worked for my parents and pretty much did everything and anything for them. He was a good man and had a way with children that most adults don't. Like he didn't talk down to you or treat you liked you were stupid the way most adults do when they're around children. I loved Chuck very much. He was big in everything - in heart, in size, in living. He treated me like I was his own son, and I'll never forget that feeling. Never."

"He sounds amazing," she says.

"He was," I say. "Sometimes he and I would play hide and seek. It was more one-sided, because there wasn't really a time he wasn't busy working for my parents, but every now and again, he'd stop what he was doing and play with me. And it was always fun when he did. My parents aren't like that. They have never been, and when I lost my leg, they became so cautious. Every little thing I did was scrutinized. They were afraid I was going to get hurt."

"That's understandable," she offers.

"I guess, but it didn't help. It actually made the healing process a lot worse because I fed off of their anxiety and their fears." I pause for a moment, thinking back to that day. The infamous day my life changed. "The day it happened, I begged Chuck to play hide and seek. Bugged him mercilessly until he relented. I remember jumping up and down with joy. It didn't take much to make me happy at that time. Something as simple as playing a game of hide and seek seemed like a slice of cake."

"I miss being a kid," she interjects. "Life was simpler then."

"You sound old," I tell her.

"That's not bad, right? Old people are usually smarter because they've lived longer."

"I don't know." I roll one shoulder. "If you're born dumb, you won't all of a sudden get smart because you're old. Besides, things weren't so simple, were they? You lost your dad, and I lost this." I tap on my leg.

"That's true," she says and chews on her lip, thinking. Her eyebrows arch in such a vulnerable way that I'm tempted to pull her to me and hug her.

"If I'd known that day would be the last time I'd ever jump up and down on my own two feet, I would have cherished the act, but that's the way life is I guess - you never relish what you have until it's gone. Now I pay attention to the good things. Like that kiss, for starters," I say with a smile, which for once, she actually reciprocates. I nudge her. "See, you liked it, too, didn't you?"

"Arrogance is not attractive."

"I'm just fishing."

"Reel the line back in," she says.

"Fine," I sigh. "It was worth a shot."

"You're relentless."

"I have to be. When you lose a part of yourself, you never give up."

"Oh," she breathes. "Well, when you put it that way…"

"Don't go feeling sorry," I tell her.

"I do not feel sorry for you. Trust me."

"That's part of the reason I like you so much." It's out in the open now: Trip Wentworth is all swoony for Millicent Huxley. Swoony? Ha! That's a laugh. It's called love. Cupid has struck his arrow right into the center of Trip Wentworth's beating heart.

"Well, it's nice to be appreciated for a quality most don't appreciate."

"Trust me, Millicent, I appreciate all of your qualities."

We're both quiet for a moment, letting what I say sink in. I don't know where I'm getting all of this nerve from. It's not like I've ever had game with the opposite sex before. Maybe I'm not afraid of taking risks anymore. Maybe going on this godforsaken mission was exactly what I needed to make me grow a pair.

"It's strange how you can remember some things so clearly and others fade. How bad memories seem to stick and good ones disappear. I can't ever get that day out of my head, no matter how hard I try. I remember it minute by minute, every detail," I tell her. "I remember hearing Chuck count out loud, shouting, 'Ready or not, here I come.' I remember the smell of juniper in the air and hearing the buzzing of honey bees as they fed off our flowers. It's clear as crystal." I pause to take a breath, then continue. "I hid in one of the dog kennels. I thought he'd never find me there even though it was probably one of the most obvious places."

She gives me a strange look. "Dog kennel?"

"Their kennels aren't the kind you see on those sad dog commercials where the musician sings some sappy song asking for money because the emaciated dogs are going to die unless you pay up. Their kennels are, shall we say, pimped out. Air-conditioned. Indoors. And big enough that one might refer to each kennel as a tiny house. My parents splurge on those furry beasts. I'm surprised they haven't installed plumbing for the little balls of fur to use at their leisure."

"You hate them," she says.

"The dogs or my parents?"

"The dogs."

"I know." My lips slightly curl up. "Actually, I like my parents but don't go around telling people. Aren't we supposed to loathe them at this point in our lives until we get our act together, then all of a sudden we determine that they aren't so bad after all?"

"I like my parents, too," she says. "They annoy me, but I'm willing to bet I annoy them, too."

"You?" I feign disbelief, teasing. "I don't hate the dogs; I'm indifferent to them."

"Indifference is worse than hate. It means you stopped caring. I hope I don't ever become indifferent."

"You, my dear, never have to worry about that." I rake my hands through my hair again, then take a deep breath. "You sure you want to hear this? It's not a pretty tale."

"I don't like pretty things," she says. "But you don't have to tell me unless you want to."

"I want to tell you so you can understand me. I mean, I want you to know where I'm coming from."

I don't tell her it's because I want whatever we have to go somewhere, and I'm smart enough to know you can't start something without knowing where you're trying to get to.

"They had this one dog, Remy, who'd been a little bit of a problem, but not so much that my parents were concerned. He barked a lot and growled at you if you came near his food. Real territorial. He nipped my mom one time, but she balked at the notion that he was vicious. To her, every dog can be trained. Even dogs like Remy, but in this case she was wrong," I say.

"Remy was an alpha dog, and there's nothing worse than an alpha dog who thinks you're trying to take over its territory. I hid in the wrong kennel that day, and I didn't know Remy was in there until it was too late. By the time I rushed to the gate to escape, he'd dug his canines into my leg and wouldn't let go."

I close my eyes for a second, remembering the terrifying, unimaginable pain from his sharp teeth piercing into my leg down to my bone, tearing at my leg like it was a chew toy. Cutting into it like a knife to a steak. His razor-sharp teeth tore at me like a chainsaw, slashing my muscles like they were jelly. Me kicking and screaming. Fighting him as best as I could. Trying to survive. To stay alive. To get out of there.

I open my eyes to see tears trickle down Millicent's face, and it kills me to see her so upset. I don't know if I should continue.

"It's okay…" she tells me, pressing her hand against mine.

"I was screaming so loud. The pain was…unimaginable," I say, purposely being vague. She doesn't need to know all of the details. That I suffered from nightmares for years because the pain was so intense. That it took years for my parents to have dogs again because I was frightened of them. We'd be out, and I'd see a dog or hear one bark, and I'd turn blue, huffing and puffing from lack of air. I'd go into a panic, and we'd have to leave where ever we were because I was having a panic attack.

"Chuck was the first one to show up. He didn't think twice about going in that kennel and shoving Remy off of me. I thought I was safe and sound. Chuck was a big guy. A strong guy and he'd just pushed Remy off of me like it was nothing. But when an alpha is challenged, and in Remy's case, I was his dinner, he strikes back. Chuck had his back to him for one second. He was reaching over to pick me up and get us out of there to safety. Remy leaped onto Chuck and bit him in his neck, hitting an artery. There was so much blood. So much. I was covered in it."

Millicent gasps. Her face is flooded with tears. She sobs but says nothing, squeezing my hand tight.

"Remy came back at me again. This time with a strange ferocity. Like he was trying to prove a point. I don't know." I shrug, trying to keep my cool as I tell her, but talking about it conjures the feelings - emotions I'd had stored away - that I thought I'd overcome. But no one ever gets over a traumatic event. Ever. Sure, they go to therapy and do all these things to heal, but it's still in there.

I suck in a lungful of air so I don't cry. The last thing I want to do is tear up while I'm telling her.

"He was a dog or a demon in disguise," I say. "I was losing so much blood and had almost blacked out. I wish I had so I wouldn't have had to see what happened to Chuck," I say.

That was the worst of it: seeing him die. It's an image I've never ever been able to get out of my head. No matter how hard I've tried. I have nightmares about it. Even now. When I think I've forgotten, the images come back to haunt me like it was yesterday.

Millicent gets up from her chair and comes over to me, sits on her knees and lays both her hands on mine. I offer her a thankful smile and try to fight back my tears, but it's hard when I see her crying like she is. When I see her tears are from me. From what I've told her.

My eyes well up with tears. I clear my throat and take a deep breath. "My parents came running into the kennel soon after," I choke back tears. "Dad had his shotgun and shot Remy. The sound was deafening." I take another deep breath. "I couldn't hear, and even days later, there was a strange buzzing sound in my head. I passed out shortly after Dad shot Remy, and I don't remember being taken away in an ambulance or being rushed into surgery. All I remember was what happened before and then the after."

She lowers her head to my knees and silently weeps. I run my fingers through her hair. My voice grows quiet, "I didn't wake up until a day later. Until after the surgery. Until after my mom told me they had to take my leg," I say. "When I looked down and saw it was missing, I screamed. It was the last sound I made for years."

She looks up at me, giving me a puzzled look. "What do you mean?"

"My parents sent me to every therapist under the sun to find a cure. The truth of the matter was, I couldn't get the image of what had happened to Chuck out of my head. I felt like I was to blame. That I was the reason he died and that losing a leg wasn't enough penance. When your mind is set and you are filled with all this guilt, no one is going to change it. Not your parents. Not a bunch of therapists. No one but you. So, they diagnosed me as a selective mute, which, I guess I was, but there was such little knowledge about this when I was a kid, so my education at first was nontraditional."

She looks at me expectantly, waiting for me to continue.

"I was in a special school for a couple of years before my parents finally had enough sense to pull me out and homeschool me. But, when you're in a special school, and you don't have a disability, other than a physical one, it's frustrating to be labeled and treated as such. I'd lash out. I was very aggressive when I was a little boy," I say, thinking back to those years of anger and rage. The years when I didn't know how else to express myself. What I was feeling inside. Everything was all bottled up. "I'd punch doors and once lit my parents living room rug on fire. I didn't know how else to cope with all of the things I was feeling. Guilt can consume a person and drive them to the brink of insanity."

"What made you change? How'd you get better?" she asks with a shaky voice. She wipes her wet eyes with her forearm and stares up at me patiently.

"Music," I answer simply, because it is that simple. Music saved me. "When my mom had Josie, my music teacher, come to our house for the first time to play the piano, I knew I wanted to learn, too. All it took was watching her. Hearing music fill the house. Seeing that I could create something beautiful without saying anything. And when my fingers touched the keys, I forgot everything. It was as if all of the pain had faded away."

"What you've gone through…" her tone is full of sadness and sympathy. "Anyone who has heard you play would say you create beauty in this world."

I cup her chin with my hand, letting my fingers brush away the dampness. "That's one of the nicest compliments you've ever given me." I bring my hand back to my lap. "Thank you."

"I mean it; you have a gift."

"I'm just better than the average person. I'm not so sure I have a gift," I say.

"I mean what I say," she says.

"Well… thanks."

"Why did your parents keep raising the dogs? Doesn't it bother you having them near you?"

"Not now. It took years for me to be okay with them. They didn't have them the first few years, but I can't fault my parents for wanting to do something they love."

"It's still kind of messed up, isn't it? Don't the dogs make you remember what happened?"

"They aren't the trigger. The kennel was, and I still don't go near the kennels for obvious reasons. Would a farmer quit farming if his son lost his leg from a tractor?"

"I don't know, but…"

"It's the same thing. They can't give up their livelihood because something unfortunate happened. They have to keep living, just like I do," I say, and she relents. "I didn't tell you to have you feel sorry for me. I told you because I think you should know."

"It was a horrible accident. A tragedy," she says with a choked sob. "But it wasn't your fault. You have to know that."

"I know that now. Finally. It took a long time and it wasn't an easy path," I say and suck in a lungful of air; when you confess everything, you feel like you can finally breathe. Like you can be free again. Like a huge weight has been lifted off of your shoulders. Cliché but it's so true. It does feel like something pressing you down but lifted once you confess. "I've had twelve years to deal with this. I deal better now than I did last year and the year before."

"Do you resent your parents?"

"Why would I? It's not their fault it happened. Believe me, they blame themselves plenty. My mother especially feels a lot of guilt. It makes me feel bad, but what can I do? I can't make her feel any other way than the way she does. We all have to go through the motions and heal in our own time."

She springs up from the ground and pulls me into a tight, lingering hug, then slowly releases me. She reaches down and places both of her hands on my cheeks, gently grazing her fingers against my stubble. "You amaze me Trip Johnson Wentworth."

I feel heat rush to my face. "It's actually Beckett Johnson

Wentworth."

"Beckett," she says and becomes reticent for a moment. "I know it's important to you. Thanks for feeling I was important enough to share it with."

"I know it's a hard tale to hear, but knowing you care helps," I say. "For a long time, there wasn't a day that would pass when Chuck Gosnell didn't cross my mind. When I didn't go over what I could've done differently so that he would still be alive. And the guilt is still there, but not like it used to be. Every day is better than the day before."

She inhales a sharp breath, and she takes a few steps away from me. Tears form in her blue eyes, then she begins sobbing uncontrollably.

I'm not sure what to do or what to say, so I reach for her hand to console her.

"I didn't mean to upset you," I say in a quiet voice.

She continues to bawl.

"I'm… I'm sorry."

She looks up at me with surprise. Her breath hitches. "You," she says with a choked sob, "shouldn't be sorry." She lets go of my hand.

I stand there awkwardly. I could try to hug her. I could tell her everything is going to be okay. I could try something but I don't know what that something should be to fix things. "Millicent?"

She swipes away her tears and wipes at her runny nose with the back of her hand. It's red like the rest of her face. "I…I just don't handle things like these very well. Everything has just hit me all at once. First with Luca, and then all of the bad things that have happened to us since we left."

"But there have been good times, too," I say. Even the bad things haven't been so bad.

"And hearing your story…" she pauses momentarily. "I feel like I shouldn't have probed. It was personal, and I pushed you to tell me, and I know it was painful for you to tell me. I'm so sorry."

"I wanted to tell you. I told you that."

"I know," she says, but I hear the uncertainty in her voice. She brings her palm up to my cheek once more and says nothing, letting out the softest of wistful sighs. "And I know how much trust I have earned from you for being able to hear it." She stays quiet for a moment, staring at me. Finally, she says, "We should get some sleep. We have a long day ahead of us."

"I'm not tired," I tell her. I hear the desperation in my voice.

I wait for her to say something, anything, but she shakes her head as if she's arguing with herself, brings her hand back to her side and heads toward the gate.

CHAPTER 25

I'm jostled awake and drenched in sweat. The sheets are soaked. I'm awakened by the touch of her hand and the bright shining light coming from the bedside table lamp. Millicent is standing over me with a look of concern and is nearly panting. "What's wrong?"

Her chest rises and falls flat. "You were screaming," she breathes.

I sit up. BB stirs, rolls over and barely opens his eyes. "Everything okay?" he asks all groggily. He glances down at the sheets. "You didn't pee the bed, did you?" He makes a disgusted face and shirks away from me.

"No," I say with annoyance. "That's my sweat, dumbass. Go back to sleep."

"That's a relief. Piss is where I draw the line," he says, then closes his eyes, rolling back over on his side. Must be nice to sleep so easily. I haven't had this luxury since before the accident.

"I'm okay," I tell her.

"What... what happened?" She sits in the chair adjacent to the bed and places her hand on top of my arm. My eyes dart down to her hand, which she immediately notices. She moves her hand back to her lap, which is a major disappointment because any type of touching with her is fine by me.

"Just a nightmare. I have them from time to time."

Her face falls.

When I had the accident, I had nightmares every night. PTSD will do that to you. I reached a point where I hated to go to sleep because I knew it'd be a reenactment of what happened: how I lost my leg and Chuck dying. Not the best images for a little boy, or anyone for that matter. I don't know how the soldiers cope when they come home from war. How can they sleep at night after witnessing all of that bloodshed? There are some images your brain can't unsee. If I was granted one wish in my entire life it wouldn't be to have my leg again. It would be to wipe that one awful day out of my mind.

I went to some New Age hypnotist who tried to help me, but it felt like weird hippie voodoo to me, and I was too young to understand the concept anyhow. My mom refused to allow me to take sleeping pills even though the doctors were pushing the issue (but doctors don't always know what's best), so I worked my way through it with the help of one very good therapist.

I lost a lot of sleep my first few years after the accident. So much of my world was upside down - from losing my leg to watching Chuck die to learning to walk again and trying to function in society. Sleeping was only part of the problem. It took years to get back to a normal routine. Now, I usually sleep through the night, but every now and again a nightmare - the same nightmare I've had since it happened - creeps right in there and hits me with a big whammy. Like tonight. Of all of the unfortunate things.

"Not a big deal. I'm a big boy," I try reassuring her.

"You were screaming so loud. I...I didn't know what was wrong. And you're sweating." She places her palm on my forehead. "Do you have a fever?"

"Maybe you just make me hot," I tease. I wink at her, which is strange because I'm not a winking kind of guy - it's more of a 1980s guy with a hairy chest and gold chain kind of move, but I can't stop winking at her. "You're concerned about me," I say, bringing my hands behind my head, feeling the sweat. "You do care about me."

She brings her hand back to her side. "Well, yeah," she says, all breathy. "We're friends." I hate that word: friends. I want more from her, doesn't she know that? What guy would want to just be friends with her? She bites on the corner of her lip and squints at me. "Do you have a lot of nightmares?"

"Not so much now. I used to. It's probably the bad diner food that caused it. Greasy foods wreak havoc on your sleep."

She shakes her head and lowers it, not making eye contact. "I shouldn't have pried..." she mumbles.

I touch her knee with the tips of my fingers. "Hey."

She doesn't look up.

"Hey," I say again. "I'm fine. It was a bad dream. It happens. I can handle it."

Silence.

"Promise," I say. "Now if you'd like, you can tuck me in so I sleep better. It might help if you sit right here and read me a bedtime story, too." I smile at her, but she doesn't reciprocate.

"Is that all you think about?"

"Yes, you're on my mind constantly."

"That's not what I meant," I hear her breath catch. I'm making her all flustered. Yes! Points for me!

"I think about food and taxes and my future and the injustice in the justice system. I think of everything and anything, but most of all I think of you," I tell her.

She smiles, but I can't tell if it's out of flattery or pity. She brings her hand close to mine but second guesses her action and drops it back to her side. "If you still have nightmares like this, maybe you should see a counselor like Willie does. He mentioned it helped him," she offers.

"I've been there and done that. You don't just get over a tragedy. You learn how to survive and glide through life with the wheels you have been given," I confess.

"I...I wish I could help you somehow."

"Well...you can't and don't need to anyhow. I'm not a fragile package needing to be handled with care," I say. "We can't let things get weird between us because I happen to have a bad dream every now and again, right?" I smile, trying to soften the mood, but Millicent is a deep thinker, a reader of people's emotions, and she knows this isn't some trite superficial experience I'm having. What I go through is a lifetime journey. Either she's game for being a passenger or she's not. I'm hoping she's game, because I can't imagine a better wingman.

"If you're okay…" her voice trails off. "I'm going to go to bed."

"I could use a goodnight kiss." I lift my brows and curl my lips upward, looking at her expectantly. "It'll help me have pleasant dreams."

She sighs through her nose, failing to respond, then ambles to her bed. Not the kind of reaction a guy wants when he's just laid his heart out there. BB rolls on his side, encroaching on my space. I try giving him a shove, but he's like a brick and doesn't move one inch. Nice. Not who I wanted to be cuddling up with tonight.

"Thanks for caring about me," I tell her.

"I'm sorry…"

"For what?"

"That you went through so much pain."

"Pain is life, right? You've had your share of sadness, I've had mine. BB has had his, but we don't let it define us. So, don't go feeling sorry for me because I have a bad dream every now and again."

"I wasn't," she lies.

"You were," I say.

"I…" she begins then pauses. "You were screaming," she whispers.

"And you were crying earlier in the bathroom. I heard you; BB heard you. But you came out of that bathroom wearing that mask of yours so we didn't budge. Sooner or later that facade is going to crack, and you'll have pushed anyone who cares one inkling about you away," I snap.

***

BB is a restless sleeper. He's shifty. Back and forth, over and over - throughout the night. One leg kicks here. The other there. I think he might suffer from restless leg syndrome or whatever it's called where the person has a leg twitch. Thanks to pharmaceutical company commercials and WebMd, I am now a savant in medical terminology.

I was struck by BB enough times throughout the night that I didn't get any sleep. Meanwhile, he's sleeping just fine: snoring it up and dreaming of beef jerky and salty potato chips.

The sun's rays are peeking through the window. I'm not ready for morning yet. I'm tired and cranky from lack of sleep. I glance over at the other bed and see Millicent is still sound asleep. Last night was strange. First, we fought (the usual). Then we kissed. (Which was nice. Actually, it was better than nice. It was amazing. Yes, I just said that). Then I laid it all out on the line by telling her about the leg (This was hard). Then she became really upset and got all aloof. Then she said we're friends but gave me the pity smile. I don't know. Maybe I freaked her out. It's a hard story to stomach, but she's a strong girl. Maybe I'm being too sensitive. Maybe I need to quit laying here in this uncomfortable bed thinking about all of this because I sound whiny.

I slip out of bed to take a shower, hoping the hot water will help quell my sleepiness and overly sensitive thinking. Put on some aftershave. Beat my chest. Shout like Tarzan. Feel like a man.

I head to the bathroom, take off my prosthetic and lay it against the wall, then hop into the shower, holding on for dear life. I'm hopping in the literal sense. This takes skill and finesse— two things I'm not gifted with— but after years of practice, I've become an expert of sorts at doing things on one foot.

At home, there's a rail on the wall in my shower and a bench. It's hard to stand on one leg for any given amount of time on a slippery surface, so we had the rail and bench installed a long time ago. This motel is old, so ADA regulations don't apply here. Yes, believe it or not, there are businesses that do not have to comply to make things easier for people like me. We don't matter to them, I guess since we're not part of the vast majority of able-bodied people who don't need to hold on for dear life just to do something as simple as showering.

The water coming out of the shower head is lukewarm at best, but that's okay since a cold shower will do me some good. The shampoo the motel provided is the cheap kind, the stuff that doesn't wash away. Even though you've doused your hair in water forever, there are still suds.

I'm gripping the shower curtain, which is a very bad idea. I'm trying to be quick and get in and out in a hurry, but I feel dirty. I haven't taken a shower for two entire days, which is a milestone for me. Not a milestone I want to go around bragging about, but there it is.

I pick up the bar of soap, which is as shoddy as the shampoo, and lather it all over my body. I'm still holding onto the shower curtain with one hand while cleaning myself with the other. I feel like a juggling act. What else can I do? Give me some apples while I'm at it, and maybe I'll be a regular on the circus circuit!

I'm almost finished showering when I feel my grip loosen on the shower curtain. I look up and see it's torn and is still tearing at the silver rings. There are two rings left in tact, but the rest of the white plastic curtain has fallen into the shower. I reach up for the shower bar, clasping my hands around it, but my hands are wet and so is the bar. My fingers start to slip.

THUMP!

"Ahhhhh! Shit! Shit! Shit!"

My butt hurts. I mean, there's some cushion back there, but not enough to spare me the pain when colliding against porcelain. The water from the shower head is pouring down on me. The tattered curtain is barely covering me.

The door swings wide open; Millicent stands over me with a look of frenzy.

My face immediately turns red, so does hers.

"Are you okay?" she asks, nearly out of breath. "Are you hurt?"

"Perfect," I lie. "Just a sore butt."

She bends over to turn off the water and looks back at me. I notice her eyes glance downward, toward the nether region. My nether region. So, it's a two-way street after all. Too bad it's not in its full glory. Then she'd see that yes the rumor about shoe size is true.

"I caught you looking," I tease. I pull on the curtain, trying to cover myself better. It's white. How much more can I cover myself? And, I'm not so shabby if I do say so myself. I work out.

I catch her watching me, then when I make eye contact with her, she blushes again.

"So, I'm a sex object, am I?" I continue.

She lets out a long sigh. "Don't press your luck."

"I'm riding the wave while I can," I say. "Can you hand me a towel and get my leg for me?"

She pulls one of the towels off of the rack and hands it to me, staring at the pink and green tiles like they're a marvelous painting in one of those stuffy museums. Then she grabs my prosthetic. She leans it close to the tub, trying hard to focus on the wall. It's hard to hold my laugh because she's stiff as a board, and I keep seeing her blue eyes darting in my direction.

"Those tiles pique your interest?"

She sighs through her nose.

"Do you need my help?" she asks with a hint of concern, still gawking at the tile like it's the most magnificent piece of art.

"No, but you might want to leave because I'm about to be sans curtain in a second and you'll get to see me in all of my glory once more." I grin wide at her. If I think of it, it's ironic I was worried about her seeing my leg but don't care that she's seeing me completely naked. Maybe I don't feel vulnerable around her anymore because I've told her everything? Maybe when you really like a person that's what happens: you shed everything because you trust.

She rolls her eyes, then steps to the threshold. She stops and turns to look at me. "You're really okay, right?"

"Yeah," I say. "Falling isn't something new."

"Do you need me to help you out of the tub? I'll close my eyes," she says in that same tone of worry and, I don't know, something else. It's like she feels guilty about me falling. She's not the owner of this non-compliant ADA motel, so what is the problem?

"I'd prefer you didn't...help me that is. I don't care if you close your eyes or not," I say, hoping she'll smile, but nope, there isn't a hint of one at all. "Look at these guns." I flex for her. It's a lame, desperate attempt, but you have to use what you have, especially in a situation like this. "I can get out on my own." I grasp the edge of the tub and start hoisting myself up.

"I'm going," she says and closes the door behind her.

***

Nearly broke. Tired. Hungry. Smelly (mostly BB). We're quite the threesome. There's no luggage to load into the truck since that was stolen. So, here we are wearing the same clothes we had on yesterday. BB seems to think that spritzing the Glade spray on his clothes makes him smell better.

I roll the windows down in the truck because BB's stench is powerful. It's like a mixture of lavender and poopy diaper. The scent wafts through the truck despite the fresh Wyoming air.

We ride west, weaving in and out of caverns and canyons. We stop to pee and stretch our legs. I catch Millicent taking a picture of the scenery with her phone.

She cups her hand over her eyes, trying to avoid the sun's direct rays. "It' so different from the Appalachians."

We're in the middle of a gorge. A body of water flows downstream. "Different good or different bad?"

"Different is always good," she says with a slight smile.

"I think so, too. Who wants normal?"

"Boring souls," she says.

"I'd say we don't suffer from the boring syndrome."

"No," she says. "Too bad we're the only ones our age who don't."

"Ah, three's a crowd," I say.

My phone vibrates in my pocket. I see it's a new text from my mom. My battery is low. We've got one charger between the two of us since the thieves took Millicent's, too. So, trying to be the gentleman that I am, I let Millicent charge her phone first.

Mom: *How are things at home?*

Me: *Quiet. Enjoying your mini-vacation?*

Mom: *No. We're coming home sooner than anticipated, so don't get too comfortable with our absence.*

Oh crap, oh crap, oh crap. What does "sooner" mean?

Me: *So, you'll be home tomorrow?*

Please say no.

Mom: *Yes. If your father had his way, we'd leave tonight.*

Tomorrow marks the end of my life.

I text her back with a typical sarcastic reply so she doesn't realize things are amiss. *Ticker tape parade or the usual fanfare for your arrival?*

Mom: *Ticker tape. Are you eating?*

Me: *No. I'm protesting the war in Afghanistan.*

Mom: *How is school going? Still making friends?*

Me: *Oh, I'm making friends alright.*

Mom: *Good. Love you. See you soon!*

This is the part when I'm supposed to feel guilty, but I'm too worried to feel guilt. They'll be home tomorrow night, and guess what they'll find? Not me. No truck! A bunch of charges on their credit card.

I furrow my brow as I squint down at my phone, pondering the inevitable: their fury when I come home. Goodbye life; hello cruel world.

"Are you okay?" Millicent asks.

"Just thinking about the ways my parents can inflict pain on me."

"I mean, you're not still hurting from the fall, right?"

I look away from my phone and look into her eyes, seeing her genuine concern. "What's with you?"

She shrugs me off. "I just want to make sure you're okay."

I don't know where this is coming from, but it's going to get old quick if she keeps it up. "My butt's sore. You want to pat it and make it feel better?" One side of my mouth lifts up.

"Ugh," she groans and marches away, toward the truck. She climbs into the driver's seat and honks the horn. Guess the love pat is out of the question.

BB jogs toward it, rushing to the passenger side. I get stuck in the back, 'cause I move too slow to compete. Once I climb up inside, she turns the ignition, and we head further west.

CHAPTER 26

We pay the park ranger an enormous fee to enter Yellowstone National Park. I don't know why, but I naively thought it'd cost less than ten dollars. I guess the park has to charge a butt load to stay afloat since the government keeps making cuts, which doesn't make any sense because if we don't have our parks we have nothing but a concrete jungle without any ecosystem. What's the point of living on this planet if there's nothing beautiful left to appreciate?

It's late in the afternoon, and there's a slight wind coming from the north. The temperature has dropped, and we've got the heat cranked up in the truck, fighting the cold. Dad keeps a Chicago Bears blanket (which is blasphemy to the fine folks of Indiana) in the back seat, and I have it draped over me, but I'm still shivering. We committed a minor crime and stole the blankets from the motel. BB says it was retribution for the break-in, but I still felt bad about the thievery. I'm just not made to be a criminal (Says the guy who plans to break into a funeral home).

He has a blanket draped over him in the front seat and is back seat driving Millicent, who is behind the wheel, driving like she's on the Daytona Speedway. She keeps tailing the tourists, then slamming on her brakes, muttering some new-found curse words each and every time they slow down to take snapshots of the beautiful scenery. There's a line of cars in front of us. The road is clogged with cars parked off to the side and eager tourists are busy taking pictures. Lots of people are taking selfies, which is strange considering they are in the middle of gorgeous scenery. Why would they care about a picture of themselves when they're here? Some people are so attuned to themselves they can't see beyond of their own reflection. Meanwhile, I can't stop turning my head from right to left at everything around me, and I'm taking as many snapshots as I can.

"You drive like a maniac," BB complains. "Where are we headed?"

"To the Old Faithful ranger station," she says. "It's where Luca was stationed."

"I've always wanted to see it," he says.

"It erupts every ninety minutes," I add. "It's the most famous of the five hundred geysers but not the most impressive in the park even though it's the most visited."

"Do you do nothing but read all day?" BB asks.

"I eat and sleep, too," I say. I tap Millicent on her shoulder. "Maybe you can stop so we can take a picture."

"I guess."

"Maybe we need to get you some sustenance, too," I say. "Since you seem to be suffering from hanger."

"He's right. You're grouchy."

"Look in the brochure and see if there is a restaurant near Old Faithful," she says to BB, who flips through the brochure and taps on it with a wide grin.

"Yep. There are restaurants in the two hotels." He rubs his hands together. "Let's take some pictures and get some grub."

"We're not lollygagging. I'm on a schedule," she says.

"We are well-aware of your schedule, time Nazi," he says. "Just pull over so me and Trip can take some more pictures of this here prettiness."

***

After taking several pictures of Yellowstone Lake—which has to be the most beautiful body of water I've ever seen in my life, with its jade water and snowy peaks filling the horizon— we drive on, stopping to take a picture of some bison who are too busy eating to notice our presence. Millicent even joins along, taking as many photos as I am.

We gather around for a selfie at BB's insistence, who says we need to have a group shot. Millicent stands in between BB and me. I wrap my arm around her shoulder, and thankfully, she doesn't shirk away since she's been treating me strangely since the big kiss. It's not like we had a one night stand. Not that I would know what the feeling is like, but I assume it's awkward because that's how it's described on TV and in books. It's not like I can go up to her and ask her if we're boyfriend and girlfriend, but I sure want to. Being a novice when it comes to love really sucks.

Old Faithful erupts right on schedule. It isn't that impressive given its popularity with the tourists (there is a crowd). After it is all said and done, we head to the nearby cafe to grab a sandwich and tea, then have a seat at a high top.

"That's it," BB says with disappointment. "What a letdown."

"Yeah," I shrug.

"Too much hype," he says.

The place is buzzing with poorly dressed tourists who don't know the first thing about color coordinating. I've never seen so many people in fanny packs in my life. Millicent keeps checking the time on her phone. I hear it ring, and she clicks on it, ignoring the caller.

"Your mom?" BB asks her.

"Yeah." Guilt floods her face. "By the way, she's threatened to keep me locked up in my room for the remainder of the year, so y'all might not see me after this."

"You need to talk to her."

"I texted her to tell her I went camping with BB and not to worry."

"Telling someone not to worry makes them worry," I say.

"And I'm sure they think it's strange that you left at the crack of dawn to go camping with me," BB adds.

"They know I don't deal well with death," she snaps. "What about your parents? I'm sure they're concerned they haven't heard from you."

"They couldn't care less about where I am. You know that. Anna and Mama Sauce are different," he says with a frown. "They care."

She tosses her napkin into the trash can and jumps off her chair. "Let's go to the ranger station."

"I guess we're through with this discussion," he murmurs.

"Yep. We're through," she says.

"I'm getting some ice cream. Maybe you should have some, too, Mellie. It might help your mood," he says. "Can I borrow a few more bucks, Trip?" He looks at me with those puppy dog eyes. I reluctantly hand him a five dollar bill, noting inwardly the lack of cash we have.

"Get your ice cream. I'm headed that way without you." Millicent points to the exit and marches outside. I give BB a look, but it does little to affect him since hunger tends to dictate his life choices. If only my life were that simple. It seems that one feisty blonde dictates my moods. Wherever she goes, I follow. I've got it bad. There, I said it. She has me hooked like Wonder Woman with her magic lasso. I'll let you in on a little secret: I read comic books. It's a guilty pleasure. And Wonder Woman, well, what guy wouldn't like her?

"Hey!" I call. "Wait up."

She keeps walking fast.

"Gimp right here. Unable to run!" I shout.

She stops in her tracks and spins on her heels, waiting for me. I catch up to her, a little out of breath - the girl can move fast. "You're in a hurry."

"I didn't tell you to follow me," she says.

"I thought the food would help, but evidently it hasn't."

She doesn't laugh. She doesn't say anything. She just keeps on marching with her left arm swinging (this is her irritated stance) and heads directly toward the ranger station. I lag behind because walking fast isn't my thing. It's just not my skill. I guess I should be thankful she's not one of those types who waits for me to catch up. That's the worst: knowing that you're holding someone up when she really wants to keep moving.

I push open the doors and scan the perimeters, searching for my moody pseudo-girlfriend. She's off to the left, standing at the ranger desk, waiting. No one is there to assist her. I'm surprised she hasn't stood on top of it and shouted for someone to come help given her lack of patience and irritated mood.

I turn to look the other way and spot a ranger trying to help an Asian woman and her sobbing child. He's using a soothing voice, but given her clueless and frantic expression, they're not speaking the same language and his tone doesn't seem to be offering much consolation. I move closer, trying to hear what she's saying to him. I catch a few words - my Mandarin is rudimentary. Something about the little boy being stung.

I get a better look at the crying child and see his one arm is ten times the size of his other, and it's red.

"He was stung by a bee," I tell the ranger.

The ranger looks away from the mother and child and gives me an unbelievable look like I've just discovered uranium on Mars.

"I know some Mandarin. He was stung by a bee. He might be allergic," I tell him.

The ranger inspects the child's swelling arm and furrows his brow, realizing I might not be as dumb as I look.

"Do you have Benadryl? It helps for bee stings," I offer.

"Ask if he is allergic," he says to me.

"I'm not that proficient," I say. What have I gotten myself into?

"Can you at least try?" he says desperately.

I think back to my one course in Mandarin wishing I'd been a better student because learning things like "I like the library" doesn't mean shit in the real world. I ask the woman if her son needs medicine because I can't think of a word for allergy.

She nods emphatically and points vigorously to his swollen arm, then starts speaking quickly in Mandarin. I don't understand a word she's saying but given her expression, my guess would be something like, "Hurry it up now, you dipshits!" Her son's cries are hurting my ears. You want to cure teen pregnancy? Go to a public forum of any sort and loiter near crying toddlers. It's enough to make you want any form of birth control anytime you're getting it on.

"He needs an EpiPen," I say.

The ranger moves in haste toward the back of the station.

I try to tell the woman that everything will be okay, but I can see she is too upset to hear me. The child is screaming, and my head is throbbing. I can't hear myself think. Meanwhile, a crowd has circled around us, mostly nosy onlookers who want to see what is causing such a ruckus with their phones whipped out, recording us. "Can any of you speak Mandarin?" I ask them.

They slightly move their heads side to side, mumbling quietly to each other. The ranger comes out carrying an EpiPen and does his job, saving the kid from possible death. The crowd claps their hands like we've just performed one of those cheesy acts at EPCOT, then leaves, bored by the lack of action. After it's all said and done, the mother smiles at me and reaches in for a hug, which is awkward since we don't even know each other's names; but hey, I did just save her son. A hug is better than a handshake.

"Good job," the ranger praises me. "We're currently looking for rangers who speak Mandarin. Do you have a college degree?"

"No. I'm still in high school," I say.

"Pity. We could use someone like you," he says. "Maybe you'll consider a career as a ranger when you're old enough," he offers.

"Yeah," I say without much fanfare. I have no intention of choosing such a career. The leg and all might be an issue with such a job. Or, maybe I'm just too much of a wuss to deal with snakes, bears, and mosquitoes.

"Anyway, thanks for your help. I appreciate it."

"You guys might want to take a course from Rosetta Stone," I offer.

"I have," he says with a frown. "Look how much that helped me."

Insert foot in mouth.

"Oh," is all I can say because I did just point out his lack of intelligence in grasping foreign languages.

"Thanks again." He offers to shake my hand, and if I didn't shake his in return I'd look like a real dbag even though I cringe from the act. I admire all of the OCD types who refuse to partake in such activities, but as it stands, I do not have the kahunas to shrug people off when they offer me their possible germ-infested hand.

BB meets up with me. Ice cream covers his lips. He's got that dreamy-sugary smile about him. "That ice cream was good, and it was cheap, too," he says. He looks around the place. "Where's Mellie?"

I motion my head to her location. We trek to her and wait while she talks with an older ranger, who's sporting a 1980s pornstache and wearing a pair of big specs. I see his name tag reads Dale Fleming. It sounds like a character from a James Bond novel.

BB nudges her. "What's going on?" he whispers.

"He's trying to find out which funeral home they took Luca to," she says. Pornstache, aka Dale, is on the phone, speaking in a low voice. Millicent turns toward me. "What were you doing over there?"

"Just saving a life," I tout, wearing a confident grin. "Rosetta Stone came in handy."

"Hmm," is all she says. I thought at least I'd get a congratulatory kiss or something affectionate since I did just save a child.

"It pays to be multilingual," I add. "Good thing I speak Mandarin." I am so obvious sometimes. Why not make a banner that reads, "Trip Wentworth is desperate for Millicent Huxley's adoration!"

Nothing. She's too busy listening to Pornstache.

"I also speak a little Italian because it's the language of love."

She turns to look at me and says, "While I'm awe of your prowess in the art of languages, I'm trying to hear what he's saying and you're distracting me."

I elbow her playfully. "So, I distract you, do I?"

"Shhh."

Pornstache finishes up his conversation, then hangs up the phone.

"Well?" she says, waiting.

"He's at the Whispering Woods Funeral Home in West Yellowstone. The service is in two days," he says. "You kids related to Luca?"

"Just me. He's my uncle," Millicent says. "I'm Millicent. That's Trip and Oliver."

"I'm Dale," he says. "He mentioned having a niece," he says, but I can tell he's fibbing. People will do that sometimes: tell a tale to offer comfort.

A much younger ranger without any facial hair, dressed in a brown uniform and dorky hat, approaches us wearing a smile.

"These kids knew Luca," Pornstache explains to him.

"Luca was the best," the guy says in that way people talk when they're in awe. "We're going to miss him."

"She's his niece," Pornstache adds, pointing to Millicent.

"I didn't know he had a niece," the younger ranger says, then realizes his blunder. "But Luca was a private guy. We didn't even know he and Jordan were dating until she showed up here one day with his lunch."

Millicent moves closer to him out of curiosity.

"She works in the park, too."

"Real free spirit," Pornstache adds. "One of those peace-loving types who only eats organic and tofu," he says with twisted lips. "My shift ends in a half hour. You kids want to get a cup of coffee?"

he offers. "My treat."

"I'd take him up on his offer; he never pays," the other ranger says. "Cheapskate," he coughs as he says it, but Pornstache is no dummy and shoots him a warning look.

"Coffee sounds great," I say. A warm beverage does sound good, and our cash supply is low. I'll take a free offer when I get one.

"Yeah, coffee sounds great," Millicent adds.

I'm not sure what Millicent's motive is, but mine is to avoid the inevitable: breaking into a funeral home.

CHAPTER 27

We're seated in the Old Faithful dining room, which is filled with tourists dressed in tacky garb who are eating like they won't get another meal. Little tidbit: the average person gains between seven and ten pounds while on vacation. BB and I decide to order a slice of apple pie and a cup of coffee. Millicent sticks with hot tea and no sugary substance.

Pornstache is a bit of a ladies man. A few of the older silver foxes who work here come his way, smile, bat their lashes, stick their sagging chests out, and leave with a girlish giggle after he flirts with them in the most obvious way. I can't criticize him, though; he's got more game than I do. I bet these women don't want to just be his "friend." Maybe I'm an amateur when it comes to love, but I thought Millicent felt something for me. Now she's sending me mixed signals. Women are complicated. If I were religious, I'd consider the priesthood or become a monk. They don't have to contend with the woes of women.

Pornstache sits with his legs crossed and with one hand holding his coffee cup while the other rests in his lap. The waitress left a pot of coffee on the table, per his request.

"So, you kids came up for the funeral?" he asks.

"Yes," Millicent lies.

My eyes shift toward hers, but she ignores me.

"Just you three, huh? His mother and father aren't coming?"

"His parents are dead," Millicent says. "And his sister isn't able to make it. So, we came to pay our respects."

His face falls. "That's tough. I had no idea about his parents, but we never got into deep discussions," he says. "I lost my wife years ago and haven't ever recovered. Can't imagine not being able to attend her funeral."

Way to add more salt to that wound, buddy.

Millicent frowns at hearing this and sips her hot mug of tea. BB finishes his slice of pie and pats his belly, licking his fingers, which, by the way, disgusts me. I've grown so used to BB's habits, I just accept them now. Isn't that what friendship is? Accepting the person at face value.

"It sure is pretty up here," BB says.

"Best damn state I've ever lived in," Pornstache says. "Better than Hawaii, but my wife would have argued with you on that."

"You lived in Hawaii?" BB asks, leaning forward.

"All over. I was in the military before I became a ranger. It's been a good life."

"It sounds amazing," BB says with a look of awe.

"You're still young. You could follow in my footsteps."

"I can't join the military," he says with sadness. "I had a bad concussion."

"That won't stop you from this job. Only thing you might be tackling is a bear," he says with a rumbling laugh. He sees BB is taking him seriously and adds, "Just joshing you, kiddo."

"You have to go to college for your job, though, right?"

"Nowadays you do," he says. "But so what? Can't let that stop you from an opportunity."

"You have to be smart to go to college," BB says.

"I work with plenty of idiots who went to college," Pornstache says. "Don't sell yourself short till you've tried. There's seasonal work out here. Not park ranger or guide jobs. More in the nature of cleaning or food service, but it'll give you an idea of what it's like here. Something to think about, kiddo."

BB nods with a pensive expression. I hope it gives him hope. He needs encouragement. I can't imagine going through my days thinking I didn't have many options. It's enough to suck the life out of you. You'd start wondering what the point is.

"Where are you kids staying tonight?" he asks us.

"We haven't figured that one out yet," I say since BB isn't one to take charge and Millicent is staring off into space, thinking. She's been acting odd since last night. More odd than usual, that is. Leave it to me to be falling for a weird one like her. I'm falling - hard and fast. I'm sure to have multiple fractures and bruises that linger for weeks because this girl has my heart.

"Don't stay here in the park. The hotels are priced way too high. Unless you kids are trust fund recipients, you aren't going to be able to afford them," he says. "West Yellowstone is the closest town, but it's still high season so hotels are going to be expensive."

"We'll probably stay at a campground," I lie.

"They're probably all full. You didn't think to make reservations?"

I shrug my shoulders. "We didn't plan." We had one objective, but the other parts were lumped together haphazardly. Like a mishmash of things - kind of like the three of us. We're quite the quirky trio.

"Fly by the seat of your pants. I like it, even if it's a bit careless," he says and folds his hands into prayer formation, leaning forward. "Tell you what I'm going to do for you: I'll offer up my place if you promise not to steal my stuff in the dead of night or hack me with an ax." He notices our shocked expressions and laughs. "I got enough pistols to start my own militia, so if I hear you traipsing around my house at night snooping around, you're likely to get shot."

We all take a deep breath. Millicent's blue eyes widen. BB's mouth flings open.

Pornstache laughs. "Relax. I'd just maim you, not kill you."

This does little to comfort us.

"You kids are too serious. I wouldn't shoot you," he pauses for a moment, then adds "unless I had to." He guffaws.

A strange sense of humor this one has.

"We couldn't impose on you," Millicent interrupts his solitary laugh fest.

He waves his hand down. "It's getting late, and you're sure not going to find any available rooms anywhere. You can stay with me tonight," he says. "I'm doing it for Luca anyhow. In today's day and age, it's hard to find people who are nice all the time. Everyone is always in a hurry. Rushing around to do this or do that, but never taking the time to stop and smell the flowers. Then when they do smell the flowers, they expect the flowers to only be theirs and get mad when someone else wants to smell them, too. All the time complaining that the flowers weren't potent long enough. Or they didn't smell the way they thought. Didn't give them want they wanted," he rambles on. BB gives me a clueless look; even though this retro park ranger is talking in circles, he's making sense.

"But to some, the flowers are just right," I say.

"That was Luca." He nods with an appreciative smile because I've caught on to his metaphor. He stands up and brushes the crumbs off of his brown pressed pants. I peer down to notice his shoes are polished. I can see my reflection.

"We should get going. I don't like driving in the dark, and my show is on soon."

***

Dale's reference to distance is different than the average person. His idea of a quick trip to the store must be an hour long excursion. Gardiner is well over fifty miles away from Old Faithful. In Yellowstone distance, that means at least an hour and a half of driving. So, we've been in the truck following him to his house while the sun still shines above us and mountains tower high in the sky. The Rockies make the Appalachians look like foothills. Like me standing next to Millicent.

BB refused to let Millicent take the wheel, stating "You made me skid my pants when we drove up here."

She's in the backseat, staying quiet, while the two of us are following our trusty park ranger. This is how those horror flicks go: a trio of dimwitted teens blindly follows some deranged lunatic to his home only to find that he wants to eat them for breakfast or keep them as pets.

"We should have declined his offer," she blurts over the loud music.

BB will go deaf before he is fifty.

I turn my head, peering at her over my shoulder. "We need a place to sleep; it's free."

"So, we're going to break into a funeral home in the middle of the day? And what if he is a creeper?"

"He's not a creeper," I say with confidence. How should I know? "Anyway, we're going to the funeral home tomorrow night." I shrug my shoulders.

She sighs. "Another night. My moms are going to kill me."

"They were already going to kill you. Another night isn't going to change that," BB says.

"He's right. My parents are coming home tomorrow night, which means the shit will be hitting the fan. So," I say with another half shrug, "My life ends tomorrow. Prolonging this trip will delay the ritualistic killing of their poster boy of rebellion."

"Should we hold a funeral for you?" BB asks, teasing.

"Yes, but don't play sad, sappy funeral parlor music. I want something happy."

"Like?"

"Maybe Vampire Weekend. They're always upbeat."

"I want Taylor Swift played at mine," BB says.

No surprise there.

"What about you?" I ask Millicent.

She chews on her nail for a moment. "I don't know. I'm not that into music."

I gasp. Appalled. "Such a shame." I shake my head in disbelief. How can I be falling for a girl who doesn't appreciate the art of music?

"It's all background noise to me," she goes on.

"Maybe you need to stop thinking and just listen."

CHAPTER 28

Dale lives in a log cabin out in the woods. So cliché and fitting for a scary Wes Craven film. I was hoping he'd live in some mid-century modern home and dispel my generalization about park rangers and log home living. But as it stands, my stereotyping isn't farfetched.

The cabin has a musty scent like moss and a century-old attic bathed in dust, cobwebs and old lady perfume. The walls are covered in framed photos of Dale and his departed wife and are hanged crookedly. I'm tempted to straighten them. Furniture with weathered upholstery fills the space.

"I've got chili in the crockpot. It's bison meat," he says.

"I love bison," BB says with glazed eyes and a hungry expression.

"You kids help me set the table, and we'll eat dinner," he says. He gestures to the nearby antique buffet, indicating it's where the placemats and silverware are housed. We do our job, then sit at the table, waiting for our grub.

"The maid quit," he shouts from the kitchen.

We don't say anything. I wouldn't take him for the type to have a maid.

"Sheesh," he mutters. "I'm not serving you is what I mean."

We move in haste to the kitchen. He hands us each a dainty floral pattern china bowl so we can pour a heap inside of it. It's a bit ornate given Dale's cantankerous persona and makes me wonder if he secretly belongs to a knitting group with a bunch of old women who are named Nancy.

"It was Betsy's," he says, reading my thoughts.

"It's nice," I lie.

"It's junk, but it does its job," he says. "I got Coke and beer. Which do you kids want?"

"Beer," BB answers.

"Coke," Millicent and I say.

"I was fooling you, kiddo," he says to BB. "If you think I'm gonna serve you alcohol, you're crazy."

"Coke it is," BB says.

He opens the refrigerator door and points to the stack of cans of Coke. We each grab one after we serve ourselves a bowl of chili, then trail behind Dale into the dining room. He sits at the head of the table and stares at us, saying nothing, then proceeds to bow his head and close his eyes, saying a blessing. He opens his eyes and looks at all of us. "Time to eat."

I'm surprised we all don't pound our silverware against the table in ceremonial fashion while shouting, "Grub. Grub. Grub."

We all begin eating. With the exception of Dale slurping his chili, silence fills the space. Please note: Dale loves eating with his mouth wide open. Trying not to cringe.

"No gals and boys sleeping in the same bed tonight." He narrows his eyes to mine and BB's, then points at us with his long index finger. "Got it."

"Yeah," I say.

"Mellie's my cousin," BB says with a grimace.

"Doesn't matter. Plenty of people have married their cousins. Look at the royals."

BB makes a disgusted face. "That's just gross."

"Just stay in your own rooms tonight. I'm not playing party to kids sexing it up," he adds.

My cheeks turn red because I'm that much of a goober. He says "sex," and all I can think of is Millicent and, well, sex and sexing it up... with her.

"I called Jordan. She says she wants to meet you." He looks at Millicent.

"Oh," Millicent says and falls back into her chair. "Okay," her voice fades to a whisper.

***

After providing a tour of his cabin and showing us where our sleeping quarters are (emphatically pointing out that Millicent is sleeping in the other room), Dale has a seat in his battered recliner and turns on the television at 140 decibels. Not really, but the guy is hard of hearing, and the volume is turned up so high I can't even hear myself think.

We're seated on his leather sofa. I'm sunk down into the worn out cushion, feeling the springs against my rear end. Millicent is squished between BB and me. BB watches the television with Dale, fully engrossed.

Millicent is chewing on her fingernail and is subtly shivering. "Are you cold?" I rub her arm.

"I'm fine," she lies.

Dale peers at us. "If you're cold, I've got some of Betsy's clothes you can borrow."

"That's okay," she says.

He pushes himself forward, causing the recliner to go back to normal. He grunts as he heaves himself up, then walks to another room. He comes back into the living room holding a pink sweatshirt and sweatpants. "These should fit you. Betsy was tiny like you are."

"Thank you," Millicent says and takes them from him, carrying them with her to the room she's sleeping in.

A few minutes later she comes out dressed head to toe in pink sweats. They're a little big on her, but I still think she looks sexy. I have issues.

She plops between us and rests her arms on her chest. Her fingertips brush against my arm. I'm tempted to grab her hand, and I stew on the prospect for minutes until I finally get up enough nerve.

I reach for her hand and twine my fingers together with hers. She doesn't let go and allows me to hold it there for an entire minute! Yeah, I counted. So what. Things are looking up. It's happiness. It's everything. (I must stop reading romance novels. I'll take up karate and read horror novels when I return home. Of course, I'll be a hardened criminal so maybe the schmoozy romance part of me will disappear.) If I wasn't afraid Dale was going to kill me, I might try and sneak into her room tonight for a goodnight kiss.

"I'm hitting the sack," Dale says after his show ends. It was some cheesy cop series with an obvious plot and dead giveaway of the whodunit. "You kids don't stay up too long. I've counted my beer so I'll know if you had one." He narrows his eyes to BB's. "And I'll hear you sneaking around if you get the urge to have a slumber party." His eyes catch mine. It's like he's a mind reader. My face floods with guilt.

"Thanks for letting us stay here," I say to him, trying to change the air of discontent.

"Yes, thank you," Millicent adds.

"Thanks," BB says. "That chili was something else."

"Like I said earlier... I did it for Luca." He nods his head at us and offers us a solemn expression before heading back to his room. We hear the door close behind him.

Millicent peers around the corner, then whisper, "We need to leave tonight."

"Are you crazy?" BB shouts.

"Lower your voice," she says to him through gritted teeth. "We need to get to West Yellowstone."

I click on my phone, checking the distance from Dale's warm and cozy log cabin to West Yellowstone. "It's three hours," I say, holding up the phone.

"We need rest. Anyways, don't we need to stake the place out before we break in?" BB adds prudently.

"He's...right," I say with a questioning tone, surprised I'm agreeing with him.

"Tomorrow we'll stake the place out, then proceed with the mission," he says.

I find myself nodding my head in agreement with him. What do I know about breaking in? I guess I should ask myself why does BB.

Her face falls and she chews on her bottom lip, pondering BB's newfound brilliance. "Okay. We go with your plan."

"No sneaking out tonight and leaving us stranded," BB says.

"I would never," she defends.

"Hand over the keys." He holds his palm out to her.

She reluctantly drops the keys in his palm.

"We better get some sleep. Before you go on any re-con mission, you need rest and a full stomach," he says.

"When did you become so knowledgeable in the re-con arts?" I ask him.

"I hunt, and I watch war movies. You know your stuff; I know mine."

CHAPTER 29

We leave Dale's cabin early in the morning before he wakes. Surprisingly, Dale is not an early riser. I pictured him as the type who gets up before the sun rises and greets the day with a cup of joe in one hand and the newspaper in the other, whistling like he's on top of the world.

I insist we leave a note because it's rude otherwise. So I scribble something on a nearby pad of paper, telling him how much we appreciate his hospitality but we had things to take care of before the funeral. It sounds like a load of crap because what could a bunch of teenagers have to take care of before a funeral? But, we've been living a lie since we started this journey; we might as well stay consistent with our sins.

Millicent was the one pushing us to leave so early. BB and I would have been content to stay put in Dale's warm abode and eat more of his hearty food. I think she wanted to avoid meeting Jordan. Why? I don't know. She's been keeping to herself and is so hyper-focused on breaking into the funeral home that I can't read her. Not that I was an expert before, but now it's even harder. Maybe love is clouding my vision. Sounds prissy, but there it is.

We're sitting in the truck, casing the joint. Those are three words I'd never thought I'd utter. BB has both of his hands in a bag of salt and vinegar potato chips and keeps tossing a bunch into his mouth, then licking each and every finger on his greasy hands. I try not to cringe. The boy eats like Henry The Eighth. I think he learned his table manners from watching guests at Medieval Times.

"These are good," he says with a mouthful of crunchy potato chips.

Millicent is staring at the funeral home saying nothing to either one of us.

"You think they make good money?" BB asks. Crunch. Crunch. Crunch. Lick. Lick. Lick.

"It's one of those businesses that is always in demand," I answer. "Not too much competition, either."

His brows furrow.

"It takes sales skills. Bet I could do that."

"You have a trusting face," I say. "People would buy an air-conditioned casket from you." He smiles at my lame joke.

"Probably don't have to rely too much on a sharp memory, right? Not hard to forget the obvious."

"Good point," I say to him. "You can't think you're inhibited because of your," and I pause for a second, "issues. Someone could take a look at me and say the same, but I don't see it that way. I can do what I want, but I might have to take an alternate route to get there."

He nods. The ends of his mouth lift up into a soft smile. "Good point."

My phone lights up, and I see a text from my mom.

Mom to me: *We're home. Where are you?*

I don't respond.

Mom to me again: *Your father's truck is gone, and your bed is made.*

I know. I know. Ridiculous, right? I made the bed before I left home.

Me to Mom: *I'm out with friends.*

Mom to me: *There's also a message on the answering machine from the school stating you've been absent for two days. ???*

Me to Mom: *Hmm. That's curious.*

My phone rings. I swiftly click it to go straight to my voicemail, knowing that this act sparks the beginning of the end of my life. Mom is no dummy; where do you think I got my smarts from? She'll smell this festering rat a mile away. Fortunately for me, (or unfortunate, depending on how you look at it), my life was so pathetic before this summer my parents never felt the need to install a GPS tracking device in my phone. Why would they? Where was their recluse of a son going to go? My, how things have changed.

"Maybe we should go in," I offer.

"Who called?" Millicent asks.

"The units; they've caught on to my shenanigans. The school called about my attendance issues."

"Yeah," BB frets. "I'll be repeating Marshall's course...again." He sighs wistfully. "Lucky for me, our house phone is disconnected so the school can't call. Don't you worry skipping out on his class will hurt your G.P.A., Mellie?"

"It's still the 'withdraw no penalty' period, so it won't hurt me," she says. "I'm sorry I brought you both into this." She chews on that one fingernail again. Her jaw twitches. "Truly, I am."

"No reason to be. I've never had this much fun in my life," I admit.

BB gives me a hearty smile. "We are good company."

"You're alright, I guess. A little smelly, and you kick too much when you sleep, but I like you," I nudge him.

"Mellie, I never would have let you do this alone. We stick together. Remember our pact?"

"What pact?" I ask.

"Just something we did as kids," she answers. "Let's go check this place out. We can share stories and compliment each other on the ride home."

She exits the truck with BB and me following close behind her. The moment she pushes the door open, a man in a charcoal suit greets us with a sympathetic smile. Spa-like instrumental music plays while a fountain pumps out water, creating fake tranquil ambiance. The floors are a creamy tile and the walls are beige. Velvet mauve chairs sit in pairs every five or six feet with small tables between them, topped with brochures about grief and dealing with loss. I'm not sure how a pamphlet is going to help someone who is in the middle of grieving.

A 1990s Olan Mills photo of an old man rests against an easel. A string of flowers is draped around it, and the words, "He will be missed and never forgotten" are stamped below the photo.

"May I help you?" the funeral home employee asks. He's tall and masculine. The type of man who might have a bowie knife strapped to his leg. Why do all of the men out west look like a rough rider or a model for ranching gear? The name tag on his lapel reads "Bryan Weathers." This is not the name I imagined for him.

"We're here for the service," Millicent lies.

"Oh," he says, then darts his eyes to our less than stellar choice of attire. We're not dressed for a funeral, let alone a trip to Walmart. Well, maybe a trip to Walmart, but not any other place. BB's in ragged jeans, a t-shirt, and a ball cap. I'm wearing basketball shorts and a t-shirt, and Millicent has on Betsy's sweatshirt and a pair of denim shorts.

"It doesn't begin for another half hour. The family is in there for private viewing." He gestures to the closed double white paneled doors. "You can sign the guestbook and may have a seat over there for the time being."

He points to an open book. The pages are blank, sans the black lines. Millicent writes the name Maribelle Huntley. I decide to also use an alias since using my real name (which isn't that common) could leave a trail. I'm not too quick on my feet and struggle to come up with a name. BB abstains from taking part. Weathers gives him a curious look; I wonder how many people out there are conscientious objectors to signing funeral home guest books.

I decide to use the alias "Hector Johnson." I can't remember the laws of creating soap opera/stripper names, but I think it has something to do with the name of your first pet and your middle name.

"I'll just be back here for a moment if you need anything." Weathers exits the room to go back to whatever it was he was doing. The idea that he might be possibly messing with a corpse gives me the creeps.

We each have a seat in the velvet chairs. The fabric has a sheen; it appears as if someone has vacuumed it. BB grabs one of the brochures and begins reading it. Millicent is scanning the place from top to bottom.

"BB," she whispers.

He drops the brochure in his lap. "This might help Mama Sauce," he says. "And you, too."

"Unless a glass of wine comes with it, a stupid brochure isn't going to help anyone deal with loss."

"It obviously works or they wouldn't make such things," he mumbles, then picks it back up and folds it, placing it in his pant pocket.

"You need to stay on task," she bosses. "Be on the lookout."

He salutes her, then stands up, making his way around the lobby area. I think it's more of an attempt to steer clear of her than to scope the place out. Maybe he's thinking the same thing I am: that we're fools and this is the kind of mission a trio of rubes like us would make.

A few people trickle in while we loiter. I never thought I'd be loitering at a funeral home, but this venture has proven to be one awakening and weird experience after another.

"We should probably get going," I whisper to Millicent. The last thing I want to do is attend some stranger's funeral. It's depressing enough sitting in a place like this. She agrees and heads outside. She paces the sidewalk and is chewing on that one fingernail again.

A petite brunette woman enters as BB and I are leaving. She stares at us long and hard like she's trying to decide if she knows us or not, then, she approaches Bryan Weathers, who has miraculously appeared on cue, waiting to greet all of the mourners. "Hi, Bryan. Has anyone come in asking about Luca?" I hear her ask before the doors close behind us.

BB hits me a little too hard on my arm and murmurs, "You hear her?"

"Yeah," I answer.

"Mellie, that woman was asking about Luca," BB shouts from the top of the steps. Meanwhile, I'm still making my way down. Stairs and I are not friends, nor will we ever be.

"Say it louder because I don't think the entire town heard you!"

He jogs down to her and lowers his voice. "Maybe we should talk to her."

I reach the two of them and glance over my shoulder, seeing the petite brunette close behind me. She hesitates before she waves at us. I offer her a smile because it's rude to just stare at her blankly if she's trying to be friendly.

"We. Go. Now," Millicent says through gritted teeth.

We follow her like a bunch of mindless cretins, hearing the short brunette calling for our attention. "Are you Luca Moretti's niece?" she says to Millicent.

Millicent ignores her and walks directly to the truck. She opens the door and sits in the driver's seat, turning the ignition, drowning out the brunette's high-pitched voice. BB opens the door to the passenger's side and has a seat. I amble slowly behind them.

"Hey!" she calls again. "I'm Jordan," she says. "Luca's fiancé."

"Sorry. You have the wrong people," I lie, but she doesn't buy it.

I reach the truck and heave myself up into the back seat, then shut the door. Millicent jets off, driving above the speed limit without a destination in mind.

"She's his fiancé," I plead. I look to BB for affirmation. What can he say? "Here. Here. He's right."

"It doesn't matter," she says. "We're his family. Not her."

"It matters. You know it does."

CHAPTER 30

We're back at the funeral home, spying from across the road and trying to be inconspicuous, but given our wardrobe, I'd say it's next to impossible to be clandestine. We need to be clothed in black attire, wearing ski masks and carrying walkie-talkies. That's how it is in the movies, anyway. As it stands, Dad's ostentatious truck and our lack of expertise in covert operations make us nothing but a bunch of yokels.

We're waiting for the funeral home to close so we can get down to business. Now I'm talking like I've been kidnapped by aliens and have been transplanted with some 1930s gangster's brain. I think I've lost brain cells on this trip.

"You think this is what private investigators do all day?" BB asks.

"Yeah," I answer. "Most of their job is about waiting. I would hate it."

"You hate waiting?" Millicent asks.

"Yeah. You can't enjoy the present. You're too focused on the upcoming."

"Kinda strange you say that," BB says.

"Why's that?" I ask.

"You spent all that time holed up in your house. Weren't you just waiting then?"

"Yeah. That's why I loathe the idea now. I refuse to ever wait again," I say.

He holds his hand up for a high five, which is cheesy given our age, but I oblige and slap his palm with mine.

"That's the spirit," he says.

"What about you?" I ask him.

He flickers a look of surprise. "What about me?"

"Are you going to look into working at Yellowstone?"

He shrugs. "I don't know."

"Sure you do. Remember your pitch to get me to go on this crazy mission?"

His eyes move from left to right in thought, then a look of realization shows on his face.

"Don't talk the talk if you aren't going to walk the walk."

We watch as a funeral home employee locks the door and steps into his car, then drives off, unsuspecting of what's about to go down.

"There's our cue," Millicent says and starts up the truck, driving across the street and into the funeral home's parking lot.

The parking lot is poorly lit. One light barely illuminates the space. Really, it's like they're asking to be broken into. Not that I'm an expert in breaking into establishments, but proper lighting does deter the possible miscreant from creating any dastardly deeds. Millicent bends down and picks up a few pebbles, then tosses them up at the light bulb. It shatters, immediately causing the space around us to turn pitch black.

"Good aim," I say.

"I used to play softball," she says.

The woman never ceases to surprise me. I never pictured her as an athlete, but now my mind wanders to her in a uniform and ball cap, which is a sight I'd like to see.

They tiptoe up the steps and move to the back door. I walk up the ramp because my leg is aching from sitting so long. My other leg, the good one, isn't that great. My knee is like an old man's, and when I've been in a seated position for several hours, I feel the joint pain, the stiffness.

I meet them at the door. "Point your flashlight here," Millicent says to me. I turn my phone on (I've had it off for hours), instantly hearing the notification of a thousand texts and voicemail messages. Slight exaggeration but the endless alerts tell me my parents have called me more than a few times and have hired a hitman to inflict unbearable pain on me. I'll face that music when the time comes.

Millicent pulls a hairpin and nail file out of her short's pocket and inserts them in the keyhole. She wiggles them around, and I hear a clicking sound. She does the same with the deadbolt, but it's not as giving and it takes her a while to break into it.

"Where did you learn this skill?" I ask, half-amazed, half-alarmed because beyond the beautiful exterior of hers lurks a potential criminal.

"Youtube," she says. "I studied up on it before we left."

She pushes the door open. No alarm sounds, and we let out a sigh of relief.

"I'm surprised they don't have an alarm," BB says.

"Who wants to steal from a funeral home?" she says.

"Us," I answer. "We should still hurry."

For one, I cannot "hurry" anywhere. The leg and all makes me a bit slower than the average person. So, when I said, "hurry," they hauled ass while I ambled behind them, trying hard to keep up. Picture a turtle racing a roadrunner.

We don't know the layout of this place. It's not like the movies where a blueprint is available to study and help us in committing the most flawless crime. This little criminal adventure of ours is far from perfect and is on the verge of spelling disaster. You know that feeling you get in your gut when something bad is about to happen? That's the feeling I'm having right now. So why don't I just walk right out of here and leave them to it? Because I care too much, and

I don't want to cower anymore.

So, I trail behind them into the viewing room, seeing tall white candelabras on both sides of the room and colorful silk flower arrangements on top of small tables. I've never understood the concept of silk flowers. They collect dust and are fake. How can they provide the same feeling real flowers do?

They open an adjacent door, enter the room and loudly whisper from the other side of the wall, "This is it!"

I pick up my pace and meet them in a sterile room. Fluorescent lights flicker above us. A humming sound fills the space. The white-walled room is filled with equipment. Jars of embalming fluid sit on top of a metal shelf. A metal table centers the room. A round glass container on top of a square-shaped machine with little black knobs and black tubes coming out of it rests above the table. An image of the human body hangs on the wall next to the machine. A stainless steel refrigeration system fills another wall. This is not the type of environment I'd want to work in, but I guess people who don't want conversation excel in the mortuary arts. There's also that benefit of no one ever arguing with you. Purely one-sided conversation, though. Okay. I'll stop.

"They eat in here?" BB asks with a grimace.

"No. That's where they keep... uh... you know, them."

Nearby there is a brown tortoiseshell casket. It sits on top of another metal table. Caskets give me the creeps, but I would assume they would make most people feel that way.

"This is it," she says with certainty. She taps the casket and nods assuredly.

"Do you want to open it just to be sure?" I ask.

"No," she says. "The service is tomorrow morning. There aren't any other caskets out here. It's his."

"He's right. We should check," BB adds. "I'm not opening it, though." He backs away from it wearing a disgusted expression.

I try opening the lid but the casket is locked. "Think you can pick this?" I ask her. I shudder at the thought of what I'm asking her to do.

She squints at the end of the casket, staring at the locking mechanism.

"This is going to take a hell of a lot more than a bobby pin," she says with her hands on her hips.

BB takes a look at it. "Reckon they use a special key for this?" he asks.

"Yeah. I don't know else they'd get it open," I say.

"Why go to such an extreme? I mean, why try and lock it if it's six feet in the ground. Ain't nobody wants to go down that far just to steal a piece of jewelry," he says.

"Money makes people do crazy things," I say. So does love, but I don't say that. "We could always," my voice trails off.

She stands up straight and looks at me expectantly. "What?"

"Well, we could uh, look in there to see if he is in there," I jerk my head in the direction of the refrigerators, "and if he's not, well, that tells us he's in there." I gesture with the side of my head, pointing to the casket.

"You mean, open them and peek?" BB asks in a whisper.

"Well, yeah," I answer.

BB folds his arms across his chest. "I'm out," he says. "That's too gory for me."

"I can do it but don't know what he looks like," I say to Millicent.

"I can look," she says and marches to the cooling units or whatever they're called. I've never researched the internet for such terminology and haven't become a savant in the mortuary business.

She opens one, and it's empty. The next is, too, much to my relief. The last door opens and, it too is empty inside.

"It has to be him," she says with certainty.

She steps over to the casket and tries to lift it but it remains planted. Her face turns red and her chest is rising and falling flat. "It's heavy," she says to us in disbelief.

"That's why they usually have lots of pallbearers for those things," BB says in a "duh" kind of tone.

"The table has wheels on it," I say, pointing to the black wheels. "We'll roll it out of here."

"And just slide it in the truck," BB adds.

"This was easier than I thought it'd be."

That's what worries me.

CHAPTER 31

I stand at the rear, pushing the table while BB stands at the front towing it. Millicent stands between us, helping us glide the thing down the ramp as carefully and quickly as possible. The words "careful" and "quick" don't coincide. Kind of like sweet and sour or bitter and sweet. The list could go on.

We reach Dad's truck, panting and out of breath because the casket weighs a ton, and even though there are wheels on the table, it didn't help soften the weight of this monstrosity. No wonder the employees here are so manly. If anyone ever asks me to be a pallbearer, I might have to think twice about it.

I unlatch Dad's truck bed and let it fall flat. BB, Millicent and I lock the wheels on the table, then push the casket into the truck bed. We give it our best heave-ho, breathing heavy from the exertion. And here I thought I was in shape.

I walk to the back seat and grab Dad's Chicago Bears blanket, wrapping it around the casket. It's like putting a used bandage on a deep cut. It won't buffer it for long.

"Think it'll stay on it?" she asks.

"Hope so." I shut the truck bed door.

I see the look of worry on her face but she says nothing and makes her way to the driver's side to take the wheel.

I emphatically shake my head and open the door, looking at her expectantly.

"What?"

"You drive too carelessly, which means our chances of being pulled over by the police are even greater."

"I drive fine."

"If by *fine* you mean like a blind retired race car driver, then okay, but as it stands, I object to your presence behind the wheel," I say.

"I do, too," BB interjects.

She takes a deep breath and grunts in annoyance, then hops down, gently pushing me aside.

"Drive then," she barks. I sit down and turn the ignition, heading away from the scene of the crime.

I'm coasting on a desolate road. The moon is full, casting a glimpse of light into our dark and dreary truck. The thought of what we're carrying hasn't left me. The aspect of what we've just done isn't beyond my thoughts, either. I just broke the law. And for what? To live? For a girl? For love? I am all kinds of stupid.

I maintain the speed limit, watching the road. The radio's volume is at a record low. The hum of guitars and other instruments can be slightly heard, but I'm not sure what song is playing, nor do I care.

My heart thumps hard, and my palms sweat. Guilt clouds my heart and head. All I can see is a fuzzy picture in front of me. I'm consumed with an ominous feeling that we've just made the biggest mistake of our lives.

"What will his fiancé think?" I blurt. "She'll get there and see he's gone. And then what?"

Millicent chews on her one fingernail, saying nothing, but a look of remorse floods her face.

"It'll break her heart, won't it?" I say. "It'd break mine."

"Mama Sauce's heart is broken, too," she says.

"How can we determine whose heart has more importance?" I pound the steering wheel with my fists. "Who the hell are we to make this decision?" I shout. "What were we thinking?"

"Now you doubt?" she scoffs.

"I doubt because before we were just hurting strangers—some idiots in a funeral home who price gouge poor unsuspecting grieving loved ones at their worst and most vulnerable time. But now, what we're doing, well, it doesn't sit right. You know it; I know it. BB, you know it, too."

I have that pit in my stomach. A churning sensation. Bile rises in my throat. What have I done? I tried to prove something to myself. That I could take a risk, but at what point is the risk too much? When does it cross the line into selfishness? Isn't that what we are? Selfish. Reckless. Thoughtless.

"You can't have it both ways," she says. "And now is the most inopportune time to have a conscience."

"There's never a right moment."

"Will y'all just shut up!" BB interrupts. "You need to stay focused," BB says to me. "And you," he turns and says to Millicent, "need to stop arguing with him. You've been a crab apple since we left that motel in Casper. I don't know what's wrong with you. You two are wearing me out." He lowers his cap onto his head, slumping further into the seat.

Silence fills our space, but the sweltering air of awkwardness is out there; things have gotten ugly. This clusterfuck of ours can be remedied. I can turn the truck around and take Luca back where he belongs. Where he is meant to be. Because if he had Jordan's heart, is it right to take that last piece of him away from her just to make another person happy? Isn't this when the greater good comes into play? When we push aside our selfish wants?

"Look, I'm sorry I snapped at y'all," BB says.

"It's fine," she murmurs.

"I just can't handle all this bickering," he goes on. He points out the window as we drive by a car dealership. "Think they're your kin, Mellie?"

"Why do you say that?" I ask him.

"It's called Gosnell's Auto Zone," he says deliberately. "Gosnell was her daddy's last name."

I hear Millicent's breath hitch.

My heart races and my breathing becomes shallow. "Was his first name Chuck?" I barely utter. I gaze at her through the rearview mirror. Tears pool in her blue eyes, and her lips quiver.

"Yeah, Chuck Gosnell," BB says. "How'd you know?"

"Educated guess," I whisper, still looking at Millicent. She looks out the window, chewing on her nail. Tears stream down her face.

"I didn't know him too good, but I hear he was real a nice man," BB says. He turns and looks at her. "Whatcha crying for? Is it 'cause I'm talking about your daddy? I didn't mean..."

"He was a hero," my voice cracks.

The world around me begins to spin. I let go of the steering wheel and let my foot off of the gas. The truck slows, then stalls in the middle of the road, idling while the world moves around us. A car passes us by. The driver honks his horn and shouts at us.

"Well, he was rude. Is something wrong with the truck?" BB asks.

I don't answer him.

"Trip?" he asks. "Is the truck broken?"

Before I can reply, I hear the screeching sound of a police siren and see flashes of blue lights whirling in motion.

"Popo," BB frets.

A police officer dressed in a navy blue uniform moves toward us. He taps on my window and tilts his head to the side, staring at me peculiarly.

I let the window roll all of the way down.

"You having car problems?" he asks us.

I'm too stunned to answer him. Chuck Gosnell is Millicent's father. I can't stop looking at her, trying to read her, but she keeps averting her gaze, refusing to face what is right in front of her. "You have to talk to me," I murmur to her.

"Everything okay here?" the police officer asks us. I hear the tone of concern in his voice; the skepticism. What's a trio of teens doing out at this time of night? Anytime a group of people is out late at night, there's always the assumption that they're up to no good. Why does night equate to shenanigans? Maybe because in the dark, it's easy to do the things that are unspeakable. If no one can see, it's easier to lose your moral code.

"We're fine. The truck stalled, but it works now," BB answers too eagerly. Who are we kidding? We're not crooks.

The cop moves closer, glaring at us with an incredulous expression. "You alright, young lady?" he asks Millicent. "You look upset."

She nods, offering a faint fake smile. "I'm fine," she croaks.

"License and registration, please," he says to me.

I can hear him. I can see him. But, I don't move. I don't do anything. Shock does that to a person.

BB nudges me in my ribcage, and I quickly come back to the present.

"Give him your license, man," he says.

I fumble for my wallet and reach over to pull out Dad's

registration, silently praying the cop doesn't notice what is in the back of the truck, but even Helen Keller could sense something was amiss.

He treks to his police cruiser and sits inside, probably checking my record.

"You didn't tell me," I say to her.

She sobs, saying nothing. Her cheeks are blotchy, and her blue eyes are bloodshot.

"Why?" I ask her.

"I think we're up shit creek," BB says, oblivious to my realization of Millicent's secret. Doesn't he know? Can't he see? Isn't it obvious? "Oh, shit. He's searching the truck bed."

The cop charges to the driver's side and aims his firearm at us. I feel nothing. Not fear. Not shock. Not panic. I should be crapping in my pants - a gun is pointed at me.

His order sounds like a distant echo. I feel as if I'm submerged in water. The sound of my heartbeat echoes loudly in my ears.

"Get out of the vehicle with your hands above your head."

I can't move.

"Trip," BB says through gritted teeth. He shoves me hard so I wake up from my stupor. "Get out!" He pushes the door open, and I stumble out of the truck.

The officer shoves me against the truck, and I lose my footing, tumbling to the asphalt. "Get down on the ground with your legs and arms spread. All of you."

I lay on the concrete road, scraped and bloodied - humiliated, aching from the internal heartache of knowing what I now know. There's nothing I can do to change the fact that the one person I am in love with is related to the man who died trying to save me. I turn my head, looking into her eyes. Does she see me as the cause of her father's death?

CHAPTER 32

We sat in a room for hours being interrogated, then left alone, only to be badgered once again.

"Why," I asked her one of the few times the cops left us alone in the room.

But I never got an answer from her.

The cops tell us Dad's truck was reported stolen. Add that to my list of crimes. I guess my parents want to teach me a lesson. I should be angry with them for screwing me over, but I'm not. Didn't I take advantage of them? Didn't I do them wrong by lying to them and making them worry? Didn't I break their number one rule: trust?

The casket was even more evidence of our deviances. The funeral home reported a robbery when the silent alarm tripped, sending the police out searching for the delinquents who had broken into a funeral home and stolen a casket.

They give us each the opportunity to make one phone call. I hesitate to contact my parents but do so because I don't know anyone else who loves me enough to rescue me from my own self.

"I'm sorry," I tell them, weeping into the phone like a frightened little boy.

"We're dropping the charges for a stolen vehicle," Mom says on the phone. "We will talk when we get there."

I'm thankful for their unconditional love. Without it, I'd be locked in a cell for who knows how long, giving me plenty of time to contemplate my choices this week. I should care that I'm in trouble, but right now, all I care about is talking to Millicent.

Once I hang up the phone, I am taken back to my holding cell, which is reminiscent of something you'd see on *Andy Griffith*. Only this isn't a vintage TV show with a pleasant sheriff and bumbling deputy who'll laugh off our crimes. It's real life. Sometimes what you ask for, you get—and then some. I wanted to live and now I am, but at what price? What have I paid to live?

BB sits like Rodin's <u>The Thinker</u> on the cot across me. He couldn't get a hold of his parents because they were working, so Anna and Mama Sauce are making the trip up here for him and Millicent. I can't help but think we were trying to save them money by going on this fool's mission, and now they're having to find a way to come up with the funds to rescue Millicent and BB.

Millicent is in the cell next to ours, curled into a fetal position and laying on a shoddy cot. A wool blanket is draped over her petite body.

"Why didn't you tell me?" I say to her.

She rolls onto her side and slowly sits up right then pads to me. Her eyes meet mine.

"I didn't know until two nights ago," she admits.

"But you could have told me then," I whisper.

"I...I didn't know what to do," she says. "I was in shock. I'd always thought Dad died from a car accident. That's what they told me, and to discover how tragic his death was… it was too much."

"We can handle this."

She shakes her head solemnly.

"Please don't blame me."

"Blame you?" she repeats in disbelief. "I don't blame you. It's not your fault, but you still see it that way even though you say you don't. I know that guilt like that lingers. And I worry that everytime you look at me, I'll remind you of that tragic day."

"Remind me?" I am taken aback. "When I'm with you, I forget. All I want when I'm with you is to move forward. You're my silver lining."

"You can't forget this."

"I can because I'm willing to. I'm sure lots of others have loved despite the obstacles."

"This isn't a minor obstacle."

"Any obstacle is a minute hurdle we can learn to jump over if we do it together."

She wipes her tears and sucks in a breath of air. "I'm not so sure it's that easy, Trip. I want it to be so bad. My heart aches from this."

"I love you, and I know you love me, too. If you didn't love me, it wouldn't hurt you like it does right now."

She doesn't respond.

"Now is the time to tell the truth to yourself. Let down that guard, Millicent."

"It won't change things." She brings her hand up to her wrinkled forehead, and her lips cast downward into a frown.

"It changes everything." I stand and move toward her, gripping the bars that separate us. "I love you."

Silence. Painful, excruciating, punch-in-the-gut silence.

"Did you hear me?" I shout to her when I don't hear a response. "I love you!" I bring my fist to my heart. "I love you! This doesn't change my feelings for you." I plead with my eyes, with my voice, with my body. "Don't you see we can get past this? Doesn't love conquer all?" I'm grasping at straws. I'm using all of those desperate lines from romance novels.

I wait for her to say something. To give me a glimmer of hope.

"I don't know how we're supposed to get past this."

"We can," I say desperately.

***

After I laid my heart on the line, Millicent retreated inwardly. I need to give her time. I'm still trying to wrap my mind around it. I can only imagine how she's feeling. What if something I knew to be true suddenly turned into a lie?

She's asleep, or at least I think she is. I'm not sure. She's quiet and isn't moving. Her back faces me. I watch her and wonder. Can this be repaired? I'm willing to move forward. Can she?

"What is going on with you two?" BB asks me. "You were all Buddy The Elf over there with your professions of love, and she kept talking about blame. What's she talking about?"

So I tell him. Everything. From the beginning to the end. How the six degrees of separation theory is true: Millicent and I were connected before we even met. How we'd been connected for years. How we're linked through a means of rotten circumstance. But can one chain be unlinked and joined with another?

He listens intently. Saying nothing. What can he say? *Sorry. Doesn't matter. Words don't matter.* Actions matter, and right now she's telling me she can't.

"You'll get past it," he says with certainty. "She loves you. I can tell about these things. Remember I have a better sense of the opposite sex than you do. You've got no game and the professions of love, well, it was a bit prissy if you ask me." He offers me a smile, the kind you can't help but reciprocate because that is how BB is: all things happy, but I'm not feeling so optimistic. I'm feeling the lowest of low. "You guys will work this out."

"I hope so," I fret.

"You will. I feel it in my bones. I know things," he says with confidence, then grows quiet for a moment. "Anyways, I hope I remember this little adventure we took when I'm older," he murmurs.

"You will," I say. How can I be sure? A concussion has lasting effects, and depending on where he was hit in his brain, his memory could worsen the older he gets.

"I'll remember the music, and if I remember that, I can recall every great moment."

"Music and memory have been proven…" I begin, but he holds up his hand, stopping me.

"Don't spout stats at me. I need a break from your brain," he says. "You're so smart you don't know when you're being stupid."

"Thanks," I say, offended.

"Look," he starts, tapping his fingers against his thighs in impatience. "Mellie is opinionated and headstrong, but when she loves, she gives it her all. These are the things I love most about her. She won't let go of you. Give her time. She just needs time to digest this. Isn't it freaking you out, too? It'd sure mess me up if it were me in your shoes. It's like those people who fall in love then find out the person they love is their long-lost half-sister or something."

"Not the same," I say.

"It's just as weird if you ask me."

"I loved Chuck; it makes sense that I'd love her, too."

He looks at me peculiarly.

"I'm saying, a part of me had to have known there was a link between us because there was this instant connection between her and me, a spark if you will," I say. "We are a product of our loved ones. When they die, they never fade because they live on through us. Aspects of them are ingrained in our soul, and that's true for Chuck. He's a part of her."

He lays down on the cot and crosses one leg over the other, then folds his arms across his chest like a vampire. "I ain't ever looked at it that way, but I see what you're saying," he says and yawns. "Like I say, it'll work out. Just be patient."

Patience is a virtue I've had to have since I lost my leg. I don't want to be patient now. I'm through with waiting.

I have a seat on the cot across from him, waiting in silence, giving me too much time to think. To dwell. I don't want time to think. Isn't that what I've been doing for the last ten years of my life? Thinking. Observing. Watching life whirl by.

The door swings open and one of the cops comes in. Trailing closely behind him is Jordan, Luca's fiancé.

"She wants to speak with you three," the cop says to us.

CHAPTER 33

I shout to Millicent to wake up. She jolts up in a frenzy. Her gaze meets mine. I tilt my head in Jordan's direction. Millicent looks at her anxiously. Her face is beet red, and her jaw is twitching.

"She asked to see you three," the cop says to us with petulance. He turns to Jordan and says softly, "You okay here alone, or do you want me to stay?" He rubs her arms affectionately and talks about us like we're serial killers intent on murdering her.

"I'm fine," she says. "Tommy, really." She tries reassuring him.

He gives us one last look, frowning in disgust at the three of us before he decides we're sufficiently safe to be alone with. Nevermind the fact that we're locked up in a holding cell and would have no way of inflicting any harm on her. I guess we are a bunch of hooligans in the eyes of the law. Delinquents. That's us. I, Beckett Wentworth, now have a mugshot.

She stands in front of our two cells, forming a subtle, hesitant smile. "I'm Jordan, Luca's fiancé." Her voice is soft like cotton and her complexion is like milk—white and creamy. She reminds me of Tinkerbell with dark hair. "Sorry if Tommy has been a bit rough with you. He's my older brother and is a bit overprotective of me," she says. That explains the canoodling with her and the manhandling with us.

We flit to her.

"You must be Millicent," she says. "Luca talked about you so much I feel like I know you already."

Millicent's face lights up from this comment. It's the first time I've seen her smile in the last twenty-four hours.

"He said you were the younger sister he never had," she says.

"He talked about everyone in the commune. We had planned a trip out there this summer but things," she pauses for a moment, choking back tears, "...happened."

"Everyone would have liked to have met you," Millicent says, forcing a steady voice. I see the tears pooling in her eyes. "Especially Mama Sauce."

"I would still like to meet her," her voice trails off, lingering in the air, waiting for Millicent to offer, but nothing is said, so she says, "You're BB, right?"

His bushy brows lift up into surprise. "How'd you know?"

"Luca was a keen storyteller and had a knack for describing people. I could almost taste Mama Sauce's spaghetti and feel the cool crispness of Spoonwood Lake," she says, closing her eyes and inhaling through her nose. She opens her eyes again and stares at me. "I'm sorry, I don't know you, though." She tilts her head to the side, studying me.

"He's Trip, Mellie's boyfriend," BB says. "'Course they're on the outs right now, but that'll be remedied soon." He shoots us a confident grin.

"Nice to meet you," she says to me.

"You, too," I say. I didn't know I was Millicent's boyfriend, and I'm optimistic that she didn't correct BB when he said it.

"Well, let's address this big elephant in the room, shall we?" Jordan rubs her hands together, fidgets and hesitates for a second. "I had it all rehearsed in my head before I got in here, but now that I have to say it out loud, I'm struggling. Luca would have been better at this." She wipes the dampness at the corners of her eyes. She sucks in a lungful of air and exhales. "Well...." she starts, then stops herself. She balls her hands into two fists, finding her resolve. "I've come here today to find out why you all did what you did," she starts. "I have a hunch, but I need an explanation. My uncle owns the funeral home, and I know he'll drop the charges if I ask him to, but first I want to know why."

She waits expectantly - darting her eyes from Millicent to BB and finally to me.

"We all have our own reasons," I answer.

"What's yours?"

"I wanted to live," I simply say. Easier to say; more difficult to experience. I catch Millicent's reaction when I say this, and if I'm reading her correctly, it's admiration.

"And are you?"

"Yeah," I gulp. "Yeah, I'd say so," I add with a confident nod.

"Living means feeling pain and happiness, thrills and boredom, fear and safety."

"That's me in a nutshell," I say. "Love and disagreement, too."

"Ah, fighting means you love," she says.

"Then they love each other a lot," BB interjects.

"Luca would have liked you," she says to me. "He was a big believer in taking risks and living." Her faces falls and she looks off into the distance, thinking. She brings her gaze back to me. "He said a life without risks doesn't matter and a life that doesn't matter is a waste."

"He sounds like he was a smart guy," I say.

"He was the best," she says. She turns her attention to Millicent. "So, are you going to tell me your reason, or am I going to have to stare at you the way Luca did to get you confess?"

"I'm...I'm not sure where to start," Millicent stutters.

"The beginning is always a good place to start," Jordan says.

***

This is not the reaction I would have expected. Jordan is snorting and hasn't stopped laughing for several minutes. "And you all thought," Chuckle. Chuckle. Chuckle. "That you could just walk out with a casket?" she says in between laughs. "Oh my," she brings her hand up to her chest, "Luca would have loved this." She howls with laughter once more. "This is too much."

"We had a plan," Millicent defends.

"A half-ass one," Jordan says. "But you all tried. I'll grant you that."

"We thought…" Millicent begins.

"You thought a mortuary was an easy place to rob and that the first casket you saw was Luca's," she says and laughs again. "This is the first time I've laughed since Luca passed. Thank you, I needed it."

We're speechless. You know those times when people are laughing it up at your expense and you're not sure if you should join them or not? That's us right now.

"Luca said caskets were a waste of money, and that all they did was waste perfectly good land which could be used for other things than storing dead souls," she says. She's gauging our reactions. We're not following her and give her clueless looks. "He was cremated," she explains. "That wasn't him in the casket."

CHAPTER 34

Our jaws drop. Not literally, of course, but the realization that we couldn't even steal the right thing on our crime spree just adds more salt to our wounds. We aren't cut out for the crime life. We're in over our heads. And now, the question is, "Who was in the truck bed?" Does it even matter at this point? Yes, yes it does.

"Who was in the casket?" I ask.

She snorts and shakes her head, smiling wide. "Sorry," she says and laughs. "That's the part that is so funny."

We're silent, trying to find the humor in this situation.

"No one," she says, laughing once more. "The casket was empty."

Embarrassment fills us, and the room grows quiet as we stand there letting what she just said sink in. We are buffoons in the criminal arts.

"Lawd," BB murmurs. "We aren't the sharpest tools, are we?"

"I'd say you might want to stick with your day jobs," Jordan says. "I'm going to ask my uncle to drop the charges."

We all let out a sigh of relief. Maybe someone up there is looking out for us because we're a bunch of novice crooks who don't necessarily deserve all of the second chances we're getting. But we're getting them. Left and right. That's what this trip has been about: people offering us hope and giving us another chance. Maybe Millicent will give our relationship another chance?

Jordan's expression grows serious. "I'm having Luca's baby." She glances down at her belly and rubs it with both of her hands.

"How far along are you?" Millicent asks.

"Four months," she says with a wide smile. "That was part of the reason we were planning to visit you all."

Millicent's lips turn up into a subtle smile. "Mama Sauce will be so happy."

"I think it's a boy," she says and twists the ends of her t-shirt nervously. "Well, my grandmother said I look like I am carrying a boy. Luca said if it was a boy he wanted to name him Antonio after his father and if she's a girl Maria after Mama Sauce."

"I'm not so sure we need another Mama Sauce in the world," Millicent teases. "One is plenty, I assure you."

Jordan's overzealous brother enters and says, "You okay, sis?"

"I'm fine, Tommy."

"Uncle Ryan wants to know if he should press charges." He places his hand on his pistol. "I told him 'hell yeah,' but he wants to hear from you."

"No," she shakes her head, "he shouldn't press charges."

He clicks his tongue against the roof of his mouth in disgust. "Not what I would've done, but you're calling the shots on this one."

"When can you release them?"

"If he's not pressing charges and the kid's parents dropped their charge, there isn't much we can hold them on."

"Luca's memorial is today," she says to us. She checks her phone. "It starts in a few hours." She turns her attention back to Tommy. "Will they be released by that time?"

"Yeah." He shrugs nonchalantly.

"Good." She says with a firm nod. "Luca would've wanted you all there."

***

Eulogies are deeply personal. I don't know anyone who can't

help but get choked up from hearing them. It's the fact that everything being said won't be heard by the person it's all about. From the way everyone is talking about Luca, I can tell he was a good man. No wonder Millicent and BB drove clear across the country for him. I'd like to think someone would do that for me. The selfish side of me hopes I'll get that kind of love in my life, and if I'm honest with myself, I'd tell you I'd do it for Millicent because I love her that much. Some cynics might chalk it up to my naivety with women or my youth, but I know my heart and it beats for her.

There wasn't a dry eye in this place - me included. I couldn't help but get caught up in the emotion of it all. The fact that he died too soon hasn't escaped me. The fact that his child will be born never knowing her/his father makes it all the worse. As if his tragic death wasn't enough. But Jordan keeps going because she's a fighter.

And you'd think that she would feel bitter and resentful about Luca dying, but all she can do is save a bunch of idiots who try their hand at crime and really suck at it. All she was concerned about was making sure we could attend his funeral. I think I could learn a lot from her.

I hold Millicent's hand through it all. I want her to know I am here for her. That no matter what, I'm not giving up. I'm in. I'm all in. She's not letting go. That's a good sign, right? I think this means something. It has to mean something.

We haven't broached the subject of her dad again because it doesn't seem like the right time. When will there be a right time? Can't we forget it and move on? The answer to that is, "No." I wish we could, but what happened to her dad changed both of our lives. We both lost a part of ourselves when he died. Is it right that we can share in this bond together?

After the service ends, we linger outside, watching while Jordan greets hoards of people who have come to pay their respects. Millicent stands by her side, talking to each and every person. And they hug her, weeping, telling her how sorry they are that he's gone. They're offering her comfort for her grief. I finally understand why people say funerals are for the living.

"What do we do now?" BB asks.

"We wait."

He kicks his foot against the asphalt; a few pebbles skip across the concrete surface. "I hate waiting."

"Me, too, but it's our only option right now. We did what we came here for, and now we wait for the next."

"But we had a purpose."

"So we find a new one." The question is, do we need a purpose? Can we just live our lives freely without an expectation? Won't we be happier that way in the long run?

As I debate life's complexities, my parents arrive in a yellow cab. I can't read their thoughts, but given their sour expressions, I'd say I'll be on restriction for months, maybe a year. I can pay my penance because I have no regrets. If I had to do it all over again, I would.

It feels different with them, or maybe I'm just not the same now. Of course, I'm not the same. Who am I kidding? They're looking at me like they don't know me. Maybe they don't know me anymore. I barely know me anymore. I'm not the same guy who started on this journey. He's long gone. All I know is what I feel, and what I feel is alive.

"This is Millicent," I say to them, feeling proud. I want to shout, "She's the girl I'm in love with!"

Millicent shakes their hands and tells them it's nice to finally meet them. "I'm sorry about all of this. It's my fault Trip's here," she tells them.

"He's capable of making his own decisions, but I appreciate you trying to protect him," Mom says.

Dad is tight-lipped but winks at me when Mom isn't looking. Maybe he has a bug in his eye or he's suffering from allergies, but I'm banking on it being something else. Maybe he remembers what it was like being my age, reckless and stupid because you're hopelessly in love.

"You should say your goodbyes," Mom says to me. "We have a long drive back home."

"I'd say you're in deep doo-doo," BB says, loudly.

"If I don't turn up at school in September, call the police," I joke, but there's some truth to that statement.

"Sorry we screwed up so bad, Mrs. Wentworth," BB says to her.

"I am, too," she says.

"She's going to take a while to warm up to me again," I whisper to him.

"Good luck with that," he says. "Don't give up on Mellie, either. She'll come around."

"I hope so."

I move toward Millicent. "I have to go now. Maybe we can talk when you get back home," I say, hoping I don't sound too desperate, but I know my facial expression shows it.

"I'd like that," she says, giving me some hope.

"Trip, time to go," Mom interrupts us.

"The units mean business," I say to her.

"Well, we did do a few reckless things, didn't we?"

"Just a few." I grin.

"But we're a great team," she says, flickering a grin.

"I wouldn't pick any other wingman," I say.

"Thanks for joining us on this crazy journey."

"I'd do it all over again."

"Me, too," she says. "Bye, Trip."

"Ah, it's not goodbye. We'll see each other real soon, like Mickey Mouse." I smile.

She flashes me another smile in return. "I hope so."

I slip her a folded piece of paper.

"What's this?"

"Read it later," I say.

As we head toward Dad's truck, I stop and turn around, then wave at her, BB and Jordan. It's like a bad scene from a movie. It's all kinds of wrong. We're acting like it's the end. Isn't that what this is? The end. How can it all change so quickly? I'm not letting this be my final act.

I quicken my pace and trek to Millicent. "I know you're confused about things, but know this, I love you and can get past this because you're too important to me." Before she has a chance to respond, I lean in and kiss her on the lips, feeling the world stop below my feet. I pull away and look into her eyes, searching for a sign. Something. Anything.

One side of her mouth lifts up.

"Trip!" Mom shouts.

"You better go before she decides to give the mortuary more business," Millicent says.

I've given it my all. I've done everything I can do. The ball is in Millicent's court.

CHAPTER 35

It's midnight. The crickets are chirping. I'm standing outside Millicent's bedroom window feeling like a creeper. I haven't gotten the nerve to tap on her window yet because I'm second guessing my rash decision in coming here. It wasn't a well-thought-out plan. It seems that is how I roll these days.

I came here with the intention of finding out where we stand. I haven't heard from her since I left Wyoming, and that was well over a week ago. I don't know if she's banned from using her phone or if she just doesn't want anything to do me. Either way, it's an awful predicament.

It's the silence that kills me. I wish she'd text me back, even if it was a rejection. At least I'd know. At least I could have a next.

I finally gather enough resolve to knock on her window and whisper, "Millicent. Psst. Millicent."

A light flickers on, and I see her shadow dart across the room. She flits to the window and leans into the glass panel. Her mouth opens wide, and she arches her brows in surprise.

"Trip?" Her hair is messy and her long pink t-shirt is wrinkled.

"Open up," I say.

She unlatches the window, then pushes it upward. "Can I come in?" I ask.

"I opened the window, didn't I?"

I sit down on her windowsill then pivot my way around into her room. Since I lack in grace, I knock over a few of her knick-knacks along the way, shattering one into pieces in the process. Broken bits are scattered across her rug. She shakes her head in disapproval.

"Sorry," I say.

"It was a family heirloom."

"Oh, sorry," I cringe.

"Just kidding. It was nothing."

"Nice," I say.

She laughs, and it's good to hear that sound again. I want to say something funny or do a dance just to hear her again but refrain from doing so because I don't want to mess this up. I rehearsed what I was going to say on the drive here, but right now, I'm veering off of the script.

I step down onto her floor and have a seat in her chair. This is the first time I've ever been in her room. It's clean and bright. Lots of pastels. Everything is color coded on her wall calendar filled with sticky notes. It's welcoming and cheery.

She cleans up my mess, then tosses the fragmented pieces into the trash.

"To what do I owe this honor?" she asks, having a seat on her bed.

"I haven't heard from you."

"I haven't heard from you," she retorts.

"I wanted to give you space," I say.

"I appreciate that because I needed time," she says.

Uh oh. Those words are never good. She reads my thoughts and continues, "And my moms have placed me on restriction: no phone, no internet, just hard labor for the next few months." She rolls up her shirt sleeve and points to her tanned arm. "Hence the farmer's tan. I've been tilling the garden and pulling weeds."

"Sounds like fun."

"I hate it," she groans. "What about you?"

"I've been cleaning the house," I say. "Day after day. Dusting the baseboards, mopping the floors, doing whatever my mom tells me to."

"Ha," she scoffs. "You got off easy."

I shrug nonchalantly. "Depends on how you look at it; I haven't been able to talk to you."

She offers me an apologetic smile. "Yeah. But still, cleaning is gravy compared to what I've been doing."

Enough of this small talk. I want to know. I need to know. "So, are you going to break my heart, Millicent?"

She's taken aback by my frankness. "When did you get so gutsy? That was quite brazen of you, Beckett Wentworth. Methinks you've been reading self-help books."

"Just had a change of heart these past couple of weeks," I say.

"Hmm," she ponders. "I like it."

"So?" I ask, leaning in, sounding as needy as I feel.

"I had plenty of time to think on the way home since I tend to tune people out when they're lecturing me for hours on end," she says. "My moms admire my nerve but don't respect my choices."

"Mine aren't too happy with me right now, either. They like that I'm socializing like a normal human being but don't care for any of the decisions I made on that trip."

"I guess we didn't go on that trip to please anyone."

"I can say with all certainty, you are not a pleaser."

"No, I guess I'm not, but it brings me comfort knowing the people I love are happy."

"That's because you're a good person," I say.

"And so are you," she says. "I confronted my moms about lying to me about Dad's death. I didn't understand why they hid it from me all of this time. And their response was that they thought it would be 'too painful' for me to handle. And," she sighs, "I just don't think that's right. Because shielding someone from the truth to protect them is as bad as lying. Hurtful or not, the truth has to be told because one person can't hold power like that."

"Maybe they thought they were protecting you."

"I don't need protecting."

"No, no you don't."

"I thought about us, too. A lot. About where we stand. About our unusual connection. About our feelings for each other. And, I'll be honest, a part of me wanted to run the other way."

My face falls.

"But then, the other part of me knows I can't do that because I'd only run in circles to find my way back to you."

My frown fades.

"It's all so incredibly messed up, but I can't deny how I feel about you. I can't deny the fact that I've been drawn to you since we met. That being with you has made me see what love looks like. What it feels like. I never knew its power until you came into my life," she says. "So, what I'm saying is, I want to give this a try because I love you, Beckett Wentworth."

"You do?" I ask, hearing the lilt in my voice.

"Yes. Definitely yes."

I stand and come toward her, then wrap my arms around her. I kiss the top of her head and hold back the tears because hearing the person you're head over heels for tell you she loves you is more than amazing. It's living. Really living.

"Remember how you once said I was an organ donor? Well, that's true. You have my heart, Millicent."

She squeezes my hand. "Well, how do you top a statement like that?"

"Just you wait. I have more like that up my sleeve," I say.

"In the meantime, we'll have to work on your staring problem," she kids.

"And we'll need to work on your hangry issues," I tease.

She slides off the bed and stands on her tiptoes before pressing her lips against mine. I pull her toward me into a tight embrace and tell myself to remember this feeling because it's truly one of the happiest moments in my life.

Her door jerks open, and I hear the sound of someone clearing their throat. We pull away from each other, seeing an irate Mama Sauce glaring at us with her hands on her hips. "What are you two doing?"

EPILOGUE

That day I left Wyoming, I gave Millicent a window to my soul on one piece of folded paper. I wanted her to know the depth of my love. Sometimes the written word is a more powerful way of expression. BB says guys don't write poetry, and I told him that real men do. Sometimes you just have to go for it.

I know Millicent likes my poems because she told me she keeps them in her dresser drawer. I don't write them to receive the praise; I write them so she knows that she's constantly on my mind.

This is the first one I wrote Millicent on our last day in Wyoming together.

Too much time
Spent alone
Now I see
You're my home
A bleak existence
Faded into thin air
A darkened sky
Brightened with you there
Once a wall
Standing motionless and straight
Now a door
Opening a locked gate
You're all that I want
And all that I need
Take hold of my hand
And go on this journey with me

I want for nothing
Except to be by your side
You make my life something
And one amazing ride

My parents have threatened that I won't get off restriction for
at least three more months - depending on my behavior. And the
thought of only seeing Millicent at school frightens me, but every
choice I have made over the course of this month was worth every
repercussion. To live is to face all of the obstacles.

Today, I've been given a momentary reprieve from my penance
because my parents decided it wouldn't be right to keep me from
attending Luca's memorial service at the commune.

"You will go there and come right back," Mom says.

I salute her and smile.

"I mean it." She wags her finger at me.

I reach in to hug her and get a whiff of her floral scent. "Ah,
Mom. You're the greatest, you know?" I form a lopsided grin.

She stares at me incredulously. "Flattery doesn't charm me."

"I'm not trying to charm you. I just want you to know I love
you."

Her lips slightly curl up from my comment. "Go on and get
out of here before I change my mind about you going," she says,
but I don't believe her. She might be irritated with me for my
irresponsible behavior this summer, but I know she's thrilled I
finally have a girlfriend and a friend. That I'm doing all of the
things a guy my age should be doing.

I grab the car keys and place my wallet and phone into my
short's pocket, then head to the door. I wrap my hand around the

door handle. "I'm happy, you know. Really happy."

Her lips lift up into a wide grin. "I'm glad."

I open the door.

"That doesn't mean you're off of restriction, though!"

"I figured not," I say.

I drive to the commune, picking up BB along the way. He collapses into the seat and turns up the volume on my radio, then bops his head along to the beat of the drum. "Think they'll let you go hunting with me in the fall?"

I shrug my shoulders. Hunting isn't a high priority of mine but trying something different is. I've got a list a mile long I plan to check off before I turn twenty-one. I'm living each day like it's my last.

"We'll see."

"I'll teach you to shoot," he says.

"Maybe I already know how."

I feel his eyes on me. "Wouldn't surprise me. You probably read a book on it."

"I've been known to read from time to time."

We blare the music as we drive down the two-lane road to the commune, singing ineptly at the top of our lungs. It's a breezy summer's day. The sun shines, and there isn't a cloud in the sky.

When we arrive at the commune, the hippies are standing next to one another by the lakeshore. Millicent hears the roar of my engine and turns her head slightly, glancing in my direction. She beams and says something to her mom, then walks away from the group, heading our way. Her long braid flops against her back as she treks in the tall blades of grass.

"You're late, Beckett Wentworth," she says to me. I love it when she says my real name.

"Blame him," I point to BB.

Everyone in the commune waves at me, which is a relief because just last week I was on the chopping block when I showed up late in the night to profess my feelings for Millicent. I guess they remember they were young and crazy in love once.

Now that they know I'm not going anywhere for a very long time—not until Millicent grows tired of me—I've become an honorary part of their family. But that's what love is: you accept without question.

BB rushes to the group, hugging Mama Sauce and the rest of the gang. I spot Jordan among the group, holding a wooden box in her petite hands. She decided that some of Luca's ashes should be scattered here because this was his home, too. They say home is where your heart is. Luca's heart was so big he had two homes. I hope to have that much heart and grit one day.

Jordan waves at me, smiling. And it strikes me as odd that she can be happy on a day like today, but Millicent said we were celebrating Luca's life, and a life worth celebrating shouldn't be a sad occasion.

"I'm glad you're here," Millicent says to me. She takes hold of my hand, and I intertwine my fingers with hers.

"Me, too," I say. I reach down to kiss her on her lips.

She slowly pulls away from me. A hint of pink pops up on her cheeks.

"You're ruddy," I say.

"Because it's warm out," she argues.

"Whatever you say." I hand her a folded piece of paper.

"What's this?"

"Just thoughts."

"I like your thoughts."

"Because they're all about you," I say.

"No, because they're beautiful like you," she says.

THE END

OTHER BOOKS BY THIS AUTHOR

OTHER BOOKS IN THE SPOONWOOD LAKE SERIES

It Started With a Whisper

Five simple words: That's all it takes to change the course of 18-year-old Josie Graham's life in the summer of 1989.

Josie is a musical prodigy: She can sing, play guitar and is a natural on the piano. Instead of spending her last summer before college traveling the country with her rock star father, she's made a last minute decision to spend it working at her Aunt Bernie's inn, in Ambler's Fork, North Carolina. But what could have turned her life-long passion for music into a hatred for an industry she's worked so hard to get into?

Her aunt's inn seems like the perfect place to escape, to clear her head and figure things out, but on her first day there, she almost drowns before Chic Hobbs saves her.

Chic wants nothing more in life than to leave Ambler's Fork and his sordid past behind—at least not until that day Josie Graham swims into his life. The problem is, Chic's got a secret. It's a secret he's keeping from Josie, and he's worried if it gets out, it'll ruin everything, and she'll judge him for his past mistakes the way everyone else in town has.

Josie is carrying a burden of her own. One that made her run to

Ambler's Fork — away from her family and everything she's ever known.

Chic saved Josie once. Can he save her again? Or will Josie rescue him this time?

THE HEARTS OF HAINES SERIES

Kiss Me Hard Before You Go

Every summer, Gray Barnes and his eighteen-year-old daughter, Evie, open up their farm in the foothills of South Carolina to Kip Kierkin's Carnival of Wonder. The carnival attracts hordes of locals and out-of-towners, and it brings in the extra cash that Gray and his daughter need to keep the family estate running.

Evie decided long ago that she wants nothing to do with the carnival or the farm that her dad so desperately works to keep afloat. She doesn't understand her father's appreciation for the land or the work that it takes to maintain it, but that's all about to change when she meets Finch Mills.

Finch is a lifer — a carny since birth. He's spent all of his twenty-two years on the circuit and longs for a different path. He's never paid much attention to Evie, not until this eventful summer of 1978.

Like All Things Beautiful

In this sequel to *Kiss Me Hard Before You Go*, Evie Barnes is living day-to-day, trying to keep her father's land and his cattle business afloat. She is adjusting to his absence and to living with Finch and the rest of the carnies, which is creating quite a stir amongst the locals in Haines.

As Finch and the others learn a new way of life that doesn't involve the carnival, they're dealing with prejudice from almost everyone in town. A string of suspicious incidents occur, prompting all fingers to point the blame at them.

Just when Evie and Finch learn to deal with the mountain of obstacles facing them, the unexpected happens, causing them to question if their relationship can survive it all.

This is Where We Begin.

In this sequel to *Like All Things Beautiful*, Katie McDaniels is unemployed, pregnant, and relying on Evie and Finch for a place to live. She is trying to survive. Nothing seems to be going right for her until Preston Dobbins steps into her life and an unexpected gift comes her way, finally giving her a chance at happiness.

Preston Dobbins is fighting his strong feelings for Katie McDaniels. He guards a well-kept secret, one that consumes him with guilt.

As an old foe threatens Katie's happiness, Preston risks everything to save her from tragedy.

OTHER BOOKS BY SHANNON McCRIMMON

The Summer I Learned to Dive.

Since the time she was a little girl, eighteen-year-old Finley "Finn" Hemmings has always lived her life according to a plan, focused and driven with no time for the average young adult's carefree experiences. On the night of her high school graduation, things take a dramatic turn when she discovers that her mother has been keeping a secret from her—a secret that causes Finn to do something she had never done before—veer off her plan. In the middle of the night, Finn packs her bags and travels by bus to Graceville, SC seeking the truth. In Graceville, Finn has experiences that change her life forever; a summer of love, forgiveness and revelations. She learns to take chances, to take the plunge and to dive right in to what life has to offer.

The Year I Almost Drowned.

In this continuation of "The Summer I Learned to Dive," nineteen-year old Finley "Finn" Hemmings is living in Graceville, South Carolina with her grandparents. She's getting to know the family that she was separated from for the last sixteen years. Finn and Jesse's relationship seems to be going strong until they're forced to deal with obstacles that throw them off-track. As Finn prepares to leave for college, she has to say goodbye to the town, her friends and family, and the way of life that she has grown to love.

At college, Finn tries to acclimate to a new setting, but quickly falls into an old pattern. Just as things start to become normal and Finn begins to fit in, something unexpected happens that takes her back to Graceville where she is forced to deal with one challenge after another. Her world nearly collapses, and she finds herself struggling to keep from drowning. Through it all, Finn discovers the power of love and friendship. She learns what it means to follow her heart and to stay true to what she wants, even if what she wants isn't what she originally planned.

The Days Lost.

On the heels of her high school graduation, Ellie Morales is spending her summer vacation in the mountains of Western North Carolina with her dad and brother, Jonah. Having lost their mother only months earlier, all of them are trying to cope with the loss in their own way.

Part routine, part escape, running is Ellie's way of dealing with her grief. Shortly after sunrise each morning, Ellie and her dog, Bosco, set out for a lengthy run on the path that passes by her house and leads deep into the woods of the Blue Ridge Mountains. One fateful morning, Ellie is lead off of the trail and discovers a secret that will change her life, as well as the lives of the family she meets, forever. One member of this mysterious family is Sam Gantry, who seems unlike any guy she's ever known.

This meeting sparks a series of events, causing Ellie to question everything she's ever known and believed. The more she learns about Sam and his family, the more she wants to help him find the missing puzzle pieces.

ABOUT THE AUTHOR

Shannon McCrimmon was born and raised in Central Florida. She earned a Master's Degree in Counseling from Rollins College. In 2008, she moved to the upstate of South Carolina. It was the move to the upstate that inspired her to write novels. Shannon lives in Greenville, South Carolina with her husband and toy poodle.

Did you enjoy *Confessions of an Organ Donor*? Please consider supporting the author by writing a review on Amazon.com or Goodreads.com.

Learn more about upcoming projects by becoming a fan on Facebook at www.facebook.com/shannonmccrimmonauthor, follow me on twitter@smccrimmon1 or instagram.com/writermccrimmon

Sign up to receive my http://bit.ly/Ma0iSJ

ACKNOWLEDGEMENTS

Jacob Farley: Thank you for sharing your personal story with me. Your thoughts, impressions, emails and videos about your journey mean a lot to me. I hope I've made you proud. You truly are an inspiration. Who would have thought that one interaction at Art and Light Gallery would have led to this book? Thank you!

Laurin Baker, aka The Editor: You knew how important this book was to me. You cheered me on and encouraged me when I needed it most. Thank you.

Bloggers Mandy Anderson from I Read Indie, Cora Page from Black Hearted Book Club, Lisa Anthony from My Indie Author Fix, Paula Phillips from The Phantom Paragrapher, Toni Lesatz from My Book Addiction, and Melissa from Books Are Love: thank you for your continued support and enthusiasm for my books. Dalene Kolb: You're not a blogger, but I thought you deserved special recognition. You're always eager to read and review my books, and for that, I'm so thankful.

Mandy Anderson: Thank you for scheduling blog tours and cover reveals, for your constant support and love for my writing. Sheila Lutringer: Thank you for the beautiful cover. You are so talented.

Mom and Dad: I miss you and love you with all of my heart. Mom, I finished this one for you. Even though y'all aren't here to share in the excitement, you're always with me and forever in my heart.

Lastly, and most importantly, to Chris: Thank you for your constant support. You are my creative sidekick and my wingman. I wouldn't be the writer I am without you by my side. I love you!